"Like I said, think hard about whether there's someone who might have something against you. A neighbor or coworker who's mad at you. A driver you cut off. Whatever."

"Why?" she demanded. "What's really going on?"

He pursed his lips. "Yeah, I think you should know, though I was asked to keep it quiet. Amber, for one, was choosing to ignore it. But this break-in here..."

"What?" Elissa repeated.

Doug looked straight into her eyes. "The night of your interview at the K-9 ranch, and before you came back up to give your demonstration, this was found on the fence there." He pulled his phone from his pocket, fiddled with it some, then thrust it toward her.

A photo was there depicting the front gate up the driveway to the main house at the K-9 ranch.

And on it was a sign: Be Careful Who You Hire.

* * *

Don't miss upcoming books in the K-9 Ranch Rescue miniseries!

* * *

If you're on Twitter, tell us what you think of Harlequin Romantic Suspense! #harlequinromsuspense

Dear Reader,

As I said here in the introduction to *Second Chance Soldier*, the first in my K-9 Ranch Rescue series for Harlequin Romantic Suspense, I'm a dog lover. *Trained to Protect* is the second in that series, and it involves both therapy dogs and police K-9s...and their people.

In *Trained to Protect*, Elissa Yorian is a therapy dog handler as well as a nurse. After hearing about a part-time job being offered at the Chance K-9 Ranch for someone to provide classes for other therapy dog handlers, she jumps at the opportunity to apply for it. She gets the job—but she also becomes the target of some strange threats. Fortunately, she meets Officer Doug Murran, a K-9 cop with the Chance police department, whose job includes helping to protect the ranch in his town—and it soon includes attempting to protect the lovely and vulnerable Elissa.

I hope you enjoy *Trained to Protect*. Please come visit me at my website, lindaojohnston.com, and at my weekly blog, killerhobbies.Blogspot.com. And, yes, I'm on Facebook, too.

Linda O. Johnston

TRAINED TO PROTECT

Linda O. Johnston

HARLEQUIN® ROMANTIC SUSPENSE

Recycling programs
for this product may
not exist in your area.

ISBN-13: 978-1-335-45661-8

Trained to Protect

Copyright © 2018 by Linda O. Johnston

Printed in U.S.A.

Linda O. Johnston loves to write. While honing her writing skills, she worked in advertising and public relations, then became a lawyer...and enjoyed writing contracts. Linda's first published fiction appeared in *Ellery Queen's Mystery Magazine* and won a Robert L. Fish Memorial Award for Best First Mystery Short Story of the Year. Linda now spends most of her time creating memorable tales of paranormal romance, romantic suspense and mystery. Visit her on the web at www.lindaojohnston.com.

Books by Linda O. Johnston

Harlequin Romantic Suspense

K-9 Ranch Rescue

Second Chance Soldier
Trained to Protect

Undercover Soldier
Covert Attraction

Harlequin Nocturne

Alpha Force

Alpha Wolf
Alaskan Wolf
Guardian Wolf
Undercover Wolf
Loyal Wolf
Canadian Wolf
Protector Wolf

Back to Life

Acknowledgments

I love the idea of therapy dogs—pets who are taught to help people with physical and mental issues by providing loving visits with them—and very much appreciate the friends and acquaintances who have given me insight into many of the aspects of training them and getting them officially qualified to provide that kind of help. Thanks to all of you, in particular Karen Saunders and Bonnie Schroeder, who provided lots of answers to my many questions.

And thanks, too, to the K-9 officers who have also answered my recent questions or given demonstrations of how those wonderful K-9s work—most especially Officer Maribel Feeley of the Glendale Police Department's K-9 Unit.

Thank you all!

Of course, as before, *Trained to Protect* is a work of fiction, so if anything seems untrue that's because I've modified reality to fit the story.

And, as always, many thanks to my wonderful editor, Allison Lyons, and my fantastic agent, Paige Wheeler.

Dedication

Like *Second Chance Soldier*, *Trained to Protect* is dedicated to all dogs and those who train and work with them, most especially police and military K-9s... and therapy dogs and their handlers.

And, as I always do, I dedicate this book to my wonderful husband, Fred, as well as our dogs, Mystie and Cari, who in their ways are my therapy dogs.

Chapter 1

Elissa Yorian stepped through the door into the Chance Coffee Shop and looked around.

This was her first time in Chance, California, and she was eager to see how this meeting turned out. If things went well, she could land a part-time job teaching people to train and work with therapy dogs. And giving lessons at a really renowned facility. Therapy work was something she loved, and she'd been doing it for a long time.

This place appeared like nearly any chain shop that specialized in coffee drinks, with a counter where patrons could place their orders and a long glass-fronted display case with food inside. It was noisy with conversations from the many people sitting at small tables, a busy place, which wasn't surprising since it was nearly lunchtime. Elissa had planned her drive well from her home in San Luis Obispo—sometimes referred to as SLO. It had taken her nearly forty-five minutes to get here, with traffic, as she'd assumed.

Depending on the schedule of classes she'd hold, her commute wouldn't be especially fun if she landed this job, but her commitment would only be part-time.

And it would be worth it.

She remained at the doorway, searching through the crowd. She knew from the Chance K-9 Ranch website and other online resources what Amber Belott looked like. That didn't mean she would recognize her, though, in all the faces of people sitting at tables, talking, sipping their drinks and munching on pastries and sandwiches in this place filled with the aroma of coffee.

No, she would rely on what Amber had told her in their telephone conversation yesterday. For one thing, she'd watch for a woman in a Chance K-9 Ranch T-shirt. Amber owned the ranch along with her mother and, from all Elissa had read online about the noted dog training facility, was the one in charge.

And her? She had dressed up as if this was a job interview—which it was. She hadn't overdone it but had put on a knee-length gray dress and black jacket, not to mention higher heels than she ever wore on a work day at the hospital where she was a nurse.

There. At a table near the counter, Elissa spotted a woman who had just stood up. She appeared slender, of medium height, with wavy reddish hair. And yes, she was wearing the anticipated T-shirt.

Smiling, her small purse slung over her shoulder, Elissa began making her way through the tables. In less than a minute she had reached her goal. "Amber?"

"Elissa!" Amber reached out and gave her a brief hug, as if they were already friends.

Elissa, hugging back, hoped that was a harbinger of what was to come.

"Let's get you something to eat and drink," Amber said after stepping back. Elissa noted there was already a brown coffee cup on the table, as well as a paper plate with a half-eaten croissant on it.

"Sounds good." Elissa was rather surprised that she had to argue a bit about who would pay for the café mocha and scone she ordered, but allowed Amber to treat rather than cause even a small rift between them to start with.

If she got the job, she would be glad to treat her boss to coffee or whatever in the future.

In a few minutes, after the barista had done her thing, Elissa sat on the vacant seat at Amber's table. Her view was of a few occupied tables between where she sat and the order counter.

Amber began their conversation. "I already know the basics from our phone call, but please tell me more about your work with therapy dogs and training their owners."

Elissa couldn't help grinning. She pushed her shoulder-length blond hair away from her face as she tried to get serious. But that was impossible, considering how much she loved what she did.

"Well," she began, "I've been at it for around three years. I'm a nurse, too. When I saw how therapy dogs who were brought into hospitals cheered patients so much, actually helping them improve faster, I had to give it a try."

Not just a try, but much more. She had chosen her

dog Peace, a golden retriever, after watching many skilled breeds and rescue dogs. Goldens performed really well as therapy dogs, following their owners' instructions and giving lots and lots of attention and love to sad and needy patients.

She described how qualified therapy dog handlers had worked with Peace and her from the first, teaching her all she needed to get started. Then she began doing it on her own.

And recently she had paid it forward and begun working with other potential therapy dog handlers in the hospital where she was primarily a full-time pediatric nurse. She had even provided a few classes for would-be handlers and their dogs, even though formal schooling wasn't generally necessary for therapy dogs. If they had the right personalities for it, their skills could be learned as people worked with their dogs at appropriate locations with expert handlers. But her students had all been appreciative—and had done well, some going on to become certified handlers themselves.

"Yes, we're aware that most therapy dog handlers learn how to do it by working directly with others at various facilities," Amber said. "But we want our Chance K-9 Ranch to expand into many different avenues for teaching dogs and their owners. We're also looking for a basic pet trainer or two, but we especially would like to hire someone who provides therapy dog training—though I realize that it's mostly the owners who need schooling. We want to start with basic classes at the ranch, then provide some of that hands-on training when the students are ready."

"Sounds good to me," Elissa responded.

"And your experience teaching other handlers sounds

good to me," Amber said as she took a sip of her drink. She was an attractive woman with assessing brown eyes and an expressive mouth. Would she be a good boss?

Heck, she and everyone else at her ranch most likely worked with dogs. That certainly spoke well of her, along with the ranch's reputation.

"Thanks," Elissa said. "And if you'd like, I can give you contact information for several more people who'll act as references for me." She'd asked some of her fellow therapy dog handlers before taking this meeting. She wasn't attempting to keep her ambition here secret, although she'd also made it clear to those she'd spoken with about it that she would limit her time in this part-time position, if she got it, so it would not affect her full-time job.

Or at least not much.

"Good," Amber said. "And as I mentioned on the phone, this kind of class is something new around here. We want someone quickly. You've got the best credentials and recommendations of any of our candidates so far, but I'll want you to come to the K-9 Ranch and give a demonstration, preferably in the next couple of days, before we make any decisions. Also—" She stopped speaking and smiled as she gazed past Elissa.

Which caused Elissa, thrilled to hear Amber's reference to her background, to turn to see what she was looking at.

She smiled, too, as she saw two cops in black uniform jackets, a man and woman, walk into the coffee shop. But she wasn't smiling at them.

No, she grinned because these were obviously K-9 cops. They both had dogs on leashes at their sides. As

Elissa watched, they approached the table where she sat, maneuvering effortlessly through the crowd.

Amber stood. "Hi, Maisie and Doug," she said as the cops reached them. "And hi, Hooper and Griffin, too."

Elissa rose, as well, while Amber introduced the officers and their dogs to her. The two cops apparently had more in common than merely being K-9 officers. They were also brother and sister. If Elissa was correct, Maisie, with short, blond hair and an air of being in charge, was the older sibling. Her dog, Griffin, was a golden retriever who appeared older and larger than Elissa's Peace, whom she'd left at home.

"Hi, Elissa," Maisie said when Amber had completed the introductions. "So you're a therapy dog trainer. I'd like to learn more about that. I think Griffin would be a wonderful therapy dog along with his great K-9 skills—which are mostly scenting out drugs and bad guys."

Hearing his name, the dog looked up at his handler and wagged his fluffy tail. Elissa couldn't help smiling. "I'd be glad to show you," she told the cop.

She turned her smile toward the other officer, Doug. He didn't smile back as he looked at Elissa. Why not? She felt an inappropriate twinge of hurt—no, it had to be irritation—that she immediately sloughed off.

Too bad his sister seemed nicer, though, since even with a neutral expression on his face, he appeared to be one hot, handsome cop. His hair was light brown, darker and much shorter than his sister's. His chiseled features were dominated by the way his hazel eyes, beneath thick brows, seemed to focus on Elissa, which made her insides churn with something she hadn't felt—hadn't allowed herself to feel—for a very long time: lust.

Though he hadn't spoken after saying hello to her,

she determined to break the silence between them. After all, it wouldn't hurt for her to have additional allies in this area who clearly cared about dogs. "I'd be glad to give you a therapy dog demonstration, too," she said. "And if it's possible, I'd also love to watch a K-9 training session sometime." One that included his German shepherd.

"Then Amber has hired you already?" Doug's tone sounded somewhat skeptical—and Elissa figured he knew enough to recognize that she had just met her potential new boss.

"Not yet," Amber said. "That'll depend on how Elissa's demonstration at the ranch goes. Does tomorrow work for you, Elissa?"

She'd fortunately anticipated the possibility and scheduled the next day as another day off from the hospital—though she'd been prepared to change that if necessary. "That works great for me," she said. She turned back to Maisie, though she also would be interested in a response from her brother. "Will you come and watch the demo?"

"Unlikely." Maisie's tone sounded regretful. "We'll be on duty and there's an investigation pending that we'll probably be involved in."

"Well, maybe another time," Elissa said, hazarding a brief glance toward Doug. He was still watching her with those intense hazel eyes.

"Maybe," he said, then looked down and patted the top of his shepherd's head. "As long as Hooper doesn't mind. He provides all the therapy I need."

Doug Murran ran into a lot of women both in his capacity as a police officer and in everyday life, even

in a town as small as Chance. Some were nice looking, even pretty.

But few were as attractive as Elissa Yorian.

Maybe it wasn't only her sexy, appealing appearance in her attractive professional outfit, though. Or her
slightly unkempt blond hair framing a lovely, mostly
smiling face.

Maybe it was because she clearly loved dogs. After
all, she was a therapy dog handler and trainer. She was
additionally a nurse, another indication that she cared
about helping people.

He cared about helping people, too, though from a
different perspective.

He was a cop.

"Do you two have time to join us for coffee?" Amber
asked.

"Sure." He moved his gaze to the K-9 Ranch owner.
He'd just been about to suggest the same thing—even
though he figured his dear sis, Maisie, would balk at
the idea. They'd intended just to come in and leave with
take-out coffee. But their next meeting at the Chance
Police Department headquarters wasn't for another half
hour.

"Oh, but—" Maisie began from beside him.

"But we can't stay long," he added. He didn't look at
Maisie, knowing her gaze would be shrewd and critical.

She knew him well, for multiple reasons—as both his
sibling and coworker. But he stayed out of her way—
mostly—when she began flirting with a new guy. She
needed to learn to do the same with him.

For now, to placate her, he said, "Do you want the
usual, Officer Murran? My treat."

"Yes, thanks, Officer Murran," she responded, a

droll look in her eyes. But telling Griffin to sit, she walked off to pick up a couple more chairs.

While he, Hooper at his side, went to order their regular black coffees and mixed-fruit muffins.

Doug was glad to see that the chair remaining empty after he picked up their drinks and food was next to Elissa's. He first set Maisie's stuff on the table in front of her, then took his seat. "Sit, Hooper," he said, and of course his well-behaved, obedient—and smart— shepherd listened.

"He's lovely," Elissa said. "Is it okay to pet him?"

"Sure, in this kind of situation, when we're not on duty." He couldn't help grinning when he saw Hooper ease his head up to meet the gentle scratching that Elissa leveled on him behind his tall ears. Too bad he wasn't getting the same kind of treatment.

But good thing they were in a social setting here. If Elissa happened to be a civilian involved in some manner in one of their cases, no way could he even consider being attracted to her.

That was how it should be. It had additionally been drummed into both Maisie and him by their wonderful uncle Cy, who was also a cop.

"Like Doug said, we can't stay long," Maisie said before Doug had decided how to start a conversation. "But I've always had an interest in the possibility of having Griffin trained as a therapy dog for when he's too old to work as a K-9. He's a wonderful K-9, and he's been known to bring down a lot of bad guys, but he loves people, too."

"Well, if things work out and Elissa becomes our new therapy dog trainer," Amber said, "you're more than welcome to participate in one of her classes. No charge, either. You and your dogs have come through for me plenty in the past."

Doug shot a glance toward Elissa. Would she balk at the possibility of some students who didn't pay? He'd heard that therapy dog handlers were mostly just volunteers anyway, but Elissa was here interviewing for a job. Of course, she'd probably still get paid by Amber, who had often demonstrated what a good citizen and training supervisor she was during her fairly short career in that position here.

"Really?" Elissa said. "How?"

"I'll tell you all about it if things work out between us," Amber said.

"That gives me an even better reason to do a really good job at tomorrow's demonstration." Elissa's smile, first at Maisie and then at him, caused a slow sizzle to build inside him. That was emphasized even more when Elissa said to Amber, "Will the demo be just to you, or will others be present?" She shot a quick glance toward Doug that then landed on Maisie. To his surprise, he had a real urge to be at the K-9 Ranch tomorrow. Too bad he figured it wouldn't work out.

"Oh, my mother and some of my staff might be there, too," Amber replied.

"One in particular ought to be there," Doug added somewhat slyly. "How about your head trainer Evan?"

He knew of their mutual attraction and half expected her to blush a bit, or to attempt to stick a bland expression on her face, but instead Amber's grin widened. "Oh, absolutely," she said. Then she looked at Elissa. "He joined us recently after some really great demonstrations. And now he's continued to prove himself to be both a wonderful K-9 and pet dog trainer. He's our head trainer at the ranch, our only trainer right now, actually, though we're looking for others."

"Does he train therapy or service dogs or their handlers, too?" Elissa asked.

"No, although my dad, who was his predecessor, did a little work with therapy dogs." Amber's face looked sad for a moment, but she shook her head then smiled a little. "That's why we need you for the therapy angle," Amber continued. "Assuming, of course, that all goes well."

"Of course," Elissa said.

If Amber hired Elissa, Doug figured she would give her a quick rundown about the Chance K-9 Ranch's background—probably including how Amber's dad had been murdered in a then-unsolved case, and how Amber had come home to keep the ranch going for her mother and herself, without knowing anything about dog training.

She'd held tryouts, and Evan had won.

And she and Evan had managed to figure out together who'd killed Corbin Belott...

"I gather that you two won't be there to watch my demonstration," Elissa continued, "which is a shame. My pet and therapy dog Peace is also a golden." She reached over to caress Griffin's head, and Maisie's dog wagged his tail vigorously as he leaned toward the woman petting him.

"It is a shame." Maisie did appear sorry. "But you'll see Griffin and me again, to watch if and when you start your classes at the ranch. You can count on that."

"I will."

Doug noted that Elissa again aimed a brief gaze toward him, then looked once more at the dog whose head she stroked. If she was silently inquiring if he'd be around to observe future therapy classes, too, he would have thought his response would have been an unqualified no.

Before.

Now, he wasn't so sure.

But heck. It was time for Maisie and him to go. Sure, he found this new acquaintance charming and sexy and definitely of interest for the future—but she had yet to be hired and he might never see her again.

Too bad.

Well, hopefully she would land that job at the K-9 Ranch. There'd at least be a possibility of seeing her again then, though not as his or his dog's trainer.

He rose then. "Nice meeting you, Elissa." He offered his hand for a polite and noncommittal shake. When she grasped it firmly in hers, he had to resist pulling her close for a goodbye kiss.

Ridiculous. His mind was taunting him as if he was a sex-starved teenager.

As Maisie, too, said her goodbyes to Elissa and Amber, he nodded at the K-9 Ranch owner, then told Hooper, on his leash, to heel.

And couldn't help, at the coffee shop door, turning back and looking once more toward Elissa. Who was looking at him, too.

He nodded then turned.

It would probably be a good thing if she didn't land that job at the K-9 Ranch.

He wasn't ready for a new woman in his life. Probably wouldn't be for a long time, no matter how attractive he found someone.

But the thought of not seeing her again?

"Hey, bro," Maisie said as they and their dogs stepped out onto the sidewalk outside the coffee shop. "What's with your attitude toward that pretty dog trainer? You after some time alone with her?"

"Hey, you know me, sis. I'm always looking, sometimes scoring, and that's all fine with me."

"Well, just be careful." Maisie aimed her hazel-eyed gaze, so like his own, up at him as both dogs sat at their sides. "I've got a feeling that you'll be the loser, with the lowest score, in any game you play with that one."

Chapter 2

Elissa drove her black SUV down the narrow forest-surrounded mountain roads and reached the 101 Freeway on her way home fairly quickly. The traffic was moving well. If it continued like this, she would be home in fifteen minutes.

Although she'd put the radio on, the current music she preferred didn't keep her mind off her earlier meeting.

Or off the K-9 police officers—particularly one.

Well, so what if she'd had a momentary attraction to handsome Officer Doug Murran? And so what if she admired that he worked with a highly trained dog to protect people and catch bad guys? She had other things to think about.

She had caught up with a slow-moving big rig. Putting on her turn signal and checking carefully for other cars around her, she passed it.

And forced her mind back onto what she'd been thinking about earlier, when she had started her drive down the mountain. What she needed to think about.

Her demonstration tomorrow.

She'd talked a bit more about it with Amber, who was incredibly nice and knowledgeable. The kind of person Elissa could see herself working for and loving it.

Plus, she was wise. She'd known that new therapy dog handlers were usually volunteers who received free training from experienced handlers. She had therefore obtained a grant from a charitable organization focused on helping people in need to help pay for the more comprehensive lessons she would provide, starting from the basics. As a result, she had funds toward the salary of whoever she hired as a part-time instructor—hopefully Elissa—so the student handlers in training would only be asked to pay a token amount. Not that Elissa would get rich, either, but that was fine.

And Amber had also mentioned that she was writing a book on dog training with her chief trainer Evan Colluro. She wasn't sure when it would be done or how she'd get it published, but she wanted to include a chapter on therapy dogs and their handlers, so that would be another fun thing Elissa might get involved with.

Regarding tomorrow's demo, Amber had told her there would be other people present who would act as if they were in a hospital environment and could potentially be helped by a therapy dog. That would be fine with Elissa. It would allow her to show off what she, and Peace, could do and teach.

And if she was hired, she would need to learn more

about the local hospital as well as long-term-care centers, schools for special-needs children and other similar facilities around Chance where therapy dogs and their handlers would be welcome. She needed to know where she could take her students to show them how it worked and, when they and their dogs were trained well enough, to make use of what they learned.

Would that include Officer Maisie Murran? Elissa hoped so—both because she liked the woman and what she did, and because Maisie had indicated she'd like to participate, or at least watch.

Too bad her brother hadn't seemed interested.

Enough. Elissa had to erase Doug from her thoughts. She had only just met the guy. He might actually be the kind of person she would detest or despise.

Although she doubted it. How could a dog aficionado like him be so terrible…?

Good. She saw the sign for her exit in San Luis Obispo. It was about time.

A few minutes later she drove along the nearest major road toward her house. She soon pulled off onto her street and drove up the driveway to the small, aging stucco house she had rented. She'd found it almost immediately after she had moved here and, though she had some problems with its electrical system sometimes, she had remained, considering it home. Her landlord was nice, though slow to respond to her requests, and so far he hadn't raised the rent too much—*so far* being the operative words. He'd been hinting lately that a substantial increase would be imposed soon.

Elissa pushed the button to open the garage door and waited while it creaked upward till it stopped. She drove her SUV in, picked up her purse from the passenger seat and opened her door.

And expected to hear Peace's cheerful barks welcoming her home. That was what the sweet girl always did.

But not now.

Immediately, Elissa began to worry. Was Peace there? Was she okay?

Was Elissa worrying for nothing? After all, the poor dog could just be in a deep sleep at the far side of the house and not heard her.

But Elissa wanted to find out for herself. She pushed the button on the wall to close the garage door and used her key to unlock the windowed entry door beside it. She couldn't see into the kitchen because of the taut draperies on the inside of the door that she'd installed for privacy and security.

She hurried through the door into the cramped and outdated kitchen. Peace barked and leaped toward her on the dingy linoleum floor, then crouched and looked at Elissa. No longer barking, she began circling the kitchen. Its door into the house was shut, which was unusual, but Elissa sometimes closed it with Peace inside. She must have done so this morning.

That didn't explain Peace's actions. What was going on? This was all entirely uncharacteristic of her sweet and sociable dog.

"Peace, are you okay?" There were times she wished she could hold conversations with her lovable pup and this was one of them. Instead of stopping and sitting and acting normal, Peace sprinted out of the kitchen the moment Elissa opened the door.

Throwing her small purse down on the kitchen table, Elissa hurried to follow. Peace wasn't really a puppy, but nearly three years old. She was smart. She was fast. And Elissa felt exceptionally close to her thanks to their therapy work.

Right now Peace was popping into each room of the house as she reached it down the center hallway: the living room, the bathroom, the guest bedroom and then the master bedroom. She sometimes sniffed the floor, sometimes kept her nose on the ground, all the time appearing as if she was tracking something—and tracking wasn't one of the many skills she'd learned to become a therapy dog.

"Peace," Elissa kept saying softly, rubbing her dog's soft, furry back each time she got close enough. "What is it?"

Eventually, whether because of exhaustion or running out of places to explore, Peace stopped dashing around. She wound up in the living room, on the polished wood floor, next to the tan sofa on its deep-colored wooden frame. The colorations went well with Peace's golden coat—usually. Right now, the way Peace was panting, all Elissa could do was worry about her.

She knelt on the floor beside her dog, bending to hug her tightly. "Are you okay, girl? What's wrong?"

Of course Peace didn't answer.

Or maybe she did. She put her head up and licked Elissa's cheek.

Hopefully that meant she was all right now.

Elissa wasn't sure. And she would do everything she could to take the best care of her beloved dog.

It was early morning. Elissa was back in her SUV, driving up the mountain once more toward the Chance

K-9 Ranch. This time she wasn't alone. Peace was teth-ered safely in the back seat.

The sweet dog was quiet. Finally resting. Sleeping at last.

Elissa hadn't gone to bed for a while the previous night, still trying to understand her poor pup's contin-ued restlessness.

She'd taken Peace for a walk but only a short one, since her moderate-size dog pulled on her leash a lot, despite being told to heel and to stay—something else that wasn't characteristic of her.

Back inside the house Peace had again moved from room to room, as if seeking something. The source of some scent that only she, and not her concerned owner, was aware of?

That's what Elissa had guessed. And of course that worried her.

So neither of them had slept well. Each time Elissa had woken, which was often, she'd heard Peace stirring on her fluffy bed on the floor beside Elissa's.

Elissa used that as her reason to get up even earlier than she'd originally planned to walk Peace once more. The quiet residential area had seemed normal to her, with a few well-recognized neighbors outside, some also walking their dogs.

Peace had seemed somewhat calmer but still did more pulling than was usual for her.

Returning back inside, Elissa had showered, changed into the outfit she'd planned to wear for her demonstra-tion, then fed them both a quick breakfast and gotten on the road.

And made herself concentrate on how she would perform her demonstration—or, rather, the best way to encourage Peace to show off how wonderful a therapy dog she was.

It was early enough that traffic wasn't heavy, although, as always in this sometimes busy southern California area, she wasn't the only one on the road, either. She stayed just above the speed limit, though now and then another car had passed her on the freeway—less so on the narrower mountain roads.

Finally she reached the turnoff toward Chance. She decided to take a quick drive through downtown, past the local hospital.

As she slowed, Peace awakened and sat up. "Good girl," Elissa said, glancing in the rearview mirror. "Are you okay now?"

Peace was quiet and calm, and appeared like her usual self. Elissa took that to mean a positive response.

She soon stopped at a traffic light and turned onto the street that would take her past the hospital. When she'd looked it up on the internet and gotten the address, she had seen that there was an entire floor devoted to pediatric patients, and another area dedicated to seniors—both age groups that were excellent focuses for therapy dogs.

If all went well and Peace and she were hired, she would definitely introduce herself to the hospital administration and offer to do some demonstrations there soon.

The streets downtown seemed a bit crowded that morning but she had no problem navigating her way to the road to the Chance K-9 Ranch. She checked the time display on her dashboard.

"Looks perfect, Peace," she said and headed along the road.

She wondered then if Officer Maisie Murran would find a way to visit the demonstration even briefly despite her indication yesterday that she couldn't.

And her brother? He was even less likely to attend.

The road narrowed even more and Elissa kept an eye out for signs indicating addresses. As soon as she passed a large property labeled Chance Resort, she saw a signpost at the next driveway for the Chance K-9 Ranch.

They had arrived.

The ranch property was surrounded by a large plank fence that probably wouldn't keep anyone out but perhaps helped to keep dogs inside. The gate was open. Elissa drove through it and up the driveway. She saw other vehicles parked at the top of the rise near what unsurprisingly seemed to be a ranch house—one story high and extending for a substantial distance.

"Let's go," she told Peace after parking beside another SUV, a big black one that appeared to be an official police vehicle, with a light on top. Was one of the K-9 officers there after all? Or was it another cop?

Elissa exited through the driver's door, then opened the one behind it to let Peace out after snapping on her leash. When she turned, she was happy to see Amber exiting the house, holding the leash of a black Labrador retriever. A tall man came out after her, also leading a leashed dog, a German shepherd—Evan, the head dog trainer, whom Elissa recognized from the demonstration videos on the ranch's website. With them was an older woman Elissa figured must be Amber's mother. Sonya Belott. No surprises there.

But what did surprise her was that this group of anticipated people was followed by another person with a dog on a leash.

Officer Doug Murran and his German shepherd, Hooper.

What was he doing there? And why did Elissa's heart both soar and sink at the idea of his watching her initial therapy dog demonstration?

There she was—the reason Doug had brought his dog to the Chance K-9 Ranch early this morning, even though he had determined yesterday not to come here at all.

And his presence was definitely not for the reason he'd even considered coming.

No, he was here on official police business.

A sign had been attached to the front gate near the road that had worried the Belotts enough to call the police and request that he or Maisie be sent to the ranch that morning. Maisie had already left for their previously assigned case, so it had fallen on him.

He'd just finished talking to Amber Belott and her mother, Sonya, as well as chief dog trainer—and Amber's fiancé—Evan Colluro inside the house. Now he followed as they strode out to greet Elissa.

He couldn't help liking the big grin on her face or the way she stepped forward and hugged Amber. Her hostess and potential boss introduced her to her mother and to Evan as well as to their dogs.

He saw her eyes shift slightly in his direction more than once. He didn't think her smile was for him, which was fine. He kept his expression blank.

But he was looking forward to seeing her reaction to the reason he had been called out to the K-9 Ranch.

Still, the decision had been made to proceed with the

demonstration that had brought Elissa to the ranch and to ignore, at least temporarily, the reason he was there.

He'd been asked by Amber to not only observe but to also help in the demonstration. He would pretend to be someone recuperating from an injury who was under a lot of psychological stress and needed soothing, perhaps by a therapy dog. Amber had said that Evan and her employee, ranch hand Orrin Daker, who was sometimes used as an agitator in K-9 training situations, would also participate.

That didn't mean Doug shouldn't at least be polite and greet her. "Hi, Elissa," he said after the other introductions had ended. "And hi, Peace." He'd heard her introduce her dog to the others, too, but he didn't bend to pet her. Not when he was soon going to act like he needed some canine TLC from this therapy dog.

Besides, he now had even more reason not to allow his initial attraction to this lovely woman turn into anything. She was potentially involved in the case he'd just been assigned to handle.

But he felt a surge of warmth inside when she returned, "Good morning, Doug. And Hooper, too."

Interestingly, her dog Peace got up close and personal with Hooper, her tail wagging furiously as she sniffed his shepherd's face. Hooper seemed fine with it, sniffing and wagging back a bit. Good thing he wasn't officially on duty at the moment.

"Okay, we'll get started," Amber said. "I'd planned to have some neighbors' kids come over, but…well, things have changed. We'll just do a demonstration with adults. Come this way." She led them all back into the house.

With Hooper, Doug stayed back and held the door open for Elissa and her dog. "So you need the warmth

of a therapy dog today?" she asked with a smile as she
went past him, but he also saw puzzlement in her deep
brown eyes. Yesterday she'd been somewhat dressed
up. Today her outfit consisted of a blue plaid shirt over
jeans—a look that seemed comfortable for her but might
also help put stressed people at ease. Or at least that was
what Doug assumed.

Soon Amber got the three men lined up in the living
room, leaving her mother holding the leashes of Hooper,
Evan's dog Bear, and Amber's Labrador retriever Lola
at the far end of the room. Fortunately they were all
well trained. Doug wasn't sure how Sonya, a somewhat fragile-looking senior, would do with aggressive
or even eager dogs.

"Okay," Amber said to Elissa. "Assume these three
guys were in the military and suffer from PTSD." She
looked toward Evan, who smiled at her. Doug knew
that the statement was accurate as far as Amber's guy
was concerned. "They need a bit of TLC and soothing
from a really good therapy dog. Show me how you and
Peace would handle it."

As far as Doug could tell—without knowing more
about how therapy dogs worked—they handled it well,
including him. First, Elissa knelt and tied a blue scarf
that said "Therapy Dog" around Peace's neck. Then,
on direction from Elissa, Peace went up to each guy
individually, sat before him on the floor to be petted,
walked carefully around him while sidling against his
legs, and acted wholly engaged and pleased, even wagging her tail, as each of the men knelt and hugged her—
or, in Evan's case, pretended to ignore her until the last
moment.

There was more to it, too. Doug was impressed, especially as Elissa explained with each movement, each command, just how that was intended to help calm a nervous, scared or psychologically impaired person. But mostly she left it to her dog to interact with the supposed needy human.

And who wouldn't be soothed by a loving, caring dog? Especially one trained, and handled, by someone as apparently loving and caring as Elissa?

Heck, he thought as he once again sat on the wood floor and pretended to mope as Peace came over and nuzzled him. He had to remind himself yet again that he knew far better than to even think of getting involved with someone entwined in a case.

And now it appeared that Elissa was exactly that.

Even Orrin, who must be used to being given all sorts of strange things to do here as a ranch hand, seemed to enjoy Peace's attention. He was a young, strong guy wearing a red Chance T-shirt. Even as he pretended to be sad and sick, he wound up petting and hugging Peace as the dog lavished attention on him.

Then it was Doug's turn. "Okay, dog," he said gruffly. "What if I don't want your attention?"

"That's exactly why you need her attention," Elissa said softly. "She wants you to hug her."

Which Doug found himself doing with the furry, snuggling golden.

The demonstration went on a while longer. Eventually, Elissa also gave Amber and Lola a brief lesson on how the Lab could also be trained to be a therapy dog.

Amber seemed to have gotten everything accomplished that she wanted to. "Okay," she said when her lesson was finished. "Good job, Elissa and Peace. Let's go into the kitchen, shall we?"

She unobtrusively motioned for Doug and the others to stay there, in the living room, while she led Elissa and Peace through the door. In a couple of minutes she returned and requested that Orrin get back to work. The ranch hand left.

"She's good," Amber said once he was gone. "Real good. Her explanations to people as well as working well with her dog… I want to hire her no matter what."

"I don't like the idea." Evan drew himself to her side. "No matter how good she is."

"Me neither," said Sonya, staring at her daughter.

"But that sign really didn't say anything." Amber directed her gaze toward Doug. "Did it? Is it really a threat? I know what real threats are like."

Doug was well aware that Amber had received text messages not long ago containing some really nasty threats. Fortunately, that situation was now resolved. "We don't know enough yet," he said. "I'm just beginning our investigation."

"Well, we'll all be aware and be careful. But I don't intend for some stupid, unclear sign to make me change my mind regarding something I feel strongly about. She'll only be here part-time anyway." And with that, Amber pulled away, turned and left the living room.

"Then you'll really have to help us," Sonya said pleadingly to Doug.

"I'll do all I can," he promised. But he was definitely concerned—about the Belotts and others who lived at the ranch, their dogs and now also about Elissa.

He might not be able to act at all on his initial attraction to her. But neither did he want her, or her dog, to be harmed.

"For now, I'll join you while you talk with Elissa,

and just listen in. We've already secured the sign and locked it in the back of my car."

They'd wrapped it in plastic carefully so as not to obscure any fingerprints or other evidence.

The sign had been hooked onto the gate down by the road that morning when Amber and Evan had first gone outside to walk their dogs. They didn't always walk that way but Evan had noticed something a bit off at the upper driveway.

The sign read Be Careful Who You Hire. It was a small cardboard sign, hung on the gate by the road with string and not too obvious. The dogs hadn't alerted on it, either.

But it wasn't something Doug, or the Chance Police Department, would ignore.

Chapter 3

Like the rest of the house that she'd seen, the kitchen seemed utilitarian yet attractive to Elissa. A tiled floor and counters, too, lent themselves to being scrubbed clean despite the abundance of dogs undoubtedly brought in here. The metal sink and refrigerator were large, and the stove, with the microwave attached to the wall over it, was more moderate in size.

Sitting on a stiff chair at the round kitchen table with Peace lying on the floor near her, Elissa made herself look over the paperwork Amber had left for her to review. It described the Chance K-9 Ranch, its history and goals, as well as the contract she would be expected to sign if she was hired.

Interesting stuff, but she couldn't help wondering how the conversation in the living room was going.

She assumed they were all analyzing her therapy dog

demonstration as well as the brief training lesson she'd provided. That was expected since they were considering hiring her.

Or at least Amber, her mother and their lead trainer were.

But what was Doug Murran doing there? A K-9 officer didn't necessarily know anything about therapy dogs. Nor had Elissa thought he or his sister would attend today, but there he was.

She hadn't anticipated seeing him again anytime soon, if at all. Of course, if she was hired and spent more time in Chance, there was always that possibility.

A thought struck her. He was a cop. He knew dogs. Maybe she could ask him…

"Hi, Elissa." Amber strode into the room with Lola at her feet. They were followed by Sonya. Both women sat at the table, facing her, and Elissa felt her heart speed up. Would they make her an offer—or would they thank her and usher her out the door?

It was the former and she was thrilled! "We understand you have a nursing job in San Luis Obispo," Amber began, "and that works out fine with us as long as you don't mind the commute. We'd like to hire you part-time, for about eight hours a week, at least to start. That means you could spend four hours a day here for the two days you're not at your hospital each week. If you're okay with that, we'll work out the schedule, how we'll bring in students and other details."

"That's great," Elissa said. "I'll give you the general training parameters so you can decide which students might work best, and their dogs, too. We can start working with younger dogs and maybe take them to therapy venues for practice, but they have to be at least a year old before we can actually get them qualified."

"Great. We'll need your input on that." Amber made notes in a folder she was holding. "I've already posted info on social media about plans for an upcoming class and received some nibbles from potential students, so we'll be able to start quickly."

"Another thing—do you have any contacts at the local hospital?" Elissa asked. "Before branching out to other facilities, I'll want to see if Peace and I can do a little therapy work there, as well as use it as a potential teaching location once we get handlers in our classes trained enough to actually start therapy work with their dogs."

"Actually, I do," Sonya said. "One of the senior nurses on staff is a good friend of mine."

"Excellent," Elissa said.

"Now let's talk some details like salary, timing, benefits and all." Amber smiled at Elissa, who could only grin back. She wouldn't get rich at this, she was sure, even with the grant that Amber had said she'd obtained. But Elissa had her other job to pay for the basics. The main thing was that this was something she really wanted to do.

Fortunately, those details as Amber described them worked well for Elissa. Today was Friday, and they determined that Elissa would actually start working there the following Monday.

That would give her time to put more hours in at the San Luis Obispo hospital. She had already arranged to be there over the weekend, partly because she was due to work then and partly to make up for the couple of days she'd just taken off.

She had looked over the contract and found the terms acceptable, so she and Amber both signed it.

Soon, they were done. They had a deal. But they both had provisions for getting out. Nothing was etched in stone, and Elissa realized she would be somewhat on trial here at first.

Which was fine with her. She'd also have to weigh whether this new part-time job would be worth it for her.

She felt certain it would be. She had loved the idea of the Chance K-9 Ranch for a while, and now she would be part of it. And the very idea of training therapy dogs and their handlers? Wonderful!

Amber soon stood, as did Sonya. Elissa did the same, smiling as both Peace and Lola, too, stood on the kitchen floor.

"Lola's a sweetheart," she said to Amber. "I think she'd make a good therapy dog."

Amber's smile broadened. "I look forward to your training her more, too."

Soon, they were all outside on the ranch's front porch—which was where Evan was with his dog Bear and Doug was with Hooper. They were sitting on a couple of the beige sling chairs, talking.

With the two German shepherds so close together, Elissa noticed even more the similarities and differences between them. Hooper was lighter in color and appeared thinner and, perhaps, younger. Bear had more black in his fur and his ears were more pointed and mobile.

Both appeared to be alert, caring and smart dogs. Which was a good thing, especially with Hooper, who had a K-9 job to do. But she wondered about Bear's background—and his owner, Evan's, too. Military maybe? The ranch website hadn't said. But Elissa noticed that Evan sometimes seemed uncomfortable looking straight into people's faces as he spoke to them, so perhaps he had a mild case of PTSD.

The men stood. "Everything work out?" Evan asked.

"Yes," Amber said. "Elissa will start working here on Monday."

"Great." Evan strolled over and held out his hand for Elissa to shake, which she did.

She then glanced at Doug. He was nodding as if in approval, although he then aimed what appeared to be a long, questioning look toward Amber.

"It *is* great." Her tone sounded stubborn and Elissa wondered what that was about.

"Well, Peace and I will be off for now, then," Elissa said. "We'll look forward to coming back here on Monday." She turned to head down the steps toward her SUV and was glad to see that Doug and Hooper appeared to be accompanying her.

She quickly recalled the thought she'd had a while earlier. This guy was a cop. He was involved with dogs.

Maybe he would have an idea…

They'd reached her vehicle. She waited to open the rear door to strap Peace in, turning to Doug. Before she could ask him anything, though, he began talking.

"Hey, I have a couple of questions for you. Would you mind meeting me in town for coffee before you leave so we can discuss them?"

He had questions for her? Interesting. She had questions for him, too. "Sounds good," she said.

But she wondered how good it really would be.

They drove separately, so that gave Doug time to consider his approach as he navigated first the winding roads then the busier ones into town.

He didn't particularly want to hit Elissa over the head with the contents of that warning to her new employers. In fact, he wasn't sure he'd mention it directly at all. At least not yet.

But he wanted to talk to her, to get an idea why she'd decided to seek a job at the ranch—and whether there was something in her life, some*one* in her life, who'd known about it and didn't like the idea.

He found a parking spot near the front of the coffee shop where he'd first met Elissa and pulled in, not needing to use the cop card to park in a spot regular citizens couldn't. Since he saw Elissa pull into another space not far from him, he didn't have to try to preserve one for her.

Once he got Hooper out of the back, he walked to the front of the shop and was quickly joined by Elissa and Peace. "I figure K-9s are allowed everywhere," she said, looking up at Doug, a somewhat quizzical expression on her lovely face, "and I hope they'll be okay with Peace joining me, too. She's not a service dog with an identification vest or anything, although I could put on her scarf—but even so, therapy dogs aren't always given the same respect."

"Don't worry about it," Doug told her. "I've seen other dogs in this place, too. The owners seem to love them and look the other way even if the law isn't on the side of canine customers."

"And I assume that at least one particular lawman turns a blind eye to that kind of violation." She stuck a solemn expression onto her face that quickly morphed into a smile, and he smiled back.

"Maybe so." He held the front door open for her and

her dog as Hooper followed his hand signal and sat beside him. Then he followed her in.

It was late afternoon and the Chance Coffee Shop always seemed to have a crowd. Today was no different but fortunately there were a few tables near the wall that they could choose from—good locations where their dogs wouldn't get in the way of servers or other patrons. He allowed Elissa to lead the way then, as she sat, asked what she wanted.

"I'll go get our stuff," he said. "You hold this table—and Hooper will help you." He told his dog to sit, which of course he did, near both Elissa and Peace, who immediately started wagging her tail eagerly and sniffing at Hooper.

Doug wasn't surprised when Elissa requested he get her a café mocha. "But either let me pay for it or plan on getting together with me for coffee again when I can treat."

He liked the latter idea—although he shouldn't. But maybe they could get together again sometime soon to figure out the origin and meaning of that sign at the ranch, if she didn't suggest a viable explanation to him now.

That would most likely be the only reason he'd allow himself to see more of her. Unless, of course, Maisie loved learning about therapy dogs enough that she convinced him to join her.

He had to wait in line for about three minutes. During that time, he turned back often to look toward Elissa, only to discover she was watching him, too—with one hand on each of the dogs' heads.

What was she thinking?

And how was he going to approach the questions he needed to ask her?

So what was this really about? Elissa wondered. She did find Doug appealing and thought that he, too, might feel some attraction between them—but she didn't think that was why he'd asked her to have coffee with him.

What were his questions?

He soon returned to their table and placed a medium-size cup of mocha in front of her. As far as she could tell, he'd chosen the same size black coffee.

Plus, he'd brought a bowl with water in it, which he placed on the floor near the dogs.

He was a considerate guy, then, including as far as dogs were concerned.

When he sat, he looked at her as he took a sip from his cup. The expression in those hazel eyes of his looked particularly intense, especially since his brow was furrowed, arching his thick brown eyebrows even more.

Even more curious now, Elissa thanked him for the mocha, took a sip of the rich brew and then waited for him to speak.

"So what made you decide to apply for the job at the K-9 Ranch?" he finally asked. "Especially on a part-time basis, so far from your home and regular job?"

Why did he want to learn that? She didn't ask, though. Instead she replied, "Impulse, of sorts—though I'm not really an impulsive person. But the Chance K-9 Ranch has such a wonderful reputation. At least it did when its original owner, Corbin Belott, was there. And now I've seen all sorts of praise online about how it's coming back, how so many police K-9s are being trained along with their handlers—and even great pet training, too, despite its rather remote location. I love its website and the demonstrations shown there, too. When I saw they were looking for someone to work with therapy dog handlers, I thought, 'Hey, that's me,' so here I am."

She smiled at him. That wasn't really all of it, of course. She'd worked with some wonderful therapy dog trainers and handlers before but had been looking for a different direction, something even more special as an adjunct to the part of her life devoted to nursing and helping ill and injured people medically…and psychologically, which really appealed to her. And what was more psychologically helpful to those in need than therapy dogs?

If she could help a lot more caring people to gain appropriate credentials with their dogs in a setting like the K-9 Ranch, well, then, she had to do it. Providing ongoing classes sounded wonderful.

"I see," Doug said, though his expression was now somewhat blank, as if he didn't see at all. "And are all the people where you work as a nurse on board with you doing this?"

Puzzlement flooded through her. Why would he ask that? "Those who know about it seem fine with it." Would they continue to when she had to negotiate more about the days and hours she'd be available? That was unknown, but she'd deal with it.

"That's good. So all's well with you, and Peace, and you are both fine with your becoming trainers here in Chance?"

"Yes." She knew her response sounded short and frustrated—but maybe it was because his questions had started a stirring in her, a reminder of yesterday and her return home to find Peace acting so strange.

Not that it had ever really left her thoughts.

"Yes," she repeated. "Although…" She let her word trail off, knowing she should only act completely sure of herself. But heck, she was in the presence of a cop, a dog-loving one at that. Maybe he would have some ideas about how she could figure out what had bothered her dog yesterday.

"Although what?" he prompted.

"Look, this probably has nothing at all to do with my interviewing for a job here, but the problem is that I don't have a clue about the reason. Yesterday, when I returned home after interviewing for the job with Amber, my usually sweet, calm, loving dog Peace acted really strange."

Interest and concern seemed to take over Doug's expression. Did he really give a damn? "Strange how?"

She described how Peace had behaved, from her barking to roving from room to room and not even acting completely calm after they'd taken their walk and gone to bed. "I didn't see anything unusual to cause her to act that way. But it was so uncharacteristic. I wondered whether, if I brought another dog in, I'd get any similar reaction, if there was some scent in my home that was causing it, but I didn't want to alert any of my friends to something that probably meant absolutely nothing."

"Or maybe it actually meant something."

Then Doug believed her? Gave a damn?

Was his interest part of some kind of flirtation?

She didn't think so. He seemed too serious, too professional as a cop.

"I just wish I knew," she responded.

"Well, how about if Hooper and I accompany Peace and you back to your home and I let my very special K-9 have a sniff around?"

Chapter 4

Doug followed Elissa in her black SUV down the 101 Freeway in his large police vehicle and wished he'd driven her, or even ridden with her, so they'd be in the same car, able to talk. Though he wanted to check out her place to try to figure out if her dog's actions were in some way related to the sign found on the K-9 Ranch, he had no intention of staying in San Luis Obispo for long. Therefore he'd needed a set of wheels so he could leave when he wanted to.

As it was, he was stretching his claim of still being on duty, though he had reported to his commanding officer to let her know where he was going and why, as well as an estimate of the time he'd return. She'd given him permission to continue working on this matter, even if it meant he could not take on the other case he and Maisie had been previously assigned to look into.

He'd also called on his cell phone as he'd taken off after Elissa to let Maisie know where he was going, and his sister had sounded anything but pleased.

"She's caught up in a case now," she had told him. "You know better than to get involved with her in any way other than professionally."

"That's all I'm doing," he had attempted to assure Maisie. "She had a problem at her home that could be connected with our investigation at the K-9 Ranch."

"Which itself isn't much of a case," Maisie had retorted. "A possible threat with no substance to it."

"But you know the department's position about Amber Belott and the Chance K-9 Ranch," he'd reminded her. "She helped us solve her own father's murder, and the current view is that we owe her. So we need to find out if that threat is legit, and who placed it there and why. That's what I'm working on."

"Sure," Maisie had said, and they'd quickly ended the call.

Fortunately the traffic wasn't bad so they reached Elissa's home fairly quickly. "Okay, boy," Doug said to Hooper after parking along the street and getting his dog out of the back. "You're on." No need to put Hooper's official vest on him for this, though he'd be on duty—kind of.

And Doug was curious whether even a trained police K-9 would find a reason for Peace's alleged odd behavior. It was probably nothing. Under other circumstances, Doug wouldn't have given it a second thought, let alone take a substantial chunk out of his day to check it out.

But behind it all was that potentially threatening sign: Be Careful Who You Hire.

The driveway Elissa had pulled into was narrow and

led to the garage of a house that appeared to have been there for a while. Its stucco seemed worn, and it looked a lot more rundown than its nearby neighbors. That surely had nothing to do with Peace's actions yesterday—or did it? Maybe someone was trying to do something to scare this tenant away so the house could be torn down and replaced with something newer and fancier.

Doug left his jacket in the car, wearing just his white cop shirt with his uniform pants. He hurried down the driveway of the house with Hooper's leash in his hand. Elissa had exited her SUV but seemed to be taking her time getting Peace out of the back.

Because she was concerned about the dog's reaction?

Because she wanted Doug to be there when she let the dog in?

In any event, she didn't open the door to the house but motioned for Doug to follow her to the lawn. "It's been a long drive. I want to let Peace decide if she needs some outdoor time."

Which she did, and so did Hooper. When both dogs were finished, Doug said, "Okay, let's go in."

"Of course." But Elissa appeared anything but thrilled about the idea.

Still, Peace's leash in her hand, she returned to the garage and used a key to open the door into the house. Doug, with Hooper, followed—and immediately saw Peace's strange reaction as they walked into the kitchen. The golden had seemed nice and gentle and reserved... before. Now she pulled ahead, yanking on her leash so hard that she nearly pulled Elissa behind her.

Nose to the floor, she walked in circles, growling occasionally, looking as if she was tracking something down.

Beside Doug, Hooper looked up at him as if waiting for his command—which he quickly gave.

"Find," he told his K-9. He released Hooper from his leash, determined to follow the dog no matter where he went in the house.

At first, Hooper appeared to follow in Peace's paw prints, but not for long. Soon he leaped out of the kitchen before the dog who lived there, nose still to the ground.

Was he following a scent—the smell of some animal that had gotten inside?

A human animal? One other than Elissa?

One who didn't belong and emitted a scent of fear?

Doug glanced toward Elissa, who stood in the hall. Peace now appeared to be following Hooper. "What is he doing?" Elissa's whisper was loud and sounded afraid.

Doug had an urge to put an arm around her in comfort, but that wouldn't solve anything—like figuring out what was happening.

"He's following a scent," Doug answered. "That might be what disturbed Peace yesterday, although I can't tell you what kind of scent it is—at least not yet."

"But…could it be—"

"I don't want to speculate." But she looked so forlorn and frightened that he did approach Elissa and put an arm around her. "Let's follow and see what he finds."

He was impressed by the nice furnishings in this old, beat-up home. Obviously, Elissa's tastes were good, even if she hadn't rented something a bit more modern.

Maybe she couldn't afford to.

Maybe she'd hoped that working at the K-9 Ranch part-time might increase her income enough that she could eventually find something nicer.

There was a lot about this woman that he didn't know. Shouldn't want to know. But he did.

Together, they followed the dogs, who both seemed to go from room to room now—the living room, what appeared to be a guest bedroom, a single bathroom and then the master bedroom.

Which was where Hooper bounded toward one of the windows that was covered by a closed shade.

"Was this open yesterday?" Doug asked before touching it.

"No, although I did look at it and the other windows in here after Peace acted so strangely, to make sure they weren't open."

"Well, let's check it out." Doug removed gloves from his pocket and put them on to avoid messing up any prints if there actually was something wrong here, and pulled on the rope at the side to open the shade.

Nothing. The window was closed, as Elissa had said.

But that didn't stop Hooper from jumping up and reacting, indicating to Doug that whatever the scent the two dogs had been chasing, this was most likely the place of origin, at least at first.

"Hooper, sit." When his dog obeyed, he added, "Good boy."

Since Peace was still beside him, he looked at Elissa, who took her dog's leash and led her away.

Which gave Doug the opportunity to look more closely at the window.

And to find what he had somewhat anticipated on the lock at the top of the bottom piece of glass along the window frame.

It appeared that some kind of tool had been inserted

to unlock it, judging by the barely visible wearing away of the metal and glass.

Carefully, Doug worked at the window and found it opened with almost no effort at all. Opened enough so that someone outside could have gotten in—and someone who'd managed to get inside could get out.

"Bingo," he said.

Standing behind him, watching what he did, Elissa felt herself shudder in shock, though she realized it shouldn't be a total surprise.

Forcing herself into steadiness, she bent slightly to stroke and attempt to calm Peace, who also quivered, though possibly because she wanted to run and not just sit there. Elissa loved Peace, trusted her, and the dog's actions yesterday had been a loud statement of something going on around here, though Elissa hadn't known what. She still didn't.

Now another dog, trained for more appropriate ways to look into the situation, had confirmed that something was not right.

"Can you tell from Hooper's actions if someone actually came inside and what they did?" Elissa hated that her voice came out as a soft croak but she wasn't surprised.

She was stressed.

She was scared.

Doug turned and aimed an ironic half grin toward her. "Possibly. But rely on your own dog, too. I'd say whoever it was managed to walk around your entire house. Your Peace already told you that."

She nodded. "Yes," she said, "she did. But why?"

"I'd suggest you look around and see if any valuables are missing."

"What valuables?" This time she did manage an ironic smile of her own.

"Okay, then, non-valuables. Whatever you own or keep here."

She had a sudden urge to explain herself to this man, this cop who had traveled a long distance to try to help her. For a variety of reasons, mostly involving how she had been brought up by her frugal family, she tried to save more of her nursing salary than she spent—though that didn't always work. The extra income from her new part-time gig at the K-9 Ranch was bound to help a little.

But mostly, she liked helping people and using therapy dogs was one of her favorite ways to do so.

All she said now was, "I'm not really into bling, and I don't keep cash around, so whoever was here probably didn't find anything to take."

But she'd keep checking, just in case. Still, she couldn't help wondering why her house had been a target. Had others around here been broken into, too? She didn't know many of her neighbors well, but she'd have to ask them.

"Well, the person who broke in might not have known that." But Doug's expression, when he turned to look at her, suggested that he somehow wanted to dig inside her head for some answers.

Answers she didn't have.

"Possibly," she said.

"Okay, then. I'll let Hooper take another swing around the place and see if he reacts to anything else. And by the way, I will speculate now that the scent he reacted to was fear—fear of getting caught as an intruder. After Hooper's done this time…well, do you have any friends you can stay with tonight?"

She had made friends in the years she had lived in San Luis Obispo, though not that many, and none particularly close.

With the vocation and avocations she had, even she found that a bit surprising. But as much as she liked to help people, she'd learned the hard way that getting close to anyone, even friends, wasn't always a good idea.

"No," she said lightly, "but I'll be fine here. Whoever broke in is unlikely to do it again. They already know there's nothing here worth stealing. And they've already been inside, so why try it again?"

"But—" Whatever he'd started to say, Doug seemed to catch himself. "Okay, let Hooper and me do our thing. Then we'll talk."

Why did even the mention of a talk with this man make her feel uneasy? He'd come here to help her, and so far he really had. Whatever they'd talk about, it would have nothing to do with the fact that she found him attractive. More than attractive. A truly brave and genuinely kind man who clearly took his job of policing, helping people, to heart.

"Sure," she said, trying to act completely nonchalant. "Let me know when you're ready. Peace and I will wait in the kitchen."

For the next ten minutes Elissa sat at the square kitchen table sipping on a bottle of water she'd taken out of the small but adequate fridge that had come with the house. She'd get a bottle out for Doug when he joined her. She had already set out a container of shortbread cookies that she occasionally brought along to her therapy sessions with kids. The sweets sometimes made them smile and become even more receptive to interacting with a caring dog.

After checking Peace's water bowl on the scratched yellow linoleum floor near the door to the hall, she'd also retrieved some healthy dog treats. She gave her smart, caring dog a few, partly in gratitude for her having let Elissa know about the intruder in the first place, and partly because she just wanted to keep her companion happy.

But why had there even been an intruder...?

In a few minutes Hooper came into the kitchen followed by Doug, who still held the end of the leash. After the two dogs traded nose sniffs, Hooper went to the bowl and started lapping up some water. Elissa rose and got Doug a bottle of water, which she placed on the table near the seat across from her.

"Here," she said. "I've got some treats for both Hooper and you." She tried to sound like a good hostess, as if his being there was because she'd invited him—not because she'd needed him and his cop senses.

"Thanks," he said, taking a seat. He picked up the water, removed the cap and took a swig, as if it were something stronger, which sort of amused her. Or maybe she'd be attracted to anything this kind man did while in her company, particularly here at her no-longer-private house. Then he looked at the table in front of her, at the dog treats and the packaged cookies, and asked, "Which ones are for me?"

She laughed. "Whichever you want, though I'd suggest these." She pushed the shortbread container across the table to him. "Is it okay if I reward Hooper with some of these?" She gestured at the dog treats.

"Sure it is, right now. Not when he's searching, though."

Both Hooper and Peace seemed happy when Elissa gave them treats. "Good dogs," she said, and they both were.

When she had given them each their share, she looked back up at Doug, who seemed awfully quiet. He was watching her. She couldn't read the expression on his handsome, craggy, all-too-intense face, but it made her shudder inside. What was he thinking?

As if she'd said something aloud to prompt him, he asked, "Do you know of anyone who might want to harm you—or even just intimidate you?"

She blinked. "No. Not at all." But the idea seemed to increase her internal shivers. "Is that what you think it is—someone who wants to scare or even hurt me, not just try to steal from me?"

He didn't answer directly, at least not at first. "Before I leave here, I'll contact the local PD, communicate to someone there about what happened and request they send a crime scene team over right now—which they might do more as an accommodation to another cop than because of their concern about the alleged crime. They'll then probably start patrolling your street every hour or so, although if you don't have any ideas who it might be, maybe they won't. In any event, I'll make sure that the vulnerable area where whoever it was got in before is sealed up."

"Thank you." Elissa did feel a lot of gratitude to this determined police officer—that and some highly un-wanted attraction. *He's just doing his job, protecting a civilian*, she reminded herself. Even so... "Is there any-thing else I should do?" Besides scream and run away.

She would do neither.

But she would, as usual, keep Peace by her side. Her dog might not have the same kind of training as an official police K-9, but she would protect Elissa to the best of her ability. Elissa was sure of it.

There seemed to be something else on Doug's mind, though. He was studying her, watching her face as if he could see inside her brain.

For a long moment he said nothing, which made her even more uneasy. Then he said, "I'd like for you to keep thinking about whether anyone has suggested or even hinted that they have issues with you or what you do—or don't do." He reached into his pocket, brought out a business card and handed it to her. "I want you to stay in touch, let me know if you see or hear anything that seems suspicious. In any case, I'll talk to you on Monday after you come back to Chance and we'll see how things are going then."

"Okay." She wanted to disagree, to tell him she'd be fine and that there was no need for him to worry about her—but she somehow felt a little less stressed that he seemed to give a damn, just because he was a good cop, of course, and not because he seemed at all attracted to her.

And she'd have to make sure her own silly attraction disappeared.

But there appeared to be something else on his mind. He was looking so intensely into her eyes…

"What?" she asked.

"Like I said, think hard about whether there's someone who might have something against you. A neighbor or coworker who's mad at you. A driver you cut off. Whatever."

"Why?" she demanded. "What's really going on?"

He pursed his lips. "Yeah, I think you should know, though I was asked to keep it quiet. Amber, for one, was choosing to ignore it. But this break-in here…"

"What?" Elissa repeated.

Doug looked straight into her eyes. "The night of your interview at the K-9 Ranch, and before you came back up to give your demonstration, this was found on the fence there." He pulled his phone from his pocket, fiddled with it some and then thrust it toward her.

A photo was there depicting the front gate up the driveway to the main house at the K-9 Ranch.

And on it was a sign: Be Careful Who You Hire.

Chapter 5

Doug watched Elissa's expression carefully. No hint of knowledge or recognition appeared in the horror displayed by her huge eyes and open mouth.

"How terrible!" she exclaimed. "I don't think Amber was close to hiring anyone else, so that must refer to me. And yet she hired me anyway. Why? But I'm so glad she did. Who could have left that? Was it the same person who broke in here?"

"We don't know…yet," Doug answered truthfully. "Any of the answers. But frankly, that's one reason I came here to try to help you figure out what happened with Peace. You appear to be on at least one person's radar, and we need to figure out who—and why." Both dogs started barking then, and Doug figured he knew the reason. "I suspect the local cops are here."

The nearly immediate ringing of the doorbell indi-

cated he was right. He initially stepped outside with
Hooper to greet them and tell them what was going on.
They didn't seem too impressed but as a professional
accommodation to Doug one of them radioed in to request a crime scene team, then both entered to look
around and interview Elissa.

They were quick and efficient, including the crime
scene investigators, who arrived fairly quickly.

What they were not was fortunate enough to come up
with any answers. Apparently the perpetrator had worn
gloves—no surprise. No other evidence was found,
either. They promised to send patrols by frequently,
without saying how often. Then, after exchanging contact information with Doug—and patting Hooper and
Peace—the two officers and crime scene folks left.

"Let's go back into the kitchen," Doug suggested.
He needed to leave, too. But he also needed to try once
more to get Elissa to see reason.

"Sure," she said. "Only, I suspect you need to get
back to Chance to actually do some of your own police work." They both remained standing near the door,
and the look she shot him appeared ironic with a hint of
gratitude. "I'll be fine now. As I said earlier, the intruder
isn't likely to come back, especially with the extra police car patrols those officers promised. And now that
I'm aware, I'll be particularly careful. There is, in fact,
one neighbor I can call on who sometimes walks her
dog with Peace and me. I'll at least have company, and
it would be harder for someone to harm two of us instead of just me."

"Well, that's better than nothing but—"

"Look, I don't know why Amber hired me, but she's
clearly not giving in to whoever did this. Well, neither

am I. I'll try to get my landlord to have some kind of security system installed, but in any event, as I said, I'll be careful. And I'm not giving in to someone trying to scare me." But she seemed to wilt a little then. "I just wish I had some idea who it is, and why."

"Yeah, me, too." He had a sudden urge to take her into his arms, hold her tightly against him, maybe attempt to cheer her a little by kissing that alluring yet sad mouth of hers...

But of course he wouldn't do that. Never mind that he felt attracted to her, or that he wanted to fix things for her. He had plenty of reasons not to get involved with her other than as a civilian who needed help. But she did happen to be a civilian who needed help.

A vision of his uncle Cy's face flashed in his mind, encouraging him and Maisie to become cops like him—and to act like professionals at all times. And never, ever, to get involved except as cops with any of those civilians they were bound to be seeing a lot of as crime victims or otherwise.

Cy had gotten involved, more than once, and, after professional scolding and even a divorce, had learned to regret it...

"Anyway," she said, "I'll be working at my local hospital tomorrow and Sunday, both as a nurse and doing therapy dog work, so I won't be home much this weekend. Then I'll head back up to Chance on Monday to give my first therapy dog training class. I'll call you then and maybe we can catch up on what's going on here and there."

"All right," Doug conceded. What else could he do? He might be concerned about this attractive, dog-loving civilian, but he wasn't even a cop in the jurisdiction where she lived who could theoretically give her orders—or at least conduct some of those patrols and drop in on her sometimes.

And he clearly wasn't convincing her to do something else—except to walk her dog along with a neighbor. Some of the time. Without additional protection at night.

"Well, be sure to keep in touch." He recognized that his words had come out in a tone of command, which appeared somehow to amuse her.

He wanted to kiss that smile right off her lovely face…but didn't.

He motioned for Hooper to join him at the door, where he removed his dog's leash from his pocket and snapped it on his collar. "Let's go," he told his well-trained partner.

Peace also came to the door to see them off. While they stood there, Elissa petted both dogs. Then, to his surprise, she leaned toward him. "Drive carefully," she said, and planted a soft and swift kiss on his lips before backing away. "And I can't thank you enough for all your help."

You just did, he thought, but all he said was, "You're welcome. Be careful, keep in touch, and we'll see you next week."

Now, why on earth had she done that? Elissa scolded herself as she shut and locked the door behind Doug and Hooper. No matter how much she liked the guy, he was a cop. He was acting like a cop. Helping her as a cop would. Trying to figure out what was going on and how to keep her safe.

And, more important to him, attempting to learn

the origin of an apparent threat to a person in his own jurisdiction.

Shaking her head, she decided to call Glynnis Crandal, the friend and neighbor she'd been referring to when she'd spoken with Doug about having a companion to walk dogs with. It was late afternoon now, nearly five o'clock, and Glynnis, a middle school teacher, was likely to be home.

Elissa couldn't plan on taking all her walks with Peace with Glynnis, too, but a couple tonight should at least give her a sense of whether she also needed to work something out with another neighbor.

"Peace, come." Elissa motioned to her pup, who followed her into the kitchen. There, after clearing off the table and taking a few more sips of water, she used her cell phone to call Glynnis, who answered right away.

"Hi," Elissa said. "I'm looking for a little company on my walks with Peace this evening. Partially as a therapy dog training thing. Are you and Socia available?" Socia was Glynnis's smart and friendly Rottweiler.

"Sure!" There was a happy lilt to her voice, as if she was thrilled by the idea.

Elissa suspected she wouldn't be so thrilled when Peace and she arrived at Glynnis's front door and explained one of the reasons they needed company.

She had to at least mention it. Not that she anticipated putting Glynnis in danger, or she wouldn't be involving her. Still, the possibility was why she did want another person and dog with them.

They made arrangements for Elissa and Peace to come by, which they did, in about half an hour.

Glynnis's home was on the same block, but three houses down. It was two-story, with a lovely blue-siding exterior, and was in a lot better condition than Elissa's rental.

Peace at her side, Elissa walked up to the front door and heard Socia barking. Glynnis opened the door only a few seconds later, as if she'd been waiting.

Glynnis was a solid and determined-looking woman in her late forties, a divorcée whose two kids were both in college in different parts of California. She wore jeans, a long-sleeved orange T-shirt and athletic shoes, and Socia was leashed at her side.

"May we come in for just a minute?" Elissa asked. "There are a couple of reasons for our wanting company that I think you should know."

They remained in the high-ceilinged entry while Elissa explained about the break-in at her house. No, Glynnis hadn't heard of anything else like that in the neighborhood or otherwise. Elissa also told her about the sign at her new part-time employer's dog training ranch.

"So if you've changed your mind and don't want to walk with us, I'll completely understand," Elissa finished.

The look on Glynnis's round, aging face beneath her short yellow hair was determined. "Changed my mind? Heck, no. In fact, I'm even more eager to go with you. If anything strange occurs, my Socia will take care of it even if your sweet Peace can't. So let's go."

There was a lot more traffic on his way back to Chance than earlier, which gave Doug time to think. Overthink. He regretted leaving Elissa alone, with no additional protection except, possibly, a few more patrols on her street now and then.

But he couldn't have stayed. Nor had he enough clout with the local police department to get further protection for her.

And though he could have contacted some private protective services in the area—and even paid for them, since it appeared that Elissa wasn't exactly wealthy, though neither was he—he felt certain she would have vetoed the possibility.

Damn! Oh, yeah, he was overthinking this. Elissa was a big girl. She knew now about the break-in, partly thanks to Peace. Doug had alerted her to the potential additional threat in Chance. She could handle things the way she chose—which apparently was to ignore it all, or at least to do nothing more than bring some additional company into her dog walking and try to convince the owner of the decrepit house where she lived to install some kind of security system. Yeah, right.

But her bravery appealed to him, even though he considered her foolish.

"Enough of this, Hooper," he said out loud, as if his dog in the back seat knew what he'd been stewing about. He glanced into the rearview mirror to see Hooper sit up from where he'd been lying. He was tethered safely. And now he was looking at Doug with his eyes large, his ears up, as if waiting for the next command.

Which he wouldn't get in the car. Except… "Good boy, Hooper," Doug said. "Now, down." And of course the smart and well-trained dog obeyed.

Doug spoke aloud a little more, mostly so Hooper could hear him. But all he talked about was his frustrations— with traffic and with Elissa. Nothing that Hooper would understand, except, perhaps, for his handler's mood.

When Doug finally pulled off the freeway and onto

the mountain roads, he used his car's wireless connection to call his sister, needing to blow off steam—and hoping she had a minute to talk. Maisie was devoted to her job—and, of course, to Griffin. If they were out on an assignment, she simply wouldn't answer.

But she did. "So what's going on, bro?" she asked.

"Any further word about the K-9 Ranch?" he asked.

"Nothing I've heard, and they haven't called Griffin and me in to try tracking whoever left that sign."

"Not surprising. Hooper didn't alert on anything when we were there, so Griffin probably wouldn't, either. But Hooper did alert on a situation at Elissa's home." Doug quickly explained it to his sister, including his subsequent communications with the local San Luis Obispo police.

"Did Elissa give you any more idea of what's going on?" Maisie's tone sounded like a demand, as if she really did want to know if there'd been an answer—and what that answer was.

"She didn't seem to know." He knew his frustration resonated in his voice. "She didn't make any guesses about who might be doing this or why, though she seemed justifiably scared. I tried to get her to stay with a friend or do something else self-protective, but all she indicated was that she'd take her dog on walks with a neighbor for a while—at least sometimes."

"Brave lady," Maisie said.

"Foolish lady," Doug retorted then changed the subject. "So what's going on with you?"

They talked for a while longer. Maisie and Griffin were at the station. Assistant Chief Kara had set up a meeting with them tomorrow morning, though it was

Saturday. "Not sure exactly what's on her mind but she indicated that Hooper and you should join us if possible. Can you come?"

"Definitely," he responded. They talked about nothing for another few minutes and Doug said he'd see Maisie soon, at the home they and their dogs shared. It was evening, and they were off-duty that night—unless, of course, a case came in that required the assistance of one or more K-9s.

Then he hung up.

Meeting tomorrow with the assistant chief was fine with Doug. If nothing else, it would be a genuine, official distraction from the nonsense going on in his mind.

No, not nonsense. There was a civilian in potential trouble.

A very lovely and, yes, brave civilian in an apparently inexplicable situation—or at least not explainable for the moment, if she truly was telling him everything.

And he wanted to trust her. Did trust her, even though he hardly knew her. But should he?

Think with your brain and nothing else, he ordered himself. For despite all the orders he'd given himself, despite everything his revered uncle Cy had drummed into his head and Maisie's when they had, at his urging, decided to become cops, he found Elissa Yorian not only a distraction but a very sexy, appealing woman.

But he was a cop. A damn good one. And so he would help figure out what was going on with her, find a way to protect her, without getting emotionally involved.

"Yeah, right," he expressed aloud.

His tone must have startled Hooper, who sat up once again on the back seat and gave a small growl.

"You said it," said Doug with a brisk nod.

Chapter 6

"Peace, heel." It was early Saturday morning. Elissa had just stepped onto the front walkway with her dog leashed beside her and checked to make sure her house's front door was locked. She had additionally double-checked the other doors and windows. Everything seemed secure.

She'd taken Peace for a walk twice last night with Glynnis and Socia, and all had seemed calm and peaceful in their neighborhood.

But that was yesterday. This was today—after a spotty, uneasy night's sleep.

At least the weather here in San Luis Obispo was fairly cool for an August day, and not much humidity, either. Peace was doing her normal thing of sniffing the air and ground, and prancing as she walked along, although she sometimes stopped with her nose down as if checking for the right place to relieve herself, which she did relatively quickly.

She was a good dog in many respects, and that was one of them. Elissa would take her along to the hospital for the first couple of hours she was there so Peace could do her thing as a therapy dog, helping to cheer patients in whatever stage of recovery they happened to be.

She wondered what Doug Murran would think if he ever watched her actually engaged in therapy work, with real patients and not just those involved in her interview process with Amber. But why should she care?

A car drove by slowly and Elissa found herself tensing up and staring at it. But it turned out to be another neighbor, apparently leaving early for his job at a nearby bank.

Drat. Was she ever going to feel normal again?

Sure, when her mysteries were solved and she knew who'd broken into her house and left that sign up at the Chance K-9 Ranch, especially if the person or persons were arrested and prosecuted successfully.

Right, as if that was likely to happen.

Although…well, Doug Murran seemed to be one good, dedicated cop. A K-9 officer to boot. If anyone could solve this situation, she suspected it would be him.

Or was that just her totally inappropriate attraction to the sexy guy clouding her judgment?

Peace completed her usual morning routine and Elissa used a special plastic bag to clean up the grass. "Come, Peace." They returned to their house.

They were soon back in the kitchen eating their own breakfasts. When they were done, they'd head to the hospital for Peace's therapy time, then Elissa would bring her home and return to the hospital in her nursing persona.

She liked what she did, both ways of helping people.

Well, okay. She sometimes loved her therapy work even more than nursing—and she adored nursing, especially with kids. But the people needing Peace and her for therapy were sometimes stressed, even just by being where they found themselves—like the hospital or even a nearby assisted living facility. Others were damaged physically or psychologically, and sometimes their mental health issues resulted from poor physical health. Fortunately, though, those who were ill tended to be healing, though often slowly.

Since she'd started doing therapy work, though, she occasionally found that the people they interacted with were in worse condition than she'd initially thought. Some had physical or mental conditions that became more severe, so bad that they weren't aware enough to even recognize a therapy dog. One she had once worked with had even died.

But nearly always, introducing the ill or stressed to therapy dogs cheered them and helped their progress.

"Hey, Peace," she said as she finished her cereal. "Are you ready to roll?"

Peace, beside her on the kitchen floor, barked and Elissa took that as a positive response.

"Good. Let's go."

The drive to the Central Hospital of San Luis Obispo didn't take long. Elissa parked in the area reserved for staff and got Peace out of the back seat. Her wonderful golden sat immediately and nuzzled Elissa, and she bent to give Peace a big hug.

The lot was full, as usual. She rose and looked up at the long four-story building, first toward the part closest to her. That was where the pediatrics wing was, and it was her goal for now to conduct therapy work with Peace.

She let Peace do some final outside sniffing on the concrete between cars, then headed inside. She stopped initially on the first floor to clock in at the computer—and was surprised that, as soon as she'd made her entry, a message came up that she was to see senior nurse Mae Shuller right away.

What was that about? Well, she'd find out. "Come, Peace," she said, and the two of them passed through the hospital lobby to the administrative offices at the left side of the same floor.

They then went by some of the main admin areas and the doctors' section. Mae's office was the first beyond that, and Elissa soon knocked on the closed door.

It opened nearly immediately. Mae stood there in her official blue scrubs, similar to what Elissa would be wearing if she'd come here first thing in her nurse capacity.

"Elissa," Mae said. "Hi. Come in." She looked down and scowled at Peace, then preceded both of them through the room.

Her tone had seemed—well, off, Elissa thought. Unfriendly, maybe. And usually Mae seemed to enjoy gushing over Peace and other therapy dogs.

Mae was in her early sixties, and she said often that she looked forward to retirement soon—though she intended to continue her nursing in a personal-assistant capacity. She liked people, and she liked to keep busy. But she indicated she'd gotten tired of all the politics and other headaches involved with helping to run a hospital.

Now, she waved toward the seats across her desk from where she sat. Her hair was an interesting orange-ish shade that Elissa hadn't ever seen on anyone else, cut short to frame a face that looked older than she was. Possibly the stress of her admin work or nursing had helped to age her.

And at the moment, the way she was frowning, she looked even older. Elissa felt herself freeze up inside. Something clearly was wrong.

She took one of the seats Mae had gestured at, telling Peace to sit beside her on the floor. Then Elissa leaned forward, still holding the strap of Peace's leash as well as wringing her hands slightly. She waited for Mae to say something—and when she did, Elissa wished she had simply run out of the room.

"So tell me what's going on, Elissa," Mae said in a chilly but intense tone.

What did she mean? She knew about Elissa's interviewing for the part-time therapy dog instructor position at the Chance K-9 Ranch, since Elissa would only have gone forward with that after getting her full-time employer's okay.

And Mae surely didn't know about the break-in at Elissa's house, or the strange sign on the ranch fence. Immediately, Elissa thought about Doug and about how well he knew both of these issues. Had he contacted Mae for some reason? Had other cops, either from the San Luis Obispo or the Chance departments?

But why?

Elissa had to ask. "What do you want me to tell you about, Mae?" She tried to sound professional and sincere without revealing the angst squeezing everything inside her.

"Your therapy dog work here, of course," Mae responded, staring down at Peace. "And everything that's been going wrong with it."

Elissa swallowed hard. "I'm sorry. I don't know what you're talking about. Nothing's gone wrong with it." In fact, she'd had a feeling that starting out doing therapy work this day would be wonderful for her own psyche, as well, considering everything else she was going through.

Mae leaned forward, clasping her work-worn hands on top of her wooden desk. "We've had several complaints over the last week, Elissa. People have said that Peace, instead of helping to soothe them or their kids during therapy sessions, has been acting aggressive and scary. And that you haven't discouraged it but have been criticizing the patients and how they react to your dog. One of them even hinted that Peace had bitten a child, though I'm not sure of that."

Elissa felt her eyes widen. "That's simply not true," she said. "Who told you that?"

"We can't divulge names—partly because the people indicated they were afraid you'd come after them for speaking up."

"Never! And how can I prove they're lying if I can't talk to them?" Elissa felt tears sting her eyes but she refused to let them fall. "You've seen us work. Peace is the sweetest dog ever, and she gets our subjects completely relaxed and happy. And if something was wrong and she didn't seem compatible with a patient—well, you know me enough to recognize that I'd calmly but immediately take her away." She had already done that once—a good thing since something bad had happened to that child a while afterward. Now, she stared right into Mae's face with her moist eyes. "You have to believe me."

Inside, she felt sick. This had to be related somehow to the two other recent issues in her life—but how?

She had a fleeting wish that Doug had remained in SLO overnight and accompanied her here to help. But nice man though he was, he was a cop. If there was any alleged proof that she was mishandling therapy sessions, he wouldn't have been on her side.

But he could vouch for her in the other situations… right?

Well, he wasn't here. And she had just met the guy, knew he was protecting citizens of Chance and helping her, too, somewhat as a result.

But she mostly had to help herself.

Should she tell Mae what else had been going on?

Would that help her—or just appear she was making things up to protect herself?

At least local cops had showed up at her house yesterday, so there was that possible evidence.

"Mae, I don't know who you talked to or what's really going on, but somehow this week I've been hit by…well, several very difficult situations. One was a break-in at my house. The other—I don't want to get into detail but it involves my interview for the part-time therapy dog trainer job in Chance, which, by the way, was a success. I don't know that these claims are connected with each other or what you've said, but I wouldn't be surprised. And I'll never find out unless I'm able to follow up in some way and talk to the people accusing me."

Mae stood, and therefore so did Peace at Elissa's side. That made her rise, too.

"I'm sorry, Elissa," Mae said. "I honestly don't know what's going on, but I can't ignore the accusations. Nor can I violate their privacy, even though I understand what you're saying. Best thing I can do is look into it further. But for now…well, this is serious enough that I was going to terminate your employment and therapy volunteering, but to be fair I'll just put you on administrative leave until I have more information. But to protect our patients, and our hospital, I can't do nothing. Again, I'm sorry. I'll be in touch."

Elissa had gasped while her boss was talking and now the tears were flowing freely down her cheeks. "But can't I keep working and providing therapy services while you check things out? Or at least just work as a nurse?"

"Sorry, but as I said, I have others to protect." Her tone had grown cold once more. "Now, I think it would be better if you left. I'll tell your coworkers and fellow therapy dog handlers that you've taken a leave and won't get into details—unless they hear them from the people involved, of course. And I do hope for your sake that things work out. The sooner the better." She then shot a telling glance toward her office door.

What could Elissa do but leave? "Peace, come," she said, and the two of them left.

She ignored all the other people in the hallway and entry area, figuring she'd know some of them but not wanting to talk to anyone. She didn't even bother signing out.

But neither did she leave immediately. Her intent before had been to provide therapy services in the pediatrics area. Maybe she couldn't do anything like that officially, but at least she could visit—right?

No one stopped her as she got Peace into the elevator to the third floor. No one stopped her there, either, as she walked with her dog to the large room where they usually worked and provided warmth and psychological help to scared and unruly kids who needed it.

One of the other therapy dog handlers, Dianne Doriene, was present with Sparta, her Australian shepherd mix. They were working with one of the long-term juvenile patients, Marcus, who had a kidney issue. Marcus's mother, DeeDee, was there, too, along with a couple of other parents, mostly ones whose kids were scheduled to come in for some therapy work later.

Another person present was Adellaide Willmer. Elissa had been surprised to see Adellaide at recent therapy dog sessions along with Popo, the dog she was training. Elissa hadn't asked but assumed she was taking up therapy dog handling in memory of her son, Tully, who'd had severe psychological issues. He'd been the child she'd removed Peace from working with because of his particularly difficult mental illness. Sadly, he had fallen out of a hospital window and died after a therapy session given by someone else.

She caught Dianne's eye, and the other handler frowned. Was she aware of Elissa's situation?

The answer was clearly yes.

Dianne handed Sparta's leash to one of the parents and sidled over to Elissa. "I'm surprised to see you here," she said.

"Me, too," Elissa said softly. "Do you know what's going on?"

"I heard…well, as I said, I'm surprised to see you here."

Elissa had to ask. "Do you happen to know the reason I've been asked to take a leave of absence?" That was, in fact, what Mae had finally said—even though that leave might wind up being permanent.

Dianne glanced down at Peace, then looked straight into Elissa's face. Her blue eyes were shadowy, her expression grim. "It's partly about Peace. Did you let her hurt, or even scare, some of the kids here?"

"No!" The word exploded from Elissa's mouth but fortunately no one was looking their way. "No," she repeated more softly. "Who did you hear that from?"

"I can't talk about it. But—well, if you've been asked to take a leave of absence then I suggest you do it."

Dianne stalked away and again took charge of Sparta.

Elissa waited and watched for a few minutes. She waved hello to Adellaide but she and Popo were busy with a child and Elissa didn't want to interrupt. Although some of the parents shot glances her way, none observed her for long, and no one else came over to talk to her.

Dianne had been right. Elissa had to leave. Without another word, she led Peace out of the room and toward the elevator.

Soon, she had fastened Peace into the back seat of her SUV once more and planted herself in the driver's seat.

She allowed herself to cry, but only for a short while. She had an urge to stay there and fight, to ask more questions and demand answers and conduct her own investigation into who'd broken into her house and more.

But she recognized that she needed a plan. Plus, the

good thing was that she had someplace else to go, at least temporarily until she could get her mind back in gear.

Today was Saturday, and she wasn't supposed to return to Chance until Monday. Even so, she forced herself to relax, to look around for a few minutes at people coming and going within the parking lot, then she called Amber as she stared up at the building where she'd been employed, wondering when she'd see it again.

"Hi, Elissa." Her new boss answered right away, sounding cheerful.

"Hi, Amber. Look, I've gotten my schedule changed a bit and I hope to come back to Chance tomorrow with Peace. Would that work? I want to stay for a few days to get started." Maybe more, but she could get into that better once she was there. "And do you know of a good motel where I could stay?"

"We have some extra houses at the Chance K-9 Ranch for live-in employees," Amber said. "You can stay here. And it will be great to see you a bit early."

"Oh, thank you." That was one relief, Elissa thought after saying goodbye and hanging up.

And then? Unsure whether it would be a relief or a mistake, she pushed the buttons on her phone to make another call.

"Hi, Elissa," Doug said immediately. "Is everything all right?"

She almost broke down and cried again at the sound of his voice—and his apparent caring and protectiveness, even if it was just his job. "Yes and no." She tried to keep a bright note in her tone. "No one's come after me or broken into my house again." She figured she'd better assure him of that before he drove back down the mountain to check. "The good thing is that I'll be back in Chance tomorrow. Is there any possibility that we can get together and talk? I'd like to ask you something."

"Count on it," he said, and Elissa felt herself smile in a modicum of relief.

Chapter 7

So what was going on with that woman?

That brave, sexy, perplexing woman who loved dogs and apparently people, too, since she used dogs to help other humans in need.

Never mind that it was early Saturday morning. Doug was in the office he shared with his sister, going over some emails and newsletters from K-9 organizations and nearby departments that also had dogs on their teams. He was still waiting for the meeting that Assistant Chief Kara had scheduled earlier but had delayed, wondering if she'd just wanted to touch base with the department's K-9 staff or if there was something else going on.

But he kept thinking even more about the call he had just received midmorning.

What was on Elissa's mind now? She sounded as

if she was attempting to hide how upset she was. Not that he knew her well, of course, yet some of her emotions had already become somewhat readable to him, or so he believed.

Was something new wrong? And was that something new the reason she was coming back to Chance a day early?

She apparently still had no idea who had broken into her home and why, since she'd found nothing missing. She'd undoubtedly have mentioned it if her local cops had found any answers.

Same thing regarding who had warned Amber not to hire her—although that was in his jurisdiction, and so far he had no answers, either. He knew Elissa would mention it to him if she'd figured it out.

Did she know the source of whatever new issue was troubling her—assuming there was one?

Hooper, lying on the floor beside Doug, suddenly stood, his pointed ears moving and his eyes fixed on the closed office door. He'd clearly heard something in the hallway and, judging by the way his tail wagged, Doug assumed Hooper's closest friend Griffin was approaching. Therefore he wasn't surprised when the door opened and his sister strode in, led by her K-9.

"Hey, bro." As always, Maisie looked fully professional that day, even though, like him, she wore her uniform shirt and pants but not the jacket. Griffin immediately approached Hooper, and the two dogs traded sniffs as if to make sure the other hadn't gotten into something fun since they'd last been together.

"Hey back. Any word on when the assistant chief wants to meet with us?"

"How about now?" Maisie asked, though it wasn't

a question. "I saw her in the hallway a minute ago and she told me to round you up and join her in her office."

Doug immediately rose. He stuffed Hooper's leash in his pocket. Here at the station, the dogs didn't need to be vested, tethered or confined, but they almost always remained with their handlers unless there was a good reason not to.

Maisie and Griffin preceding them, Doug walked with Hooper along the clean white halls to the administration area of the building, passing other cops who greeted them, including the dogs, but knew better than to reach out to pat them unless given the okay by their handlers.

A few civilians were hurrying through the building and several stopped, their smiles suggesting they wanted to engage in a lovefest with the K-9s, but Maisie immediately corrected them, explaining that the dogs were professionals like their handlers and were somewhat on duty just by being there.

Soon, they were outside the offices of the chief and assistant chief. Maisie knocked, waited for a "Come in," then opened Kara Province's wooden door and walked in with Griffin. Doug and Hooper were right behind her.

As usual, Doug watched his sister take the lead, not because she was a better cop but because she was older—and generally insistent on being in control. Rather than fight it, he allowed his amusement to take over and let her do it.

"Here we are, Assistant Chief," Maisie said.

Kara, behind her desk, looked up at them. "Yes, here you are. Have a seat." She met Doug's gaze and smiled briefly, as if she, too, recognized he was acting, as always, like a good sibling and letting his big sis have her way.

Like the two K-9 handlers, Kara was dressed somewhat informally, at least without her black jacket. Kara's large desk had a few piles of paper on it, as usual, and her laptop was on a wheeled table to the side. The assistant chief was fairly young for the position, not much older than Maisie or Doug, both in their midthirties. She had dark hair cut professionally short, which framed her face attractively. The gaze she moved from Doug back to Maisie with her deep brown eyes looked friendly— but not too friendly.

Doug sat on the chair closest to him, facing the desk, not waiting for Maisie to make her decision. The dogs both took positions sitting on the floor next to each of their handlers.

"So," Kara said, "you want to know why we're meeting."

"Yes, ma'am," Maisie said formally, and Doug half expected her to salute—but she didn't.

"Well, I just wanted an update on any cases you're working on—and especially if there's anything regarding the K-9 Ranch that the department needs to be concerned about after that sign posted outside it."

"That's Doug's matter," Maisie said immediately, gesturing toward him. "Although I am concerned. I planned to take Griffin there to observe some therapy dog lessons and hope they're still in the works. He's already a good boy, not too old, and does his job well, but I thought that would be another good skill for him to learn for the future. Right, boy?" She reached over and stroked her golden's head. The dog wagged his tail. "And while I'm there, I'll also look around."

"Okay, then. Doug—" Kara looked at him "—what's your update?"

This was his boss. He had to remain professional and tell her what she wanted, and needed, to know. He kept it brief but told her about his trip down the mountain to visit Elissa's home to see if the break-in might be related to that sign.

He mentioned that Hooper was the one to alert on where the break-in had occurred, explaining Elissa's dog's strange reaction at their home. Also, he let her know he'd been in touch with local cops.

Sure, he'd acted fast in hurrying to a civilian's home out of their jurisdiction, while he was on duty. But he had gotten the chief's general permission to look into the apparent threat at the Chance K-9 Ranch, and the matters were possibly related.

He still hoped that investing his time and Hooper's might help lead to the information they sought.

"So you still have no answers" was Kara's correct conclusion as he finished.

"That's right," he said, "but we're still looking into it. Ms. Yorian was hired part-time at the K-9 Ranch starting on Monday, but I've received information that she is heading back to Chance tomorrow, and I hope to get any further updates from her then."

He felt his sister's wry stare but didn't look at her. She'd already told him he was getting much too interested in the woman he'd followed down the hill. In some ways, she was right. And oh, yes, Maisie was usually right.

But he saw a wry stare from their boss, too, who might also be getting the wrong—or unfortunately right—idea. "I'll keep you informed about any additional info I get from her or otherwise. The Chance K-9 Ranch is an important part of this town and I recognize our duty to protect it along with all our other critical businesses." Was he laying it on too thick?

"Of course," Kara said. "And I assume you'll be helping the other Officer Murran." This time her gaze was on Maisie.

"You can be sure of it," Maisie said. "I'll be right on top of it all."

Doug heard his sister's unspoken message. *Keep it professional, bro.*

Which was absolutely his intention. And now he needed to follow through.

She needed to leave, to start her new life—temporary or not. And so, first thing Sunday morning, Elissa packed a bag with essential clothing and more, including her laptop, then gathered items important to Peace's lifestyle, such as her food, and loaded most of it into the rear of her vehicle. She walked Peace briefly along with her friend and neighbors, Glynnis and Socia, to say goodbye for now, and got her dog into the back seat of the SUV.

She'd hoped she wasn't too tired to drive. So many things had affected her sleep last night. She'd kept listening for the sound of someone breaking into her rented home again—fortunately hearing nothing. She'd stewed about losing her job thanks to those totally untrue accusations. And of course she'd thought about what would be facing her up the mountain, in Chance— a new direction for her life, yes, at least temporarily.

But someone there had threatened her, too. Warned her new boss not to hire her… Why?

And in between all of that, she had gotten some small doses of sleep.

As she'd pulled out of her driveway nearly an hour ago, she had pushed the button to close the garage door on the house where she'd been living…and on that part of her life, at least for now. She was currently renting month-to-month and hadn't yet given notice of termination of the lease. Not till she saw how things went in Chance. If she did return, she would ask her landlord to add a security system—but right now it felt unlikely she'd even be there to ask, let alone push him about it.

Was she doing the right thing? Well, she no longer had a job to return to in SLO, even though she wanted in the worst way to hang around to see if she could figure out who had falsely accused her of inappropriate behavior during her dog therapy work. Of all that had happened so far, that in some ways affected her the most. She loved doing therapy work, helping people with the kindest of dogs, Peace. Teaching others to do the same.

To hear that someone claimed she had instead frightened needy children…that sent a knife of sorts into her heart.

As a result, to maintain her sanity, she wanted to start her new job as fast as possible, even if it was only part-time. While she did that, she could try to figure out how to find these answers along with those for the other questions hanging over her.

Now, rehashing it all yet again as they neared Chance in traffic a lot better than her journey there on a weekday, she said to Peace, "I think we'll like living on the K-9 Ranch. You've already met some of the dogs there, and we'll meet more."

And her? Well, she really liked Amber Belott, her

new boss. Not that she knew her well, nor her mother or their head trainer or other employees at the ranch, but she would get to know them better, she was certain of it.

On top of that, she was thinking of Doug. "I don't know if he'll help us find all the answers, but at least we have another new friend in Chance, Peace." The cop had already done a lot for her. And she was going to see him soon to let him in on the latest fiasco in her life. Not that he'd necessarily care—but maybe he could add this latest thing to the list of issues he seemed to be investigating on her behalf.

Rather, the Chance K-9 Ranch's behalf, but that was fine. She was involved, and he had agreed to talk to her sometime today. And she believed she could count on K-9 Officer Doug Murran to keep his word.

At least she hoped so.

She took her time on the drive, sightseeing a bit, since she wasn't going to be commuting between SLO and Chance again, at least not now. She even stopped to walk Peace often, to give herself a little exercise, too—both to boost her body and her mood.

In a while, she was driving through Chance's downtown. She decided to go past the civic center and police station.

To see Doug? It was Sunday afternoon. Might he be on duty? She doubted it unless there was a local problem requiring a K-9's help. She'd call him soon to see where they could meet.

"Let's go by the hospital instead," she said to Peace. But to get there from where they were they would have to drive by the police station.

She was startled to see Doug, his sister Maisie and their K-9s right outside the building, as if she'd told him to meet her there. But she hadn't. She hadn't known when or where they would get together, but it seemed too strange to consider stopping and saying hi now, so she just waved and kept driving.

Okay, maybe it wasn't so strange. Chance wasn't a large town. All its police officers probably spent time patrolling the streets, possibly even on weekends, including the K-9 officers—right?

Elissa's cell phone rang nearly immediately. She answered it on the wireless system in her car.

"This is Doug Murran, Elissa. Why did you just drive by rather than stop? I know you saw me. I thought you wanted to talk today." He sounded brusque and not especially friendly. Because she hadn't stopped—or because he was with another cop, even though she happened to be his sister, and wanted to sound more professional than nice?

It didn't particularly matter. With Elissa's current mood, she felt somewhat hurt. "I do," she said. "But I thought I would go to the K-9 Ranch first. I need to talk to Amber." Never mind that she'd also hoped to talk to someone at the hospital today about therapy dog work. That could wait a little longer.

"Fine. I'll meet you there in half an hour. Okay?"

"Sure." Before she could say anything else he said goodbye and hung up.

Which made Elissa wonder if she was making a mistake by coming here after all—or at least hoping Doug was as nice a cop as she'd started to believe he was and that he would continue to try to help her.

"That's probably just wishful thinking," she said sadly to Peace. "I shouldn't get my hopes up that anyone will help me." Especially a guy like that. Sexy, yes. But a professional cop all the way.

Hey, she told herself, *buck up*. Her life was about to improve. She was in Chance.

She continued driving to the ranch. Amber Belott had hired her. Amber had said she had a spare employee's house where Elissa and Peace could live, at least for a few days. She had an ulterior motive of wanting a skilled therapy dog worker and trainer to be part of the K-9 Ranch staff, but she still had acted awfully nice to Elissa, at least so far.

And Elissa would take advantage of it and hopefully stay there for a while—and in turn, she would be the best damn therapy dog handler and instructor possible.

She soon turned onto the ranch's driveway and drove up the hill. As she parked, the house door on the front porch opened and Amber came out, along with her mother and their black Lab, Lola.

"Hi, and welcome," Amber said immediately as Elissa opened the driver's door.

"Thanks so much." Elissa smiled greetings at the two women standing near her.

"It's great that you decided to come early," Sonya said.

"And to stay here," Amber agreed. "We've been working on getting a class together for you to start with tomorrow. Some potential students responded to my social media posts, and I've chosen a few to participate. It'll be a small class, but it will be a start."

And sometime tomorrow, Elissa would find a way to do as she'd hoped today and visit the hospital. See if she could conduct some therapy dog work there, as well as demonstrations and lessons once she got her classes going.

As they talked, Elissa got Peace out of the back and the two dogs exchanged greetings with their eyes and noses.

For an instant, Elissa allowed herself to believe that all the hardships she had been undergoing might just have been preparing her for the changes to her life that she was about to begin. Good changes. Wonderful changes.

She hoped.

That attitude persisted a short while later after Amber and Lola walked her to the first of the four houses off to one side of the main house.

"This one will be yours as long as you're working here and want to stay," Amber said, walking up the front stoop and using a key to open the plain wooden front door with a window at the top. She then handed the key to Elissa.

It was a single-story building, not elaborate at all, but better kept than the place she'd been renting. It felt like home immediately to Elissa—probably because she yearned for it to be, at least for now. Plus, Peace seemed right at home, too, as she began exploring the place, nose down, with Lola accompanying her.

"Not the most sophisticated building, but it's convenient for the people who work here. Evan, our head trainer, lives in the end house with his dog Bear."

Amber's smile was huge and she seemed to blush a little. Elissa figured Evan might also hang out a bit at the main ranch house—assuming Sonya could deal with that.

"Our ranch hand, Orrin, lives in the house next to

Evan's, and the house closest to this one is currently vacant. Oh, and in case you're interested, the houses on the other side are sort of like hotels for visiting students, though they can be used for employees, too. At the moment, no one is living in any of them."

"Got it." Elissa had noticed a few homes in that direction, as well.

"So...everything look okay here?" That was Sonya. The older woman appeared concerned, as if she really cared whether Elissa was comfortable in the house.

"Absolutely," Elissa assured her. "This is great. I've already started figuring the best way to start my classes, and it will definitely be easier for me to run them while I'm actually living here. I really appreciate it." She leveled a smile first at Sonya and then at Amber. "And just so you know, I've taken a leave of absence from the hospital where I work as a nurse to make sure I get started well here." Okay, that wasn't the full story, but they didn't need to know the rest, at least not now.

"We really appreciate you," her new boss assured her, causing Elissa's smile to widen even more. "Now go ahead and start getting settled here. I imagine you haven't bought groceries, so you're welcome to join us for dinner."

"She's having dinner with me tonight," said a familiar voice that wasn't entirely expected—at least not then. But Doug and Hooper had entered the house and now stood in the living room with them. Peace headed toward them, tail wagging fast, and traded face sniffs with Hooper.

Well, that answered one question—although this wasn't exactly the way Elissa would have wanted her evening plans to be determined. But she nodded at

Doug, then said to Amber and Sonya, "That's right. But thanks, anyway. And let's plan to have dinner together soon—my treat." On only a part-time salary?

Well, she'd work it out.

"We'll see about that," Amber said and then she and her mother left with Lola—leaving Elissa and Peace alone with Doug and his K-9.

Doug Hai Su Hill and Elissa, though both clearly here

heard or some thought whatever, to his listeners

that so far away break for my a good someone said

Well, right now she's that

Well, but certain that a matter Doug said she was

here but here it will receive and for Elissa said how

who knows if not he said.

Chapter 8

"So you're staying here for a while?" Doug had to ask as both he and Elissa stood near the now closed front door. "I heard you say you'd taken a leave of absence from your other job."

Which surprised him. He'd gotten the impression she enjoyed being a nurse, and though she also liked handling therapy dogs and training others, that wasn't her main focus. He figured she had come here early to get ready for her part-time job that started tomorrow, but was there more to it than that?

He was glad she was here now, though. Not because he'd wanted to see her any sooner, but her presence should assist in his attempts to figure out that sign left at the K-9 Ranch. Or at least he hoped so.

He hadn't seen her dressed quite this casually before, in a green T-shirt and jeans. She looked good that way.

Of course he figured she would look good in whatever she wore.

And he wouldn't even think about how she would look wearing nothing…

He reminded himself yet again that he was a cop. On duty. Dressed in his uniform shirt and slacks. *Be professional*, he ordered himself.

"Yes," she was saying. "I decided to come early and stay for a while as I got into my new job here."

He saw through that, though. Or thought he did. The bright smile on her face looked forced and her voice held a tinge of sorrow. What really was going on?

He would find out soon.

They were in a hall leading to the house's other rooms and he wanted to check them for their current condition. He knew what they were like because he'd been in the similar home occupied by Evan, the ranch's head trainer.

"Well, that's good," he said. "Come on. I want to see the rest of this place."

"Sure." Elissa almost sounded relieved, as if she'd hoped he would check this place out, too—to ensure nothing unusual was present here.

Like jimmied windows…

As she, with Peace, preceded Hooper and him down the hall, Doug hung back. He had a totally inappropriate urge to grab Elissa and hold her tight to keep her safe.

But there was unlikely to be anything here to harm her…and he would confirm that.

For now, he wanted Hooper to accompany him and check this house out as his K-9 had done with Elissa's other place. Not that he anticipated his dog would alert on anything unusual. They were within the boundaries of the vast fence that surrounded the Chance K-9 Ranch. Evan's dog Bear was a former military K-9 who would also let his handler know if someone was around who shouldn't be.

Although, Bear apparently hadn't alerted about whoever had left that sign. Of course the front gate was far from where Evan and Bear lived. And it most likely had been hung in the middle of the night.

Lola and the young dogs that were being trained to become police K-9s were slightly closer but mustn't have heard or smelled anything unusual while they were sleeping in the main house, or they'd undoubtedly have barked.

Which indicated to Doug that the intruder had enough knowledge of this ranch and its occupants to have a good idea how to be careful and stay off the canine radar.

"I really don't know enough about this place to give you a grand tour," Elissa said. "I walked through it briefly with Amber before but just peeked into all the rooms—and there aren't many."

"We'll take our time now," Doug told her, and he and Hooper did exactly that.

Even so, it didn't take long because the place was so small. In turn, they walked through the living room, kitchen, bedroom and bathroom—and that was the entire house.

Each room had the barest minimum of ordinary furnishings in it. Nothing in the whole place got Hooper excited. When they saw the bedroom, though, Doug could imagine Elissa sleeping there. And the image made him feel warm.

Too bad he couldn't join her. Which was another of his entirely inappropriate thoughts around this woman.

They all walked through the bedroom at the end of the hall. "Doesn't look like Hooper's too excited," Elissa said, and Doug heard the note of relief in her voice.

"No, all seems well. So… I meant it about our having dinner together. But you indicated you wanted to talk to me when we saw each other next. Do you want to talk here?"

"That would be a good idea, for privacy," she said. "But I just got here and don't have any drinks or snacks, not even bottled water."

"You don't need to feed me," he said, though the idea that she wanted to entertain him somehow amused him.

"No, but… Look, let me drive into town and pick up a few things. I'll make us a light dinner and we can talk then." She smiled down at Peace, lying on the floor near the foot of the bed covered with a pale yellow spread. "I did bring dog food, though."

"Makes perfect sense to me." Doug reached down to pat Hooper's head. As usual, when nothing was happening, his wonderful dog sat on the floor beside him, waiting. "But regarding dinner, I've got a place in mind downtown where it's usually not very crowded on Sundays and we should be able to talk. We can stop at the grocery store on the way back and get you some essentials." He liked the idea of her making him dinner— but that sounded too intimate, even more than a date.

Eating at the restaurant he had in mind would also feel a bit like a date, but at least they wouldn't be alone.

"Well…if you're sure we'll be able to talk, that sounds good to me." The smile on her attractive face appeared almost relieved, as if she, too, had reservations about hanging out alone with him here for long.

Or maybe he was just reading too much into it.

"Great." He pulled his phone from his pocket and looked at the time. "It's nearly six o'clock—maybe a little on the early side, but if we go to eat now, not many people are likely to be at the restaurant. Does that work for you?"

"Can we bring the dogs?"

"Of course," he said.

"Then let's go."

Was this a big mistake?

Oh, having dinner with Doug wouldn't be a mistake, Elissa thought as she followed him out of what was now her residence and down the path toward the parking area outside the ranch's main house.

But telling him she'd been fired? And why? It was definitely a misunderstanding. Or someone had lied about her.

Yet once again she would be crying on this cop's shoulders—figuratively only, she hoped, although her emotions were definitely overwrought about all that had been happening to her.

Doug soon helped both dogs into the back of his official cop SUV, and she wondered about the appropriateness of that. But it was up to him. He didn't seem to be on duty at this hour, even though he was still dressed somewhat in his uniform. And this small town of Chance might have completely different protocols for its cops than a larger city.

He was a complete gentleman, helping her into his SUV, too. After settling himself in the driver's seat, he turned the vehicle around and drove down the driveway, then made the turn onto the narrow street toward town.

"All right," he said. "We'll talk more later, but why don't you tell me what's happened since we last spoke?"

"What makes you think anything has happened?" She didn't mean to play games with him, but now that she was second-guessing herself she wasn't sure she wanted to tell him anything.

"Because you're here. Because you said you wanted to talk again. And because I can tell from your attitude and body language that there's something on your mind. Was there another break-in at your house? Did you come up with some idea of who might have broken in before, or left the sign? What is it?"

He sounded annoyed that she had even dared to consider backing down and keeping him uninformed.

Well, she was annoyed that he was pressing her. That he…

Heck. No she wasn't. He was a cop. He was the right kind of person to talk to, and he had already demonstrated he was willing to help her, to work with her, especially when it helped him fulfill one of his own official assignments.

Telling him what was wrong wouldn't help with that. But it just might help her. Or at least help her damaged psyche to have someone to tell about it.

"Okay," she said softly.

He'd pulled up to a stop sign and glanced at her without going forward. "What is it?"

She bit her lower lip to keep herself from doing as she'd feared and beginning to cry. "I think I need a glass of wine before I can tell you," she said, hoping to turn it somewhat into a joke.

"Coming right up." He started driving again and in a couple of minutes he parked at a space on the street in front of what appeared to be a fancy establishment, with a long, low roof and lots of lit windows. A sign on top said it was the Last Chance Bar.

"Last Chance Bar?" Elissa repeated. "Do they serve food, too?"

"Yes, some really good stuff. And they have entertainment on Friday and Saturday nights. That's why they're generally not very crowded on Sundays."

This time Doug helped Elissa and the dogs out of the SUV. She still wondered if dogs would be welcome, but the hostess who met them at the door of the dark and—unsurprisingly—not very crowded place gave Doug an effusive greeting, and Hooper, too. She seemed to give Elissa a once-over and also Peace. Elissa wondered how well Doug knew this thin, attractive woman, then decided it didn't matter. Her relationship with Doug was strictly professional.

And maybe she would get his additional help to solve the mystery about why she'd been fired.

Soon, they had made their way around myriad round tables, some occupied but many not. They were seated at a table in a corner, with the dogs lying on the floor near them. A scantily clad female server came over and Elissa wondered once more what Doug's relationship to this place was.

But she remembered her not-quite-amusing comment from earlier and immediately ordered a glass of Pinot Noir. Doug ordered a dark beer, which didn't surprise her.

When the server left, Doug started telling her about some of the performers who showed up here on Friday or Saturday nights—local singers and some imported from Los Angeles, which wasn't far away. Magicians. And more.

Soon, their drinks arrived and were placed on the table before them. Partly to set a light mood, and partly just because she wanted to, Elissa raised her glass and said, "Here's to all last chances."

Doug clinked his glass against hers, raised it to his mouth and looked much too sexy taking a swig of his brew. Elissa sipped her wine. It was slightly bitter, and fit her mood. And then she took another sip as she met Doug's hazel eyes with her glance.

He raised his own glass then and said, "And here's to answers. All of them." After they both took another drink, he said, "So tell me, Elissa, what's your latest question?"

Doug figured that, whatever it was, that question was causing Elissa some kind of trauma since she said she wanted to talk about it—but apparently didn't really want to talk about it. It had caused her to flee her San Luis Obispo home, but she didn't seem comfortable being here, despite her initial plan to come to Chance tomorrow.

He was intrigued. And concerned.

Somehow he had taken on a need to protect this attractive woman—and not entirely because it was his job.

"Well… I don't know if everything is related," she finally began, looking at her wineglass and not at him. "But—"

She was interrupted by the arrival of their server to take their order. They had barely glanced at their menus, so Doug said to Elissa, "I'd suggest their pesto pasta with chicken. It's also got a lot of veggies in it." He didn't know what her eating habits were—healthy or not so much, usual foods or vegetarian—but that was a dish he'd always liked. She could take his suggestion or not.

She did. "Sounds good," she said, then told the server that was what she wanted. Was she just being accommodating? Or not wanting to take time to study the menu more?

No matter. He ordered the same thing and was glad when their server walked off.

"So...?" he said right away.

Elissa looked around as if to check to see if anyone was close enough to eavesdrop, which wasn't the case. This corner wasn't particularly popular on show days, and even on this Sunday most people sat in the center of the room at tables where they'd be able to see and hear the shows best had there been any.

That wasn't an excuse for her not to talk.

"Okay," she said. "The thing is—and please don't tell Amber. I'll let her know soon when it seems right."

"Tell her what?"

"That I was fired from my job and my work as a therapy dog handler at the hospital where I was a nurse. Or, rather, involuntarily given a leave of absence, which I'm sure will turn out to be permanent unless I can find answers fast."

"Answers to what? Why were you fired?" With effort, Doug kept his tone soft and sympathetic. He wanted to find a way to extract everything from her quickly but suspected she was taking her time about revealing the circumstances because she found it hard to talk about them.

Elissa placed her elbows on the table and rested her head in her hands. Doug resisted an urge to go over there and throw a sympathetic arm around her as she began to speak. "My boss, the head nurse, said that someone—more than one person—claimed that Peace had acted aggressively during some therapy sessions and scared the children we were working with rather than soothed them. Maybe even bit a child. And that I criticized the patients rather than accepted any scolding about the situation. But that's all lies."

Her tone had become raspy by the time she finished, and he knew she was holding back tears. They were visible to him, though, in her dark brown eyes when she moved her head to look at him.

"All lies! Isn't it, Peace?"

She bent and stroked her dog's back. Peace turned her head to look at her handler, and the caring, concerned expression on the golden's face would have convinced him of her...well, peaceful nature even if Elissa hadn't asserted that the allegations were lies.

"Do you know who made the claims?" he asked.

"No. My boss said she was afraid I'd go after whoever it was if she let me know. But all I wanted to do was talk to them, figure out where that story had come from...and why."

"And that's the end of it, as far as she's concerned?"

"Well, when I begged her she said rather than firing me I could take a leave of absence while she looked into it further, but I doubt that she will. And when I went to observe a therapy session before I left, one of the other handlers had obviously heard the claims against me and seemed uneasy that I was there. I just... I just don't get it. And I realize I should probably not hide it from Amber at all, but…well, I hate to even talk about it let alone think about it."

"We'll tell Amber," Doug said. "Both of us together. And I'll let her know I'm looking into that along with the origin of the sign left on her property, since they're probably related. Plus, you can encourage her to watch all your therapy dog classes if she's concerned any of it can be true. That okay with you?"

He was almost surprised to see her smile at him—even though it was a sad smile. "That's more than okay with me. Thank you so much, Doug. And in case you have any doubts about the truth of those claims—"

"I don't." And somewhat to his own surprise he realized he meant it. But this woman before him clearly was a caring person, both about kids and dogs.

So who was out to get her—and why?

Chapter 9

Now that she had opened up a little to Doug, Elissa wanted to tell him everything…and hoped he could help figure out the answers she really needed.

Still, she was glad when their dinner arrived so their talk was delayed once more as she sampled the pasta dish he had recommended.

"This is delicious," she exclaimed, though she wasn't surprised. She had already learned to trust this cop a bit, so why wouldn't he be able to choose a good meal?

"Glad you like it." He took a bite then pulled a couple of treats from his back pocket for the dogs, who nibbled them appreciatively. Once they'd settled back down, Doug leveled his incisive eyes on Elissa again. "Okay, do you have any more information on those claims against Peace and you?"

"No," she said sadly, shaking her head. "And maybe

I shouldn't have run away, although I was coming to Chance tomorrow anyway. But only for the day. I could go back to SLO again on Tuesday. There's no way I'll be able to figure out what happened from here."

"No, you need to stay here." Doug's tone was firm, allowing for no contradiction. "For one thing, maybe you can convince Amber to hire you full-time now that you'd be available. And for another…"

His words tapered off as he took another drink from his beer glass. Did he want her to prompt him to continue?

"What?" she asked.

"If you're not here, I can't keep an eye on you, at least not as easily. With—"

"You don't need to watch me," she broke in. With all that was happening around her, she had to remind herself now and often that she might be depending on this cop too much and she barely knew him. She needed independence. She needed space.

And she needed…okay, she needed protection. She recognized that once again even before he said, "Yeah, I do. You may be in danger. If all that had happened was that weird sign at the ranch, maybe not. But your house was broken into and that's definitely not a good sign. Whatever was done to get you fired could be unrelated, but I doubt that. We have to assume it's all connected until we get it figured out. And even though you have a very nice dog at your side most of the time, we can't depend on Peace to take care of you the way Hooper would."

Both dogs stood again and came over to Doug as if anticipating further treats—which he gave them.

"You're right." She knew she sounded dejected.

"And…well, if only that sign hadn't been left at the ranch, I'd feel thrilled to be away from the things that happened in SLO. But whatever—whoever—it is has already figured out my possible connection here, and despite having warned Amber not to hire me will probably know she has. So does it really make a difference where I am?"

"Of course it does. I'm here, and so is the rest of the Chance PD. I'll inform the appropriate people there—including Maisie—what's going on. You won't have a cop near you at all times, but at least you'll be able to count on one coming as soon as possible if you ever call."

Okay, he wasn't promising to be her bodyguard. Why should he? But he was offering ongoing help, and that made her feel better, at least somewhat.

"In fact," he continued, "Maisie isn't the only one who wants to eventually train her K-9 as a therapy dog. At least one of us will be at your class tomorrow—me, since it's my day off. Plus, we'll learn then when the next ones will be."

Elissa couldn't help smiling at the guy, who was smiling right back at her. Cheering her—and allowing her to consider all the good things about being there, including soon providing lessons to potential therapy dog handlers.

So it was a good thing that she was there…and she enjoyed the rest of her meal in this kind cop's company.

When it was over, they stopped at a local store for some groceries. Then Doug drove her home and accepted her invitation to come into her new residence again, which sent shivers through her. Would he truly act as if tonight was a date between them?

And was there any possibility of more happening that night, like a visit to her bedroom?

Well, Hooper and he did visit her bedroom, but they were clearly only checking it out along with the rest of the house once more to make sure there weren't any surprise visitors or evidence of any break-ins. Then they accompanied Peace and her outside for her dog's final walk of the evening.

Doug wouldn't allow her to say good-night at his SUV, which he had driven down the narrow road to the front of her place. Instead, he walked her back inside.

"Be sure to lock the door behind us," he said.

"I will." She prepared to shut it—but was delighted when he reached out and took her into his arms.

Their kiss was more than friendly, yet it didn't suggest that they do anything more, now or ever. Which both relieved Elissa—and confused her.

"Good night," she called as she did Doug's bidding and locked the door behind him.

Doug's house was in a nice but not elite neighborhood on the other side of Chance from the ranch. He drove there quickly now. It wasn't very late, but he was definitely off duty and wanted to chill out at home.

As long as Maisie let him. The house belonged to both of them, and she was likely to be there with Griffin at this hour on a Sunday night.

Which she was. Doug took Hooper for a quick walk, then hurried up the couple of steps onto the front porch. With his key, he opened the large wooden door that was black and plain except for the round window at the top. He strode inside, his dog right behind him.

Hearing the TV on in the den, he went in. It was a

compact, comfortable room, and Maisie sat on one of the two, matching brown-leather recliner chairs, watching the screen mounted on the beige-textured wall. Griffin stood on the wood floor to greet first him then Hooper.

"Well, hi, bro." Maisie turned to face him. "Did you have a good evening? I didn't expect you home this early." The last was said with a smug smile on her face. She'd warned him several times of Uncle Cy's edict not to get chummy with civilians involved with cases but she knew him well enough to recognize when he was attracted to a woman.

Still, she also knew him well enough to know he would do the right thing.

Just for fun, thanks to her gibing, he said, "Oh, it was a very fun evening. We started early."

Maisie snorted as she pressed the mute button on the remote and stood, obviously recognizing that he was attempting to pull her leg. "Yeah, right. But tell me, is your new best friend Elissa going to conduct her first therapy dog class tomorrow?"

He sat on the other chair, leaning back but not moving the leg support up. "Yes," he said, "she is. You going to join me there?"

"What—you're going? You must really be smitten, brother."

Maisie knew his love of training dogs was limited to police K-9s. Or at least that it had been.

Maisie knew a lot about him, but not everything.

"Just doing my job. And a little more. But not what you're thinking, sis." He gave her a rundown on the latest information, about Elissa getting fired. "She's going to be staying here in Chance for a while, at least—full-time. If all those various barbs at her mean anything, something could happen to her on our watch. I intend to prevent that...yes, because I find her attractive. But also this seems to be a unique opportunity to stop something illegal and likely to be harmful before it actually happens."

"I get it. And I have to admit I like the idea of preventing a potentially nasty crime besides finding drugs with our dogs, rather than attempting to deal with it afterward. But—" She walked closer and squatted on the floor beside him.

Both dogs joined her, nuzzling her for attention. "Griffin, sit," she said. "Hooper, sit."

Because they were both well-trained K-9s, both immediately obeyed, causing Doug to smile at them. But the smile evaporated as he turned to look into his sister's face. Her expression was grim.

"I'll work with you, Doug. You can be sure of that. Even if you've got the hots for that woman, I recognize it's more than that urging you to get involved. She could wind up being hurt, and we need to prevent that."

"You got it, sis." He recognized that his expression must look grim—as hers did.

"Even more important, to me at least, we have to prevent you from being hurt emotionally, too."

"I know," he said—although he figured his emotions were already way too far involved.

He'd somehow have to back them off, even as he made certain that whoever was threatening Elissa in so many strange ways was caught and prevented from doing anything else.

So much to think about. So much to do.

And a therapy dog class to run that day—her first at the Chance K-9 Ranch.

Would Doug be there with Hooper as he'd suggested?

Those were Elissa's first thoughts when she woke the next morning—after getting more sleep than she'd anticipated.

She showered in the bathroom of her new home and got dressed, then took Peace outside. She'd brought the right kind of biodegradable plastic bags along with food for her dog, so she was prepared for their walk, as she'd been last night.

She had also brought hand—no, paw—wipes and spray-on doggy shampoo and other basics to use for teaching the future handlers in her upcoming classes how to keep their dogs somewhat clean when they were working with patients. Of course, some venues where they would eventually provide therapy might require recent baths and more sanitizing than that, and she would make sure her student handlers were aware of that, too.

What she wasn't entirely prepared for was to see she wasn't alone at that time. Amber and Evan were walking their dogs close to the main house, and they obviously saw her, too, since they waved—and she waved back.

Nearer to her was an area enclosed by a chain-link fence where three other young-looking dogs were confined. Those were the ones being trained as police K-9s, to eventually be sold to departments whose officers were given lessons by Evan. Elissa had heard about that and admired this wonderful facility—and its owners— even more for it.

She soon turned back toward her house, where she and Peace ate their breakfasts in the compact but nevertheless well-equipped kitchen. Elissa also made some flavored instant coffee for herself—not as good as the brewed stuff but it was what she'd bought at the store last night since it required only a microwave and not a coffeepot.

She sat at the small kitchen table but before she finished the cup, her phone rang. She pulled it from her pocket and glanced at it, half hoping it was Doug.

Instead it was Amber, which also pleased her. "Good morning, Amber," she said immediately. "Peace and I enjoyed seeing all of you taking a walk this morning."

"I was glad to see you were awake. Why don't Peace and you come to my house now and we'll talk over your class. I have it scheduled for eleven this morning and you'll have at least a few students with their dogs there for orientation. I've brewed some coffee and have a few sweet rolls, if that encourages you more."

"I was going to say yes anyway, but now I'm really psyched. See you in a few minutes."

On the walk there, Elissa again weighed in her mind what to tell Amber now and how to tell it. If she didn't let her new boss know she'd been officially put on leave—or more—from her other job, Amber might hear anyway from someone else. She'd already told Amber she'd taken a leave of absence, and that wasn't exactly a lie since her boss Mae had agreed to it, at least for now. But it wasn't the full truth.

Of course, she didn't want to come across as a whiner, either—telling her new boss about so many things out of her control that had been happening to her lately. Amber at least knew of the sign telling her to watch who she hired. She might also know of the break-in at Elissa's house, depending on how discreet Doug had been.

And now this.

Peace and she had reached the front door. She turned

to take another look at the fenced-in dogs they had passed. Then she knocked.

The door opened nearly as soon as she touched it. "Hi, Elissa." Sonya pushed the door farther open. Amber's mom, smiling broadly, wore a blue work shirt over matching jeans—not too different from what Elissa had on, although her shirt had a dog's face on the pocket. "Glad you could join us early."

"Me, too." And Elissa was glad—at least for now. She hoped they'd continue this nicely developing relationship after the discussion she was about to start.

Elissa followed Sonya to the kitchen. Lola was there, sitting on the tile floor near her mistress.

"Good morning," Amber said. "Have a seat." She, too, wore a casual outfit.

Elissa obeyed, joining Sonya at the round table in the middle of the room. Amber immediately poured three cups of coffee from the pot at the counter and brought them over, along with a plate of cinnamon buns.

Elissa wasn't surprised to see a large bowl of water on the floor near the fridge. Like people, dogs who lived here or visited were also well taken care of.

Amber joined them at the table and gave a brief description of the four locals interested in therapy training who'd be there at eleven. Those who were employed had been able to take time off work and planned to do it again for future classes.

Then she asked Elissa how she intended to handle the class that day.

Elissa described some of the exercises used to evaluate the dogs and their interactions with their people so she would know how to focus for future lessons with these owners and animals. The exercises would also help her determine if any of those dogs definitely didn't have the personality to become therapy dogs.

She mentioned she'd been in touch with both Officers Doug and Maisie Murran, and they might attend, too.

The practicalities of the day's schedule taken care of, she decided it was time to clarify her situation. Taking a long sip of coffee and half wishing it was alcohol, even at this hour, she looked across the table toward both Amber and her mother.

"Now there's something I need to tell you." The expressions on both women's faces quickly converted from smiling to quizzical. "I have taken a leave of absence from my nursing job, as I told you. But there was an additional reason besides my wanting to have adequate time to get my classes here started."

"What's that?" Sonya asked, and Elissa recognized that she wanted to protect her daughter. Her own parents acted that way about her, too, which was one reason she hadn't been in touch with them since all of her recent difficulties had begun. They still lived in Seattle, where she'd grown up, as did her sister. But as much as she loved them, she had needed to start a new life elsewhere and on her own after a rotten relationship had gone bad, which was why she'd moved to San Luis Obispo when she'd heard of a great nursing job opening there.

She forced herself to stop thinking of them now, though. She needed to concentrate on what she had to say.

"What I need to tell you could make me sound like I'm paranoid or…well, a difficult person. And I don't understand the reason for any of it. But—"

"Does this have anything to do with the sign that was

left on our fence?" Amber interrupted. She appeared as concerned as her mother, but there was something in her look that suggested warmth to Elissa.

"I don't know," Elissa responded, "but I wouldn't be surprised if it did." She then related the claims her boss, senior nurse Mae Shuller, had leveled at her regarding allegations of letting the therapy dogs under her control bully and even harm children. Elissa felt her eyes tear up as she related the story. "I realize you don't actually know me," she finished. "And I could be lying through my teeth when I tell you that I would never, ever, do that to a person, let alone a child—and no way would I allow a therapy dog I was training or working with to act that way."

"But you're not lying through your teeth or otherwise," Amber said calmly. "Right?"

"Absolutely. But I'll understand if you don't believe me and want me to leave."

"Well, you're welcome to stay but you could take a leave of absence from us, too," Amber added.

Feeling devastated by the idea, Elissa looked once more at Amber's face and found her smiling ironically.

"I could," she acknowledged, trying to smile back. "But I'd rather not."

"I figured. Oh, and by the way, I received a call from Officer Doug Murran this morning after we set up this meeting. He didn't go into any detail but said he needed to talk to you first, before the class, and then you and he might have something to tell me. Of course he knows about the note on the fence, but I assume he knows about your leave of absence, too, right? Is that what he wanted to discuss?"

Somewhat shocked, Elissa didn't know whether she

should kick Doug or hug him when he arrived…before her class. Had it been a good thing for him to prime her new boss about something she needed to know? But he had said before that they would relate it to Amber together.

"Yes," she told Amber. "He does know, and it might be the subject he alluded to. He's continuing to investigate your fence issue, and he was also helping me look into a break-in at my house in SLO that might be related, so I figured he needed to know this, too, just in case they're all related."

"Do you think they are?" Sonya asked. "And are you safe? Will we be safe with you around?"

"I do suspect they're all related," Elissa admitted. "I've no idea why, or who's doing it. And I absolutely hope you're safe—and me, too. Good thing there are so many dogs around here who can at least bark at any strangers."

"Right," Amber said. "And Evan's Bear, plus our young dogs he's training to be police K-9s, can do even more than that if something triggers their protective actions. But assuming this was what he wanted to talk about, it'll be interesting to hear Doug's take on all this when he arrives shortly."

"Yes," Elissa agreed. "It will."

"In any case," Amber said, "we'll take you at your word. At least for now. Just to feel more comfortable about the whole thing, though, any one of us here may drop in and watch you both at your classes and when you give demonstrations at our local hospital or other venues."

"I won't say anything about those accusations against you to my friend at the Chance Hospital who I'll be introducing you to," Sonya added. Her expression still remained stiffer than Amber's, so Elissa figured she wasn't nearly as trusting as her daughter. "But like Amber said, you can expect people to observe you anytime."

"I look forward to it," Elissa said. In a way she did. She craved their trust, and they'd surely come to trust her if they watched her therapy dog work and classes the way she always performed them.

"Great," Amber said. "Now let's talk a little more about your class today and what you intend to accomplish."

As Elissa described her plans for an introduction to therapy dog work, she felt herself relax, at least a little. Gratitude at the kindness of the people she had met here so far in Chance warmed her insides. Sonya might be somewhat skeptical, but she hadn't tried to talk her daughter out of giving Elissa this opportunity.

And Amber? She didn't seem mistrustful in the least—and Elissa would do her utmost to ensure Amber never regretted it.

At least here she felt that the other things that had been troubling her were far away…somewhat. Except for that sign.

Unless, of course, those allegations against her as a therapy dog handler wound up following her.

And acceptance by other Chance residents she'd met? At the top of the list, of course, was Doug.

Kind K-9 handler Doug.

Almost as if she had called him with her thoughts, he suddenly appeared in the kitchen doorway, Hooper un-surprisingly at his side. As Peace and Lola barked and hurried toward them, Peace wagging her tail wildly, he said, "Hope it's okay that I let myself in." He looked down at the table then to Amber. "Any coffee there for me?"

"Sit down," their hostess said with a laugh. "I'm surprised neither of our dogs let us know before now that you were sneaking in here, but then, neither of them are K-9s like yours, and our future K-9s next door are still in training. Besides, these two know and trust you. Anyway, there's a sweet roll for you, too, if you'd like."

Both dogs had quieted down and seemed quite content interacting with Hooper.

"I'd like." Doug sat and reached for a roll. Only then did he aim his glance toward Elissa. "Everything set for your class?"

"It sure is," she said.

Everything was definitely ready now and Elissa couldn't wait to get started.

Chapter 10

It was nearly eleven o'clock. Doug waited in the main ranch house's living room along with Elissa and the Belotts, as well as all their dogs—although the younger dogs being trained to become K-9s were still in the nearby den.

One potential therapy student had arrived with her dog, and they were waiting for a few more—including his sister.

Hooper had settled down beside Lola on an area rug on the room's hardwood floor, though Elissa kept Peace beside where she sat on a light blue chair facing the sofa where everyone else was seated. Elissa made friends with Barker, a Doberman mix brought by the therapy student—a college-aged, eager-appearing girl named Kim Boyd.

Doug, at one end of the sofa, watched Elissa. He had

almost convinced himself he had come partly for her protection and partly to observe this session to get an idea what she would do as a therapy dog instructor. He deemed it unlikely she would have any issues during her first class, even if the claims made against her were even a tiny bit true.

But he realized he was getting into a bad habit—hanging out with Elissa as much as possible.

Protecting her, at least, was related to his job, he kept telling himself. But he was doing a poor job of convincing himself.

Too bad Uncle Cy wasn't there. But he lived, and worked, in Riverside, California. He almost never visited Chance. Probably a good thing right now, at least. He'd be telling Doug to start acting more professionally. Fast.

But Doug was glad he had come—for multiple reasons.

For one thing, almost as soon as he had sat at the table, Elissa let him know that she had told Amber and Sonya about the latest issue in her life. He was pleased, and a little surprised, that she had approached it herself.

The doorbell rang and Sonya hurried to answer it. A minute later a familiar voice called, "Hi, everyone." Griffin preceded Maisie into the room, and she let go of his leash so he could greet Hooper then the rest of the dogs. Maisie spotted Doug immediately and, after saying hi to Elissa and Peace, headed in his direction.

"Hi, bro." She took the seat beside him. She wasn't wearing her uniform today, although he was—with his jacket still in his car. "So how are things?" she asked quietly.

"Satisfactory, at least for now." Though there were

some things he wanted to catch her up on, this wasn't the time or place.

"So are you really wanting to turn Hooper into a therapy dog?" Maisie's low voice not only rang with skepticism but he heard amusement, too.

"Maybe someday, like your Griffin," he said, his tone more somber. "When he's no longer a K-9. Or maybe I just want to observe Elissa in therapy-dog-trainer mode. I intend to figure out how a therapy session could go wrong enough to cause a skilled nurse who's also a dog handler to get fired, assuming that was really what happened."

"Yeah, I kind of figured that and think it's a good idea, considering everything going wrong around that particular trainer, though I question your motives."

The doorbell rang before Doug could justify his highly professional motives to his sister—or at least try to convince her, without fully convincing himself.

Sonya left the room again and, in a minute, returned with three more students for Elissa's first class, two men and a woman, each accompanied by a dog. One looked like a French bulldog mix, and another a yellow Labrador retriever mix. Doug figured they'd both be nice and friendly and potentially excellent therapy dogs.

The third was a Jack Russell terrier already pulling at the end of his leash. A kind dog who'd help soothe people in trouble or in pain? A cute animal who'd amuse them and make them feel better? Well, possibly the latter. Doug might doubt this was a potentially great therapy dog, but he'd be interested in seeing how things went.

The newly arrived dogs bounded toward those already there—a probable indication that they all required a lot of training. Griffin stood and walked in their direction, but not Hooper. Odd. His K-9 tended to be friendly except when following commands. But he sat there almost as if in alert mode—until a couple of the newcomers hurried toward where the people already in the room, dogs at their sides, now stood.

"Hi," the woman said. "Can I give your dogs some treats?"

"Me, too," the man said. He knelt on the floor, petting Griffin, then Hooper. Not good, but Doug didn't object since this wasn't an official K-9 event.

"Since our dogs aren't on duty now, that's fine," Maisie said, and Doug agreed.

The guy stood fairly quickly and both of them showed Doug and Maisie they held standard store-bought treats. By then, Hooper was standing, too, sniffing the air in their direction and wagging his tail like the other dogs.

He told his dog "okay" when Hooper looked at him, and Hooper grabbed some treats. Peace, still beside Elissa, also received some of their goodies.

Apparently this was the full class Elissa anticipated that day. Already standing by her chair, she called, "Hi, everyone. Welcome. We'll get started soon."

She glanced toward Doug. He was sure she didn't want his permission to start but the look she levied on him seemed full of poise and challenge, as if she dared him to say something contrary. He kept quiet.

He wondered, though, whether those friendly people, who apparently wanted to impress other dogs as well as their teacher by providing treats first thing, would do well in the class—and how well they'd be able to work with their own dogs.

Well, he would soon have a better idea.

Elissa first went around the room, asking everyone to identify themselves and their dogs. Kim Boyd, who'd arrived earlier with Barker, her Doberman mix, had already introduced herself to those who'd been there but she spoke up again. Jill Jacobs, the female treat-bearer, was the other woman, and she was with Astro, the Jack Russell. The man who'd also offered treats was Paul Wilson, and the French bull, Ollie, was his. The other man was Jim Curtis, accompanied by the yellow Lab mix, Bandit.

"Great to have you all here," Elissa said. "Now, just so you know, this first session will be very informal and informational. We'll discuss what therapy dogs are all about—all the many ways they can be used to help people, and how they're trained to do so. We'll also talk about how they differ from service dogs. We'll start checking your dogs for their strengths and weaknesses as potential therapy dogs, too, though that will mostly be determined in our upcoming classes. I gather they're all over a year old?"

She looked at each of the students, and they nodded.

"Good. That's the requirement for therapy dog certification. Now, Sonya has graciously agreed to provide us some refreshments—coffee and water, and some wonderful cinnamon rolls that I've already tasted. That's for today only. We won't have time to eat or drink in our more active classes—though that won't be true for our dogs in training, since they'll often be given treats. Everyone okay with that?"

Everyone was. As a result, they were all invited into the kitchen to get their drinks and rolls, and those who hadn't brought any could also pick up a few dog treats.

They were told to just leave their dogs in the living room since Amber would remain with them.

Doug held back with Maisie, and they were the last to get their refreshments, although when they got there Sonya hovered over the kitchen counter handing out drinks. Eventually, everyone had picked out what they'd wanted and all returned to the living room.

"Great," Elissa said. "Let's get started."

Elissa had pondered about how best to run a class like this since a lot of her prior teaching sessions had been with only one potential handler. But she'd held classes before, too. She'd decided that the best way to begin it would be with a description of some wonderful ways therapy dogs had been trained and utilized to help people and their states of mind.

While everyone sat on the sofa and a few extra chairs Amber brought in, Elissa stood and reviewed the notes she'd printed out.

She couldn't help glancing toward Doug and Maisie. They both watched her, and she smiled somewhat tremulously. Okay, they made her nervous, especially Doug. He helped her—but he was also studying her. Possibly investigating her.

His sister might be doing so, too, which added to Elissa's nervousness, yet she somehow didn't care as much whether Maisie believed her about why she was put on leave or anything else.

Which she recognized as foolish. Maisie was also a cop. Her belief—or doubt—about Elissa could be equally important in figuring out what was happening to her, and why.

Still, Elissa decided to begin a little differently than

she had originally planned—not just talk about how wonderful therapy dogs could be in a variety of difficult situations, but instead get a discussion going about how dogs contributed in more ways to helping people.

Starting with Doug.

"I'll begin with something a little off topic," she said. "Officer Doug Murran, please tell us about your partner Hooper and how he helps you in police investigations and other situations as a K-9."

She noticed that Evan had slipped into the living room along with his dog Bear. Elissa had learned from Amber that Bear was a retired military K-9 who now assisted Evan with his police K-9 classes…along with helping his trainer and best friend with his waning PTSD. Evan, too, was teaching dog training classes this week, as he always did—though not for therapy dogs. Maybe he could participate in this discussion.

First, though, she was both amused and pleased when Doug rose, putting his hand on top of Hooper's head as the dog sat beside him on the area rug. "What does Hooper do? Anything and everything I need." Looking into Elissa's eyes, he said, "Including investigating sites where something bad is alleged to have happened, like a break-in, and using his extraordinary sense of scent to figure out where and how."

Elissa felt herself smile fondly. "Yes, I'm aware of his skill in doing that. Very aware. What else?"

Doug continued to play along, enumerating other instances where Hooper had helped him find bad guys, their weapons, other ammunition, drugs and more.

"Griffin's good at such things, too," he finally said, looking at his sister.

Maisie fortunately seemed to be playing along.

"That's my wonderful K-9," she said, and likewise described some situations where her golden had also ferreted out bad guys and more. "He's saved my life a couple of times, as well," she concluded and then, at Elissa's urging, told about instances where some suspects had gotten the drop on her and Griffin had attacked, bringing them down before they could shoot Maisie or anyone else.

"They're wonderful," Elissa couldn't help saying, wanting to hug both dogs now lying on the floor at their handlers' feet. And maybe one of those handlers, too— No. She might need to rely on him for her safety, but that was all.

"And I'd love to add to that," she continued, "but first I'll tell you how therapy dogs are different from service dogs." She explained briefly how service dogs weren't considered pets as therapy dogs were, but were trained from early in their lives to work with people with a specific need or disability, from mental illness to physical problems like blindness. "Some even sense when their owners are about to have a seizure."

The students all seemed impressed, but it was time to move on.

"Now I'll tell you about some of the many possibilities you'll have when your dogs are trained as therapy dogs," Elissa said. She briefly described some of her own experiences at hospitals, mostly helping ill or injured children focus on something besides their pain at least for a while—on warm, loving dogs who gave attention and love and distracted the kids.

"And outside of hospitals, therapy dogs help children in many other ways, too, including even encouraging them to learn to read. But more about that later. Therapy dogs do similar kinds of things with injured military veterans who aren't disabled enough to require service dogs but may have mild PTSD or other issues where focusing on a warm, caring animal can help. There are therapy dogs who also go to facilities for seniors. They can help people get their minds off their disabilities or difficulties just by being friendly and fetching toys or even just snuggling."

"That's why I'm here," Kim said, leaning from her chair to give Barker a hug.

"Me, too," added Jill. "I'm just hoping both Astro and I can learn enough from you to slow him down. He's a bundle of energy, but also maybe the most caring and loving dog in the world."

Not exactly contradictory, but Elissa realized Astro might be a bit of a challenge in her classes. She'd do her best to try to help Jill prepare him for therapy work. But he might simply not be appropriate for it, as many dogs weren't. Therapy dogs had to care for and bond with people, even strangers. She hoped Astro would show himself to be that kind of caring once he slowed down.

"No problem with Ollie," Paul said with a shrug and a smile. "My guy is a people dog."

"Same with Bandit, despite his name." Jim also grinned.

"Great." Elissa continued her description, moving her gaze from one dog to the next. They were all behaving well—at least for now. She told the students that they could choose the type and location of therapy that worked best for them and their dogs. "We'll keep these classes general for now, but if you wind up with specific questions, feel free to ask. First, though—Evan, could you tell us a bit about Bear and his military K-9 training?"

Evan obliged and also added, "You may have heard that I returned to the US with a mild case of PTSD. Bear wasn't ever trained as a service dog or a therapy dog, but he definitely helps me when I have an episode." He even described a couple of instances that made Elissa smile.

When she started talking again, it was all about therapy dogs once more. Then it was time for questions, including getting facilities like hospitals to allow dogs inside. These days, Elissa informed them, it wasn't particularly hard since those places were now well aware of how much therapy dogs could brighten the moods of their patients.

"I know you'll help us train our dogs," Jill said, "but I want to hear more about the requirement of qualifying that you mentioned."

"I plan to get into more detail later, but here's the introduction." Elissa explained that there were a lot of well-qualified organizations, often recognized by the American Kennel Club, that tested and then, hopefully, certified a dog to be a therapy dog. "Various hospitals and other locales allowing therapy dogs generally choose which kind of approval they require, so that's always a factor to consider, too."

Eventually, Elissa believed she'd provided enough of an introduction. "How about a demonstration of how a therapy dog works?" she said. She'd noticed Evan slip out the door during the questions, which was a shame. With his admitted mild case of PTSD, she figured he'd be a good one to assist her now, too. But with him gone… "Officer Doug Murran, would you be willing to help out?" She could have chosen Maisie Murran, or even Amber or her mother, but somehow she felt Doug would do the best acting job—as long as he didn't feel uncomfortable or embarrassed.

"Sure," he said, rising. "Now, am I an injured police officer, or some kind of mentally ill fellow in a hospital for treatment?"

Thrilled that he was playing along so well, Elissa said, "You choose."

"I think for now I'll have been shot in the arm in the line of duty and feel angry and depressed."

Damn, he was good. He seemed actually to know something about therapy dogs and what they did.

Sure enough, when she had him sit on her chair and adopt the emotions he'd mentioned, he seemed to be one nasty, irritable guy till, on her orders, Peace came over and nuzzled him, distracting him, bringing over the tennis ball Elissa had given her and demanding by her actions that Doug play with her—in all, getting his attention till Doug stroked Elissa's smart and delightful dog and also tossed the ball a couple of times.

"Guess I'm therapied," Doug finally said.

"You are. Thanks so much." Elissa wanted to hug him the way he had hugged her dog. And, fortunately, well-trained Hooper hadn't acted jealous. She turned back to her class. "Now, there's a lot to learn on your part and your dog's till you can do all that. We'll start working on the basics at our next class. On Wednesday?" She glanced at Amber, who nodded.

It wouldn't have been scheduled this soon if she still had her nursing job, Elissa reminded herself. Maybe it was for the best.

Except for those horrible, false allegations hanging over her.

Well, she'd already decided what she wanted to do that afternoon. She'd check, though, to make sure it was okay for her to go visit Sonya's friend who worked at the local hospital. She would hopefully conduct a therapy dog demonstration and get the hospital's okay for further visits.

For now, though, Elissa allowed herself to feel relieved and even happy.

And to bolster that, she aimed a smile at Doug as the other students started to leave the ranch house.

Chapter 11

The class was over. This first one, at least. And, to his surprise, Doug had enjoyed it, even though the dogs were only discussed and didn't undergo any training...yet.

Maybe it was because he was fascinated by the instructor.

Too fascinated.

Now, both Maisie and he waited till the other students left with their dogs, each saying enthusiastic thank-yous and goodbyes to their teacher. Elissa, in turn, appeared happy as she told them each how much she looked forward to seeing them, as well as their potential therapy dogs, at the next lesson.

"Anything you need me to stay around for?" Maisie asked when the rest were gone. She aimed her question toward Elissa, but Doug knew she was talking to him, too. They'd walked to the door with the others but had returned to the living room. Before he left, Doug wanted to ask Elissa what she planned to do next.

"We're fine, thanks," Elissa said. "I'm so glad you came. I suspect that, if you continue to come to these classes, you'll be really pleased to see what a wonderful therapy dog Griffin can become when you're ready." She smiled both at Maisie and her dog, then bent to hug Griffin.

"Sounds great." Maisie looked at Doug. "You coming now, too?"

"I've a couple more questions." That wasn't a lie. He had a lot of questions. He wasn't sure, though, whether Elissa or anyone there could answer them. "I'll hang around a little longer."

"Okay, then. Walk us to the door." That wasn't a request but an order from his sister. He didn't have to obey her—but it was usually a good thing if he did. It saved her from gentle retaliation later.

He sent a "come" gesture toward Hooper and the four of them left the living room. But Doug intended to return momentarily.

"So what's next?" Maisie asked in a low voice when they'd walked down the hall and reached the door. "You going to continue to follow her? You're on duty tomorrow—aren't you?—so hanging around here isn't going to work."

"You're right. And you're also right that I shouldn't spend so much time on this case, but so far there seem to be no answers even as more issues keep popping up, so I hate to just walk away."

"Knowing you, you won't walk away. But let's just hope that Elissa has seen all the bad stuff she's going to."

"Definitely," Doug said. "Anyway, I'll see you at home later."

"If not before, someplace else."

Doug hoped that wasn't some kind of harbinger of strange things to come that day. He returned, with Hooper, to the living room. There, the three women were engaged in a conversation about what Elissa planned to do that afternoon, while Lola remained lying on the area rug and Peace came over to Hooper before settling down again.

"I guess you're right that the Chance Hospital also needs to know what happened in San Luis Obispo," Elissa was saying, sitting again on the blue chair. "I was hoping otherwise, but on reflection, it's better that they're aware of it up front—and how false it is."

"You can visit them this afternoon," Sonya said from the sofa beside Amber. "I'll give a quick call to my friend there, Petra Frayer—one of the head nurses—to let her know you're coming, and just mention casually that you had some bad vibes at the hospital where you used to work so now you're here full-time. Something like that. I won't go into detail except to say there were false rumors being circulated about a couple of your therapy sessions, but that you're more than happy to have your sessions here observed by anyone." Sonya seemed to hesitate as she stared at Elissa. "Right?"

"Right," Elissa responded immediately. "That might actually be a really helpful thing till I've gained the trust of the staff there...and also yours." She was glad for many reasons about the connection—including that she hopefully would now have a venue for demonstrating and teaching therapy for a while.

"We trust you or we wouldn't have you here," Amber said.

"Thanks. I appreciate that." Elissa nodded at Amber,

but then looked back toward Sonya. "I want to make sure everyone agrees."

Sonya didn't respond, and Doug assumed she had her doubts—but fortunately not enough to have talked her daughter into not hiring Elissa.

Elissa stood. "Peace and I are going to our house now. If you don't mind, please give me Petra's phone number. I'll call her in a half hour or so and work out a time to meet with her and, hopefully, give an initial therapy dog demonstration."

"Sure," Sonya said.

"Let us know that time, too," Amber said. "We'll try to go there to observe."

"I'll also be there." Doug remained curious both about how therapy dogs worked—and how Elissa would be treated by a hospital staff member who'd heard about her travails at her last hospital therapy situation.

Elissa turned to look at him from the doorway. "Really? Then you're actually interested in therapy dog sessions and how they work? I thought you were just…well, being a dedicated cop trying to help investigate what was going on around this ranch—and me."

"Both," he admitted. "But I definitely want to watch your session. With Hooper along. He can watch and learn something there."

And so can I, Doug thought.

She was used to being watched during therapy sessions with Peace. Sharing with others, including friends and relatives of the patients, was part of the enjoyment.

But with all that was happening around her, she felt particularly nervous about this one.

After parking in the lot behind the Chance Hospital,

she walked around the front with Peace on her leash. The hospital was smaller than the one she had worked at before, yet it seemed pleasant, with lots of windows visible on each of its three elongated floors. The facade looked like gray stone, and Elissa got the sense of the place being both inviting and clean, a good place for people to heal.

She tied a scarf around Peace's neck that designated she was a therapy dog and blotted her paws with a cleaning wipe. Then they walked through the front door and stood in the lobby in front of the greeting desk. Lots of eyes were on them—or at least on Peace. People of all ages and ethnic groups, some in white or blue medical jackets, hurried through the reception area. This hospital appeared to be a bustling place.

"Hi," Elissa said to the young woman behind the desk. "I'm Elissa Yorian, and my therapy dog Peace and I have a meeting scheduled with Nurse Petra Frayer at two o'clock."

It was five till two now. Elissa had, as she'd promised Sonya, called Petra as soon as she had returned to her house at the ranch with Peace, told Petra who she was, and set up this time to meet with her and demonstrate some therapy dog skills.

"Very good," Petra had said. "I just spoke to Sonya about you. She said you were hoping to give more demonstrations and therapy lessons here in conjunction with some classes you're going to teach at the Chance K-9 Ranch."

Elissa was certain that wasn't all Sonya had told her. And she had little doubt that Petra, or someone assigned by her, would be with them today at the demonstration and maybe at all future sessions, too, and would perhaps even call her prior employer for references.

They would see Peace and her perform well. And they wouldn't see anything harmful resulting from the therapies she would provide. Elissa's new contacts here with Sonya and Amber would hopefully outweigh any criticisms anyone heard.

The receptionist had gotten onto her phone immediately and now she hung up. "She's expecting you. Go on up to the second floor. The pediatric wing is to your right as you get off the elevator." The young woman, clad in a dark blue dress with a pin on the pocket identifying her as Rona, stood and looked down toward Peace. "Is that a therapy dog? I heard we were going to have a demonstration and that I should allow the dog in."

"Yes, that's Peace." Elissa smiled. "She's a certified therapy dog and I hope we'll work things out here for her to help soothe a lot of people."

"I hope I'll get to watch her sometime," Rona said.

"I do, too." On impulse, Elissa led Peace around the reception desk and told her to sit. Rona's grin was huge—and it got even bigger when Elissa said, "Peace, shake," and her dog offered her right paw to the receptionist.

"How cute!" Rona left her chair enough to bend down and shake the offered paw. Then she looked up again at Elissa. "I don't know how therapy dogs are supposed to work, but this one certainly has made my day."

"She does that with a lot of people," said a familiar voice from the other side of the reception desk. Doug. Behind Hooper and him were Amber and Sonya. They'd all apparently just arrived, too, and Elissa introduced them to Rona and told her they were here to observe the therapy dog session she was about to give. Peace, greeting Hooper, wagged her tail.

It was time to head for the elevators. "So, are you and Peace all ready for this?" Amber strode at Elissa's side. Of everyone, Elissa wanted to impress her most this afternoon.

"We're definitely ready. And excited about this. You'll see me demonstrate what I'll eventually teach to our students at the ranch."

Elissa knew her excitement was obvious, and that was fine.

They had to wait for the elevator and during that time Elissa moved slightly to be closer to Doug. Since Doug was in uniform, no one stopped Hooper, either.

"So you're really interested in watching this demonstration?" she asked him.

"The more I hang out with you, the more I want Hooper to learn some additional skills—like becoming a therapy dog someday." The look on Doug's handsome face appeared a touch amused, yet his eyes captured hers for just a moment as if he said something entirely different with them—like, maybe, he wanted to hang out with her even more.

But that was only Elissa's imagination. She knew that.

"I'll be delighted to help you train him this new way." Elissa spoke fast since the elevator had arrived and the four of them, plus the two dogs, hurried to get on, along with several other people who'd been waiting.

The elevator reached the second floor in no time. As the door opened, a nurse in royal blue scrubs stood there. She appeared to be in her late fifties, with short, curly brown hair and a penetrating look in her eyes that suggested she had seen everything but was still looking for more.

"Petra!" Sonya called and maneuvered her way out of the elevator first.

"Sonya, it's so good to see you." Petra held out her arms and the two women hugged briefly.

Then Sonya introduced Petra to Elissa. Petra asked to see Elissa's therapy dog paperwork, then said, "Are you all set for the demonstration?"

"I sure am," Elissa replied.

"We'll go down here." Petra gestured over her shoulder as she walked down the hall with Sonya beside her. The area looked much like most other hospitals Elissa had visited or worked at—clean, light-colored walls, with people in scrubs hurrying by as well as a few patients walking slowly in their gowns with family members at their sides—and lots of doors to patient and exam rooms.

Petra opened the last door on the right at the end of the hall, and Elissa immediately heard kids crying and yelling at each other. A familiar sound.

Here were some nervous, sad, frightened patients whom Peace could help.

The room was somewhat large, with about five nurses and a couple of doctors standing around, plus half a dozen kids inside. Two lay on mobile beds and seemed to be the ones who were crying. The others sat on chairs facing each other with plush toys in their arms. Half were girls and half were boys.

Then Elissa glanced at Doug. "I know Hooper isn't trained for this, but maybe he can help, too." She gave a hand signal to Peace, who followed her to the kids in small hospital gowns, sitting up with toys, who were shouting at each other. Elissa wondered what their illnesses were, but wouldn't bring that up now.

"Hi, guys," she said. "Would you like to meet Peace? I think she can show you a new game to play, but first she just wants to get to know you."

Peace immediately went over to the closest child, a girl of about seven, who crossed her arms belligerently— until Peace put her head on the girl's lap and nuzzled her to be petted. The girl's expression turned to confusion, then pleasure as she gave in and hugged Peace.

"She loves that," Elissa said. "Now, would you like a turn?" she asked the nearest child, a boy about the same age who was sitting there. That kid appeared a bit jealous at first, and as Peace approached he threw the teddy bear he'd been hugging. Peace immediately went after it and brought it back, making the boy smile as he threw it once more.

She did the same with the other kids sitting there, and they all seemed enthralled—and none yelled at the others, or at Peace. All seemed to be going well.

Elissa picked up one of the teddy bears and nodded toward Doug, who clearly knew what she wanted. He gave hand signals to Hooper to get the toy while Elissa had Peace approach the kids on beds. There was a boy on one and a girl on the other. Apparently, Petra had chosen the patients carefully to see how some with mobility and others with less would get along with a therapy dog—a good test, Elissa acknowledged.

Both of those on the beds didn't seem to move much even to look at the two dogs now in the room, and Elissa figured they weren't able to get up.

At Elissa's command, Peace stood on her hind legs

and placed her muzzle beside the little girl on one bed, who turned slightly toward the dog and smiled, reaching out and petting Peace's head. Elissa let Peace stay there for a while, then do the same with the boy in the other bed.

Meanwhile, while watching, she approached Petra, who stood with Amber and Sonya near the door. "There's a lot more to an actual session than this," she said, "but you can get an idea from this how comforting a therapy dog can be to a child with emotional and other issues." She looked directly into Petra's blue eyes. "I still need to actually start the training at the ranch, but will you be okay with my giving demonstrations, and lessons, at the hospital, as well?"

Petra nodded—and smiled, Elissa saw in relief. "That will be fine. I've got some other long-time patients in mind who might get a lot out of this. Let's give it a try."

"Great." Elissa grinned as Hooper brought the teddy bear to the seated boy for about the seventh time while that child and all the others watched. Hooper might not be trained as a therapy dog yet, but he certainly had a lot of potential.

So did this entire situation. And Doug, for whatever reason he'd come today, certainly seemed happy and proud of his K-9.

Soon Elissa ended the session, promising to keep Petra informed about how the classes went and when another session would be appropriate. She said goodbye to the other hospital personnel in the room, then invited Petra to come to the ranch to observe a class or two.

Soon they were all in the parking lot. Doug congratulated Elissa on a demonstration well done, and she felt happiness filling her everywhere—especially thanks to his sexy, warm smile. "Glad you came," she told him.

He told her he and Hooper were heading to the police station now. Amber let Elissa know that Sonya and she were stopping at a grocery store before going home.

"I'll just go back to the ranch now," she told them. She'd bought enough stuff the other night to have dinner later in her new home. And right now, she felt thrilled that she might remain there for a nice, long time to come.

She strapped Peace into the back seat of her SUV, and they headed to the ranch.

Elissa felt nearly ecstatic then, and her good mood lasted for the rest of the afternoon and evening. It escalated even more when Doug called early that night just to touch base, say nice things about her session—and, apparently, make sure she hadn't had anything else nasty happen to her.

Which she hadn't.

But her good mood evaporated early the next morning when she received a call from Amber. "Can you come over?" her boss asked. "I just took a couple of our young K-9 trainees out for a walk and—well, you'd better see this."

See what? Elissa wondered. But not for long.

Though she was concerned about what Amber wanted her to see, Elissa's great mood from the day before still lingered—at first—as she leashed Peace and walked her toward the main ranch house.

Until she saw Amber standing at the bottom of the driveway, still holding the leashes of two of the young German shepherds Evan was training for sale as police K-9s.

And if Elissa was any judge at this distance, Amber's expression looked grim.

Amber motioned for Elissa to join her, and Elissa, fearing what she'd see there, nevertheless obeyed.

She quickly saw what had disturbed her new employer.

There was a new sign on the gate.

It read You Hired Her. You'll Pay.

Chapter 12

It was early in the morning, just after seven—the time Doug always started getting ready on days he was on duty unless there was an earlier meeting he needed to attend or a crime scene to visit. He'd thrown on jeans and a T-shirt and was outside walking Hooper. In a few minutes, he'd return inside, shower and put on his uniform. Then they'd head to the station.

Maisie was also up but she followed a slightly different routine. She'd already walked Griffin and Doug believed they were both eating breakfast. Which he and Hooper would do, too, just before they were ready to leave.

He was glad they'd be on duty today. Fewer distractions. More like his usual life, the way it used to be.

Not that yesterday wasn't enjoyable. Who'd have thought he would find therapy dog training so interesting? So captivating?

Or maybe it wasn't just the idea of therapy dogs, but one particular trainer…

He'd just stepped back into the house when his phone rang. He pulled it from his pocket. Well, speak of the devil. Or angel. He swiped it to answer. "Good morning, Elissa. How—"

"Doug," she interrupted, and her voice sounded choked. What was going on? "Could you please come here to the ranch?"

"Sure. A little later." But as he listened, he thought he heard…was Elissa crying? "What's wrong?" he demanded then realized that was no way to help her. "What's wrong?" he repeated more gently.

"Sorry. I don't mean to be paranoid or stupid about it…but whoever left that horrible warning about hiring me here? They've done it again. Apparently sometime in the middle of the night. And they're threatening—"

"I'll be there right away," Doug said. "Be sure to stay with Amber or Evan or Sonya. Don't do anything by yourself. And of course keep Peace with you, too."

"I will." He could barely make out her soft words.

He wished he were there already, holding her. Soothing her. And taking Hooper on a walk to track whoever had dared to do such a thing.

"Good. Now, don't worry. We'll figure this out. I promise."

"Thanks," she managed to say, and then Doug hung up, wondering if he'd made a promise he'd be able to keep.

"What's going on?" Maisie strode down the hall from the kitchen toward him, Griffin at her heels.

"Another warning sign at the K-9 Ranch," he said. "Someone left it overnight."

"And none of the dogs barked?"

"Don't know yet. I'm heading there as soon as I change clothes. Please let Sherm and Kara know where I'm going and why." Police Chief Andrew Shermovski and Assistant Chief Kara Province would both want to know right away about this latest threat at the Chance K-9 Ranch. They'd both been eager to have the murder that occurred there before solved as quickly as possible, and they now had an ongoing good relationship with the Belotts. His going there right away without checking in at the station would be fine with them.

Maisie, already dressed to go on duty, pulled her own phone out of her pocket. "I'll call and let them know. Griffin and I are coming with you."

Pushing the button to end the call with Doug had been difficult. Having even the distant connection with him had helped Elissa feel a little better.

But just a little.

With Peace still standing at her side, she turned to look at Amber, who was also talking on her phone—remaining near the fence, staring at that miserable sign without touching it. To Elissa, that eyesore closely resembled the last one: block letters on a small rectangular piece of cardboard attached to the fence by string. Last time, Elissa was aware that the Chance Police Department had checked the sign for fingerprints or anything else that would help identify the elements of it—which then could help identify who'd left it. But as far as she knew, they'd found nothing useful.

This time? If she had to live with the fact of another threat relating to her—but directed at her new employer—she really hoped it at least provided an answer.

"I... I just spoke to Doug," Elissa said, probably unnecessarily, when Amber hung up. She had remained close enough for Amber to have heard the brief conversation if she'd wanted to while also speaking with someone else.

She had also no doubt witnessed Elissa's near breakdown. But Elissa realized that, to keep her job—to keep her sanity—she needed to gather her resources to try to figure out what to do next to solve this increasingly horrendous situation.

And to protect Amber and her mother, since they'd been the ones to hire her.

Could Doug help? Would he help? Surely, as a local cop, he had reason to get involved again. But Elissa didn't know how the local PD worked, and whether, even if they did start a new investigation on this sign—which surely they would—they'd assign the same officers to do the work.

Almost immediately, Elissa saw movement from farther down the small lane where her house sat. Evan was striding quickly in their direction, with Bear at his side. Since he was former military and now trained police K-9s, maybe he could figure this out. But he hadn't with the last threat, apparently leaving the investigation to the local authorities.

Not for the first time Elissa wondered why Evan didn't live in the main ranch house, or why Amber didn't live in the employee home where Evan and Bear stayed. They were clearly a couple—but as she'd also wondered before, perhaps Sonya's living with Amber made their staying together too awkward.

They seemed really, really close. Too bad Doug and she had no chance at that kind of relationship. As nice as he was to her, he was just doing his job. Besides, she didn't really want to be close to anyone. Not again. And especially not now. She needed to get her life settled without any additional drama.

But life wasn't letting that happen.

Evan reached them quickly. Like Amber and Elissa, he was dressed informally in jeans and a T-shirt. He immediately joined Amber at the fence, staring at the sign. "When did you first see this?" He put his arm around her and pulled her close.

"When I came out to walk Lucy and Hal." Amber pointed to the two young shepherds on leashes beside her. "I saw something on the gate and went down there. I thought about trying to get these young dogs to search since they're starting to learn how, but didn't want to get in the way of the cops—or Bear." She paused. "You know, I'm getting really tired of threats around here."

Elissa certainly understood that. She's also heard that these fence threats weren't the only ones her boss had been faced with recently.

"I get it," Evan said. "Well, let's try to figure this one out now." He walked Bear up to the fence, let his dog sniff the area, then said, "Bear, search."

Elissa was fascinated to see the way the German shepherd obeyed by sniffing the fence, then the ground around it as if whoever had done this has left a unique and identifiable scent. Bear headed toward the driveway—just as a black police SUV drove up the incline and parked at the top.

Doug and Maisie got out immediately, and soon had Hooper and Griffin leashed beside them.

Bear, meanwhile, kept on the move at street level with his scenting rather than going up the driveway to greet the newly arrived dogs and people. Elissa had heard he'd been trained to find explosives as a military K-9. That might not help to determine who'd left that sign.

Doug and Maisie came down the hill with their dogs and joined Elissa and Amber where they watched Evan work with Bear. "We'll observe for a few minutes and then get our dogs to search, too," Doug said. He had drawn up close to Elissa but didn't touch her. She had an urge to reach over and hug him, to hide her face on his chest while she cried—but she wouldn't allow herself to show the angst she felt inside.

"Sounds good," she said. "Thanks to you both for coming. Will there be an official investigation by the Chance PD?"

"We'll make sure of it." Maisie smiled grimly at Elissa. "Any ideas about when and how this happened?"

Elissa shook her head. "I haven't a clue."

Doug looked to Amber. "How about you? Did Lola or any of the youngsters bark at any time last night?"

Elissa had wondered that, too, and was glad Doug asked.

"Not in any unusual way that would signify a prowler," Amber replied. "We often play a game of fetch just before bedtime to tire them out after their final walk of the night."

"We let them bark then for fun sometimes." Sonya had just joined them from the top of the driveway and now also stared at the fence. "Where did that come from?"

"That's what we hope to find out," her daughter said.

"Hey, cops," Evan called from the other side of the driveway entry where Bear was pulling on his leash as if he wanted to walk along the road. "Let's get your dogs working, too."

Neither Doug nor Maisie hesitated while they had Hooper and Griffin start out much as Bear had done—and they, too, appeared to alert on some kind of scent near the sign that led them toward where Bear was, as if wanting to go down the road.

Elissa kept watching, fascinated, keeping Peace near her.

Were all three dogs telling them that someone had parked a car some distance away and walked to the driveway last night—probably after dark? Maybe the person had come when Amber was playing with the dogs in her house so barking wouldn't be a giveaway as to their presence. Or they'd been so quiet that the dogs hadn't noticed. There was, after all, a distance between the gate and the ranch house at the top of the long driveway.

Too easy? Maybe. But even if all the dogs did now smell the scent of the person who'd posted the sign, that wasn't an identification of who it was. And other people could have walked along the road recently, too.

All three handlers soon relieved their dogs of their duty.

Then Doug, Maisie and Evan all led their dogs back up the driveway. "Well, no surprise, but it seems fairly clear how the suspect got here," Maisie said. "Too bad we don't know more."

"Yeah," Doug said, and the look he leveled on Elissa appeared both concerned and angry. He was undoubtedly the kind of cop who wanted answers. Fast.

The fact that he seemed to give a damn about what

was happening around her made Elissa feel a little better, sure—but she still worried about what was to come.

Maisie went to her car and returned with a large
plastic bag and some rubber gloves. Doug and Maisie
walked back down the slope with their dogs, then placed
the sign in the bag, and Maisie took it to transport to
the police station for a forensics exam.

Which would probably yield no more than the last
time. Elissa figured that would be the case. Same person, same way of dealing with the sign, so why would
they be any closer to being identified?

When they were done, at Amber's invitation, everyone went into the ranch house. Sonya brewed fresh coffee, and they all sat at the kitchen table with the dogs
near them—but their conversation felt stilted. Amber
was clearly worried, and Evan was concerned about her
and her mother. Doug and Maisie were friendly enough
but now acted distant. Professional. Watching all the
people around them as if studying them for answers.

Elissa understood—but she wished on some level
that she could get Doug to join her at her house so they
could just talk. But soon he would say goodbye and
most likely head back to his station. Without Elissa.
Without answers. Without—

"Are you teaching any classes today, Elissa?" Doug
asked, aiming an unemotional glance at her.

"No, we'd planned on the next one for Wednesday,
and this is only Tuesday."

"Good," Doug said. "Right now, I'd like for you to
accompany Maisie and me to the police station."

Chapter 13

Doug sat nearly motionless in the driver's seat of his police vehicle, driving them quickly, but cautiously, to town.

Well, motionless except for his head, which turned enough to ensure safe driving—and to steal glances at the woman beside him. Elissa sat in the passenger seat. She held her body stiff while she stared out the window. She looked nervous.

And she wasn't talking much at all.

Maisie had graciously volunteered to sit in the back with Hooper and Griffin. Or maybe she'd just wanted to eavesdrop on what he and Elissa discussed.

Which so far was nearly nothing. Not even any questions—not even from him, though he had plenty. But his inquiries could wait till they were at the station—and within the scope of the official investigation.

Elissa hadn't objected when Doug had essentially given her an order to come along. She'd even offered to drive herself to the station so he wouldn't have to get her back to the ranch, but he didn't want her alone at the moment. Maybe ever. Not with the strange, different kinds of threats being aimed at and around her.

She had chosen to leave Peace at her house—and Evan and Amber had promised to check on her often. "I think she'll be safer there," Elissa had said somewhat vaguely.

Did she anticipate the threats against her would increase into something worse at the police station? Or, perhaps, that others would consider her guilty of something that could lead to her being detained at the station for some long period of time?

She didn't elaborate.

In a short while, Doug pulled into his space behind the station. "Here we are," he said unnecessarily.

"Yes, here we are." Elissa didn't sound thrilled about it. "Could you tell me a little more about what I can expect?"

"There may be others besides Maisie and me who have questions about those signs left at the ranch—and we should also make sure our investigators know about the additional things going on with you." Doug glanced behind them where Maisie was getting out of the car, with Griffin leashed beside her. Doug also exited but went around to the passenger side first to help Elissa out.

Instead she got out herself—and looked up at the rear of the station. If he read her expression correctly, she felt doomed. Or at least resigned. To what?

To the investigation, at least. But was there more?

He needed to know—especially because his urge to protect her might be way out of line. But right now, he didn't think so.

By the time he got Hooper out of the back, Elissa had followed Maisie through the rear door of the station. Several other uniformed cops approached from different parts of the parking lot. Doug accelerated his pace and Hooper's.

Sure, he knew those other guys. They were legit. Even so, not knowing where the threats to Elissa came from, he didn't want anyone to come between him and her, at least not now.

Inside, Maisie, with Griffin remaining beside her, and Elissa behind her, approached Ed, the uniformed officer on duty behind the reception desk. She must have explained why they were there, since she turned slightly to gesture toward Elissa. Ed, nodding, picked up the desk phone receiver—evidently calling to inform the assistant chief of their arrival. Kara had indicated previously that she wanted further information, which was one reason Doug had told Elissa to join them at the station that morning.

Doug, Hooper at his side, immediately joined them. Elissa's gaze roved through the station's large entrance lobby, probably taking in the few groups of civilians talking among themselves or with a police officer or two. Her eyes were troubled, but even when he made a slight movement to attract her attention she didn't look at him. He felt an urge to comfort her, to tell her everything would be all right. But he had no genuine sense yet that it would be. Even though he would do all he could to get this situation figured out.

"Okay, she's expecting you," Ed said to Maisie, who nodded.

"Thanks." She must have known Doug was there since she turned and gestured toward the hall to the station's administration area. "Let's go."

Only then did Elissa's gaze seem to focus—on Maisie, not on him. She nodded.

Doug followed them toward the main hallway, Hooper with him. They quickly passed the groups of people he figured Elissa had been observing for the few minutes they were there, then entered the hall and walked down it nearly to the end.

As they reached the office, Maisie knocked on the wooden door. Kara called, "Come in," and Maisie pushed the door open, gesturing for Elissa to precede her inside.

"Hello, Elissa," Kara said. "I'm Assistant Chief Kara Province. Thank you for coming." The assistant chief rose from behind her desk and offered her hand for a shake. There seemed to be fewer piles of paper on it than usual today, but her laptop remained on the small table beside her tall desk chair.

"Hi," Elissa said. Despite her demeanor a minute ago, her voice sounded strong. "Thank you for inviting me here. I really want to figure out what's going on, and I'm hoping you can help me."

Doug found himself impressed with her attitude. Was it real—or was she just assuming it to try to impress the assistant chief?

"I hope we can, too." Kara aimed a glance with slightly raised eyebrows first toward Maisie then toward him. He elevated his brows a bit, too, but without otherwise changing his mild expression. It would be interesting to hear how Kara played this game. "All of you, please have a seat. But before we begin—" She lifted her phone receiver, pressed a few buttons then talked briefly before putting it back down again. "I'm having a detective join us."

Which was fine with Doug. Maisie and he were detectives of sorts, too—but with constant assistants who helped stop or solve crimes with the use of their noses and ears.

All of them sat—including Hooper and Griffin on the floor beside their respective handlers.

In a minute, another knock sounded at the door, and Detective Vince Vanderhoff, one of the department's senior detectives, entered before Kara could invite him in.

Vince was moderate height, with a receding hairline of brown hair over a narrow face overpowered by large glasses. He wore a suit, as usual. "Hi," he said first to Kara, who introduced him to Elissa and asked him to sit, as well. Her office had more chairs in it today than usual, so she had been clearly anticipating this meeting.

"Elissa," Kara began after settling herself once more behind her desk. "You may be aware that I've discussed your situation with Officers Doug and Maisie Murran. I've also mentioned it to Detective Vanderhoff. We're concerned about you since you've apparently just moved to Chance, and we're particularly concerned about what's going on at the Chance K-9 Ranch. Why don't you describe it all, to make sure we're on the same page?"

Doug had managed to take a seat beside Elissa. Now, he looked at her, expecting her to begin. Which she did, but only after glancing at him first. He half wished he could say something to make this discussion—and everything surrounding it—easier for her. But he was here on duty.

Besides, he wanted to hear her latest take on it, too.

"There have been things happening around me. To me. I really don't understand any of them." She started by describing the break-in at her San Luis Obispo home—how Peace had acted oddly when Elissa had returned home after spending hours away from her during her first visit here to Chance. "I happened to mention it the next day when I was here, and Officer Doug Murran was nice enough to come to my house with Hooper—who found where a window had been jimmied open. But I guess there wasn't any evidence that identified who it was." She looked at him again, this time less covertly, and smiled sadly.

"Was that around the time the first sign was left at the K-9 Ranch?" asked Vince.

"Yes," Elissa said. "The next thing that happened to me was that I was...well, given a leave of absence from my nursing job at a hospital in SLO where my dog and I also provided therapy sessions for patients. Someone...someone claimed we had done it in a way to scare or harm children. And now...now this latest sign at the ranch." Her voice broke slightly. "I don't understand any of it," she said more strongly. "Can you help me?" She was looking at Vince as she asked this, which somehow made Doug angry—and even slightly hurt.

He'd already stepped in to try to help her—as part of his job, of course. But he'd failed her, at least so far.

Well, Vince could do whatever he could do as the detective now assigned to the case. But that wouldn't prevent Doug from continuing to do what he could, too.

"We'll try," Vince responded in a kind voice. But that

was the last time he sounded kind, to Doug. He immediately started grilling Elissa about her work at the SLO hospital, both as a nurse and a therapy dog handler. He particularly pushed about anything she knew regarding who'd made the claims against her therapy dog work—which still wasn't much, apparently, although her boss at the hospital had made a big deal about it without notifying her of her accusers' identities.

Nothing new to Doug came out of this discussion.

It certainly didn't feel new that he had an urge more than once—maybe all the time—to shout out to end this intense interrogation. Or maybe to help Elissa through it by drawing his chair closer to her, putting an arm around her, being as supportive as he could. But he was on duty, and one of the people in the room was the assistant police chief.

Kara seemed to sense, at least somewhat, what was going on in his head since she kept glancing toward him, a frown on her face.

A frown that somewhat mimicked the one his sister was levying on him.

Heck, he was a professional. Sure, he felt something toward Elissa. Pity. Nothing deeper—or at least nothing he'd allow.

But as much as he'd wanted to get this situation, and all of its aspects, resolved as fast as possible for Elissa, that urge was even stronger now.

Eventually, Vince ended his inquisition, but that didn't stop Kara from adding more questions, largely about how Elissa had first heard that the Chance K-9 Ranch was looking for dog trainers, including those skilled in teaching both the dogs and their owners what they needed to know for approval as therapy dogs and handlers.

That was an interesting question, one that had occurred to Doug, but he hadn't followed through with Elissa. How she'd heard of it wasn't likely to be as important as how she'd decided to apply.

"It was online," she said. "I'm always checking for posts relating to therapy dogs, since it's something really important to me."

"More important than your nursing of people?" Kara asked wryly.

This time Elissa's smile appeared genuine. "Oh, I love people, so I'm happy to help care for them both with the skills I know as a nurse, and for cheering them up a whole lot more by having my dog provide therapy."

Kara smiled back. Maisie raised her eyebrows, but she, too, seemed amused and more relaxed now. Even Vince nodded and shot her a small grin.

And him? Doug couldn't help but send a much bigger grin her way, and Elissa met his gaze as she took it in.

Looking first at Vince, then at Kara, he said, "Despite all the stuff going on around her, Elissa is one heck of a good therapy dog trainer. I've already heard her explain it and saw a demonstration at the hospital. Hooper and I hope to go back for more." He grew more serious. "Of course, I'm wondering now if Elissa's appearance at the hospital, in public here in Chance with the owners of the K-9 Ranch there at first, too, is what notified whoever's leaving those signs that she was hired by the ranch."

"Which could have then triggered the second sign," Vince acknowledged with a nod of his head. "That's one of the things I'll be investigating, including who was there and whether anyone heard someone else say something against therapy dogs in general or Elissa and her dog in particular."

"Good idea," Doug said. He had wanted to do that, too, but if he did, it wouldn't necessarily be in his capacity as a local police officer—a K-9 officer. For now, he intended to keep probing on his own when he could—and also to stay in close contact with Vince to learn what, if anything, he found out.

It was over—for now. And this police interrogation wasn't as bad as it could have been, Elissa thought as she rose and thanked the people in the room. She couldn't pet the dogs since they were on duty here at the station, but she certainly appreciated their presence. They, at least, hadn't acted as if she was somehow on trial.

And the cops? She'd gotten the impression they were looking for a reason to investigate her rather than try to find whoever was creating such havoc in her life.

Or maybe that's what they always did—make assumptions against people involved in difficult situations to try to learn enough to eliminate them from their suspect lists.

Had it helped to have Doug present? He, at least, had acted before as if he was willing to help find out who was behind all this.

"You okay?" she was asked the moment they were in the hallway outside Assistant Police Chief Province's office. Kara remained inside with Detective Vanderhoff.

But it wasn't Doug who asked. It was Maisie. She stood right outside the door, Griffin at her side.

"More or less," Elissa said as Doug joined them with Hooper.

"Hey," he said, "if you've got a few minutes, let's grab some coffee before I take you back to the ranch. I'd like to dissect a little of what Vince asked—and also figure out what comes next. Okay? Maisie, you can come, too."

"Thanks, but I've got another assignment I need to start working on. You can fill me in later." She looked at Doug and the two of them shared a glance that Elissa could only interpret as amusement on Maisie's part and maybe irony on Doug's.

"I'm fine with getting some coffee," Elissa said, "as long as I get back to the ranch soon to check on Peace— though I'm sure she's fine with Amber and Evan looking in on her. Maybe we can figure out how I should handle my classes and hospital visits now that I know I'm being spied on by whoever's doing this."

"We'll definitely talk about it," Doug said. "Let's go."

Chapter 14

Elissa wasn't surprised when Doug suggested they go to the Chance Coffee Shop. It wasn't far from the police station, so they could walk. And he'd invited her for coffee, so it made sense to head there.

But she knew full well that he didn't just want to sip coffee and talk about the nice August weather in Chance. She wasn't certain what he did want to talk about, though. Since he'd been there for the grilling she had been subjected to about all the issues she'd been facing, he should feel certain that he knew everything she did—right?

Now, with Hooper beside him, he led her through the hallways at the station, past a few other uniformed cops and a civilian or two, and back to the reception area. He gave a slight wave to the same guy at the reception desk who'd been there before, then led her through the small crowd to the front door.

He opened it, and when Elissa walked outside she took a deep breath—and not entirely because she was outside in the fresh air again. No, she somehow felt relieved that she had been permitted, finally, to exit the station.

They turned to the right, in the direction of the coffee shop. There wasn't much traffic on the street, nor were there a lot of pedestrians on the sidewalk near them.

"So how are you doing?" Doug asked without looking at her.

She glanced toward him and managed a brief laugh. "I feel like one of those characters on television interrogated by a star who plays an important cop—verbally ground into the dirt. The audience may know the character is innocent, but the point is to display the cool intelligence of the star in his role. Of course that cop eventually comes up with the right answer and he and his innocent interrogation victim become buddies."

"But you don't think you'll become buddies with Vince?"

"No, and not Assistant Chief Province, either. But I'll like them a whole lot more if your department actually figures out what's going on."

They'd reached the coffee shop and once more Doug opened the door for her before he and Hooper walked in. It was approaching noon and the place was busy, but they still managed to find a table along the wall beneath the windows facing the sidewalk. Doug had Elissa sit to save the table, along with Hooper—or so he said. That way she couldn't object much if he treated her to the mocha she wanted.

The line was short so he came back soon with cups for both of them, along with a plastic plate holding a few finger sandwiches on mini-croissants. "In case you're hungry for an early lunch," he said. They looked good, possibly with tuna salad and roast beef.

He sat, gave Hooper a couple of treats from his pocket, and took a few sips of his drink before beginning.

That gave Elissa an extra minute or two to feel him out. Was he, too, going to interrogate her today? Again?

Was there anything he was looking for that his colleagues hadn't approached and he'd neglected to ask her about previously?

"Okay," he finally said, "I mostly wanted to apologize. Sort of."

That surprised her. "I figured the questions and pressure were all part of what police on a case need to do."

"True." His hazel eyes gazed at her with what appeared to be amusement.

She took another sip of her sweet and bracing mocha. If that was his opinion, was he just using his apology to try to get her to relax—so she'd divulge something else?

As if she had anything she hadn't already told him or, now, the others, too.

"So what's next?" she finally asked. He had something on his mind, or why get together to talk again now?

"I've been considering that." He reached over and picked up one of the small sandwiches. "I'm glad Maisie and I were invited to be there when Vince questioned you. You and I have talked about the incidents, but I also wanted to get the take of others with a lot of experience in crime solving, even more than Maisie or I have. I was hoping they'd come up with a different direction, a course of questions or actions I hadn't considered yet."

"I wouldn't say they did that," Elissa said dryly. "Same stuff, but just more detail than you provided."

"Right. That's kind of my point." He grasped her hand, which had been reaching for her cup once again. "They asked about preludes to each situation, who you knew, who you suspected—pretty much what we've already talked about. So maybe we need to figure out another approach."

His hand held hers firmly and she reciprocated. His was warm and solid, and she had a sudden urge to hang on to it forever. Yeah, right. His touch might help her feel safe for the moment, but there was no way he would stay this close to her for more than a few minutes.

"Sure," she said as casually as she could. "Do you have any suggestions? I've been thinking about it, too, but with a civilian's mind, not a cop's."

"I'm still mulling that over," he said, draining the sudden hope she'd felt at least a little. But he wasn't through. "There's only so much time I'll be able to hang out with you, since Hooper and I still have to go about our regular job. If I have no specific assignment but I'm on duty, I usually need to stay around the station. But I'd like for you to schedule what classes you can to coincide with my off-duty hours. And when you hold classes or go anywhere, let's try to ensure you're accompanied by someone trustworthy. Me or Maisie or even Amber—or better yet, Evan, with his K-9 training and military background. We'll need to make it seem coincidental and informal, in case the person menacing you is hanging out nearby."

"No privacy then," she grumbled but she didn't let go of his hand.

"Not as much as you're used to, probably. But there's a good reason for it."

"Yes," she said sadly. "There is."

"There's more to it than that," he continued. "I want to know about everyone you come in contact with, no matter how you run into them. I'm familiar enough with all the folks at the K-9 Ranch, even their ranch hand Orrin, to feel you're okay with them. But anyone else—students, people who work at the hospital where you'll be conducting therapy sessions, other therapy dog handlers, even the people who are your therapy patients and their family members—we need to figure out who they are and why they're in contact with you."

"That could take a lot of time and effort," Elissa said.

"Yeah, it could. Some info is available online, and I have access to websites especially for people in law enforcement that could give me even more information than civilians like you can find. I'll be delving into them myself when I can, count on that. And you, too, can check out some sites available to the general public."

"Okay," she said. "Let's do it. But, Doug, I hate to take up so much of your off-duty time like that." She meant that—and she didn't. She craved answers.

She also craved being with him, as foolish as that might be.

"That's my decision," he responded. "And I can get some technical help at the station. We'll figure this out, Elissa. I promise. And if there's any way I can get my partner here to help, you can be sure Hooper will do all he can to bring down the person who's harassing you."

"Sweet dog," she said, bending to ruffle Hooper's fur on top of his head.

Sweet man, too, she thought, but kept that to herself.

* * *

Were they approaching this from a better direction now? Doug certainly hoped so.

But what if there was something—someone—else? Someone in Elissa's past, maybe, and not a current friend, student, coworker or whatever.

She might consider him a nosy SOB, but if so, she'd just have to live with it.

He picked up the last of the small sandwiches and said, "Under other circumstances, I wouldn't consider it any of my business, but tell me a bit now about where you grew up, whether you're close to your family, what friends you have from your past—just in case we're going in the wrong direction to figure this out." He took a bite, watching her.

Her eyes widened—those beautiful brown eyes—even as she scowled. "I'd rather not answer. No one from my past could be involved with this." But then her expression grew a bit puzzled.

"So who are you thinking about?" he prompted immediately.

"No one, really, but—"

"Tell me. In fact, give me a rundown of how you came to be a nurse and a therapy dog trainer in San Luis Obispo. Did you grow up there?"

Her glare returned, but only briefly. Then she said, "No, I didn't. Okay. Here's the short version, and that's all you need. It's not relevant."

She briefly described how she had grown up in Seattle. That her parents and older sister still lived there. Her dad sold real estate and her mother and sister were in retail, managing different clothing stores.

"I wasn't interested in following in any of their foot-steps."

"I figured. But you were interested in nursing, right?"

"Right. And we had dogs as my sister and I were growing up, so the therapy dog idea was a natural re-sult." She described going to college and nursing school locally and landing a job in a hospital near her home.

And then her somewhat lighthearted attitude seemed to change.

"No details necessary," she continued, seeming to focus more on her nearly empty cup of mocha than anything else. "But suffice it to say that I had…well, a relationship with a doctor on staff. A pediatrician."

That doctor, she told him, also had an outside prac-tice. They'd been together for more than a year before she'd realized that he'd become a doctor more because of the potential for a high income than to truly help kids. "Not my way of looking at things, but since he helped kids, too, I could live with it. He also wasn't wild about dogs, but I'd already gotten Peace and started therapy dog training, and he let me work with some of his patients."

Her former guy-friend was irrelevant to Doug, or so he told himself, unless this somehow led to Dr. Kids-Mean-Money coming after Elissa now for some reason.

But just hearing about her relationship, over or not, gnawed at his insides.

"Sounds good," he lied.

"Well, it wasn't." Her tone grew sharper and she glared at him for a moment till she shook her head and looked down again. "I thought we meant something to one another, but…I learned that wasn't true. For one thing, nurses didn't earn enough money to make him happy." She described how she'd learned he was also having an affair with a well-paid and generous cardiologist. "That was more than enough."

Just quitting her job there, even though she still had family in town, hadn't been enough. She'd done her research and found a job that sounded good to her in San Luis Obispo. She'd gone there to interview and secured it, then faced down the miserable doctor, quit her old job and moved with Peace to SLO.

"That was that," she finished. "And in case you're going to tell me that my ex, or his girlfriend, has to be behind what's happening to me now… I've considered it, but there would be no reason for it. He clearly didn't want me any more—no more than I wanted him after I learned the truth. And even if he dumped his new friend, he didn't try to come back to me, so there'd be no reason for her to try to get vengeance in any manner."

Doug bought that, although he would look into the situation anyway—but he'd wait till another time to ask her for the names of those involved. He would also check records of people with the last name of Yorian in Seattle, but unless her parents or sister were so determined to get her to run home that they'd resort to these scary tactics, it was unlikely they were involved.

Still, he asked, "Are you in close touch with your family?"

"Don't go there," she ordered. "I don't want them worried. They're wonderful people. Supportive. Would like me to come home but understand that my life is my own. They're definitely not involved."

Hopefully not. But Doug knew better than just to assume things were what they seemed.

Like love affairs gone bad. He recognized too well

how much that could hurt. He'd had one, too, back when Maisie and he still lived in Riverside, where they'd grown up—and their parents had split. Their divorce was one reason he and his sister were so close with Uncle Cy, who was always there for them. Plus, he was a cop and taught them to appreciate law enforcement enough to follow it as a career.

They'd both decided to become K-9 officers and heard of an excellent opportunity here in Chance— at a good time, as it turned out. Doug had been dating a woman he'd met in college, but the relationship had started going sour. She'd kept getting more and more demanding—and he hadn't been obedient, at least not to her. Leaving had definitely been the best option.

And Doug had come to appreciate his sister—and the K-9s he worked with—even more.

"Okay," he finally said. "We've got our work cut out for us checking into people you've been in contact with recently, maybe for the past month or two. I'd like you to make a list of everyone you can think of—friends, acquaintances, neighbors, whatever."

"Fine. I'm going to ask Amber more about hiring me full-time and what I can do for her and the ranch. I'll want to give the therapy dog classes I'm already scheduled for, but maybe also provide some additional general dog obedience classes along with Evan, though he'll need to teach me the way he wants it done. Even if that works out, I should have enough free time to get on my laptop and work on my list. I might even do a little checking on some of them if I think they might have something against me, although I doubt I'll find anything on general websites. I don't suppose you can get me access to some of your official ones, can you?"

"No," he said. "But, as I said, I'll make the time to do some checking on my own, and I might be able to get our department's techie to help out." He looked at her cup. "You want more mocha?"

"No, and I've taken up enough of your time. Could you take me back to the ranch?"

"Sure."

He felt glad, as he and Hooper led Elissa back to his SUV, that they'd accomplished something—maybe.

Would their search lead to results? He certainly hoped so. He had to stop whoever was harassing Elissa this way—and before anything accelerated.

When they were all settled in the vehicle and on the road to the ranch, he glanced at Elissa and found her watching him. Smiling slightly.

"I can't tell you how much I appreciate your help in all this mess," she said softly. "I know it's your job to help civilians, but you're surely going above and beyond all that's expected of you."

"I don't like unsolved cases," he told her. "Or hearing of people with troubles I want to fix."

"I figured," she said with a slight laugh. "And I thank you."

The ride back to the ranch was pleasant. More than pleasant. With their discussion at least temporarily behind them about ramping up the investigation of people in case they were behind her harassment, Elissa was able to change the subject.

She wanted to know more about Doug. Just because he was a nice guy and helping her, she told herself. There was no more to it than that—at least nothing she would allow herself to feel.

For now, she latched onto a somewhat neutral yet very interesting topic. She wanted to hear how Doug—and Maisie—wound up as K-9 cops here in Chance, and he told her. It had something to do with a cop uncle they both respected and cared for, their joint love of dogs, and combining their career interests by diving into training as K-9 officers.

About the time they'd completed that training and acquired Hooper and Griffin as partners, they'd started looking around for the right situation for them. Relatively quickly, Maisie had found an opening for a couple of K-9 officers in Chance. It was somewhat unusual, since most often the K-9s were acquired by the police department where they worked, but things could go differently in a small town like Chance.

"You've certainly got a wonderful sister," Elissa said.

She enjoyed Doug's rascally grin in response. "Yeah, but don't tell her I agreed with you."

As more questions filled her mind, she realized this wasn't the right time to ask them—assuming there'd ever be a good time. But they were now on the road near the ranch.

Doug slowed as they reached the driveway. Elissa's gaze aimed involuntarily toward the open gate where both signs involving her had been hung.

Nothing there.

She breathed a sigh of relief. And was well aware when Doug, now nearly stopped, was looking at her. "Looks like all's well," he said then accelerated up the driveway.

"I hope so." But she reached for the phone in her pocket and quickly called Amber. "I'm back now," she said. "I'll come by the house soon. Everything okay?"

Like, did you or Evan check on Peace and confirm she's all right?

Amber heard what Elissa didn't say. "All's fine— including Peace. Evan and I had her out for a short walk, along with Lola and Bear, around twenty minutes ago."

"That's great. Thanks so much."

"You're definitely welcome. I assume you're all set to provide your first training class tomorrow, right?"

"Right." Elissa considered whether she should invite Amber over for breakfast to discuss some of the other things on her mind, but she didn't have to.

"Good. I've set it up for around nine with your students. Why don't you join my mother and me for breakfast again first so we can discuss logistics?"

"Perfect."

By the time Elissa ended the call, Doug had parked his police vehicle in the driveway right off the narrow lane where her house was located. He looked over at her.

"Everything okay?"

"Definitely. And my first actual training class is at nine tomorrow morning, in case Maisie or you, or both of you, want to attend."

"I'd like to but I'll have to see how things stand tomorrow. Meanwhile, Hooper and I will come in for a minute to say hi to Peace."

Elissa heard what he wasn't saying. He wanted to check the place out and make sure all was well there. Which she appreciated, even though she wished there was no reason even to wonder such a thing.

Bad enough that he'd helped her that way before she'd moved from SLO. But her problem had followed her here, and she had no idea yet of how to solve it.

She popped out of the vehicle before Doug had a

chance to hurry around and open the door for her. His old-fashioned gentlemanly behavior made her feel warm and mushy inside, but that wasn't appropriate.

Besides, she had to remain in charge of her own life, even if she appreciated his "protective police officer" demeanor.

Almost immediately when she walked up the first step, she heard a soft "ruff" from inside the wooden door. She considered glancing inside using the glass window at the top but instead hurriedly used her key to open it—glad to hear Doug and Hooper behind her on the short stairway.

"Let me." Doug attempted to move around her, but after hearing her dog right inside sounding eager to see her and not upset, she figured all was well.

"I'm okay," she said and went in. She was immediately greeted by Peace, who nosed up to her and acted as if, had she not been such a well trained dog, she wanted to leap on Elissa and hug her.

Elissa instead did the same thing, bending and grabbing her dog around the neck and giving her a big hug.

Which also caused Elissa to stay right near the door as Doug and Hooper maneuvered around Peace and her. Looking away from Peace, Elissa watched them hurry down the hall. Doug peeked into each room as Hooper dashed inside then returned to the hall. Apparently, neither saw nor sensed anything amiss.

Which allowed Elissa to breathe normally again.

But heck, here inside the fence of the Chance K-9 Ranch, surely she was safe, despite those horrible signs left at the front gate…right?

It didn't hurt to have someone and his dog check,

just in case. Especially this particular police officer and his wonderful K-9.

"Okay." Doug had returned to the entry. "Everything seems fine, but remember that Hooper and I can't be here every time you come inside. Be careful. Have someone with you whenever possible. And listen to Peace. She was smart enough to alert you to the break-in at your old place."

"She certainly was." Elissa gave Peace another hug, then stood, knowing it was time to say goodbye—at least till tomorrow. *If* Doug was able to come to her class... She had a thought. "One more thing. Would you take a look at my laptop?" She had it stowed in its case in her bedroom.

"Sure, if you'd like."

"I don't have much to do this afternoon so I'll do as you said and start looking up the names of some people I've been around lately."

She liked his pleased expression as he nodded. "Good. I'll be interested in the results."

She led him down the hall and motioned for Hooper and him to meet her in the kitchen while she went to grab the laptop.

In a few minutes she was back and got it set up on the table. "Here's a test of whether I can find interesting info on anyone I choose to check on." She looked Doug's name up on a search engine.

Yes, he was there, listed on several sites including those connected with Chance, its government and the police department.

There were a few other references, too, and Elissa knew she'd go back to them just out of curiosity. The more she knew about her protector, the better, right?

"This may be fun," she said.

"Just as long as it's helpful," Doug added.

Elissa realized she'd done this to get him to stay a few minutes longer, but she knew he might have real work to do. "Anyway, thanks for coming. I'll let you know if I find anything noteworthy, and I'll keep a special file with names that I can turn over to you."

"Very good," he said as Elissa stood again.

She found herself staring up into his eyes, unable to pull her gaze away. Stepping toward him.

As if she had planned it, she found herself in his arms. His mouth lowered to hers and the hot, firm kiss they shared stirred her everywhere inside—especially in her most sensitive areas.

It lasted for at least a minute. Or two. Yet it felt too short.

Doug was the one to end it and pull away.

"Very good," he repeated huskily, then added, "I'll do what I can to make sure I attend your class tomorrow."

Chapter 15

The first thing Doug did when Hooper and he returned to the department was to check in their office for Maisie and Griffin. The room was empty, so he texted his sister. If she was out on a case, she'd see it whenever but he wouldn't interrupt if she was in the middle of something. Which was probably the situation since he didn't get an immediate text back.

Next thing was to go see Assistant Chief Province. He knew he'd been spending an inordinate amount of time on the K-9 Ranch issues—and Elissa's related ones—and now he had reason to want to expend more.

Kara, fortunately, was in her office and willing to see him. "So what's going on now with the ranch and its latest employee?" she asked drolly, looking up from where she remained seated at her desk.

"There are a couple of updates," he replied, intending to act entirely professionally and not react to his boss's gibing about what might appear like he was attracted to Elissa.

He hoped it wasn't that obvious, but wouldn't be surprised if it was.

Before continuing, he took one of the familiar seats in front of Kara while Hooper lay down on the floor beside him. "One is that I want to take a couple of hours off tomorrow so I can observe the latest class Ms. Yorian will be giving, as well as her students who are present. It can be sick time if you want, since it's for therapy work and therefore involves mental health." He gave a wholly unprofessional grin while waiting for her answer.

He had no reason to believe any student was involved with what had been happening to Elissa, but without knowing who was involved, it didn't hurt to hang out with her as much as possible.

"And if nothing happens, at least your mind will feel better and Hooper will get some training in becoming a future therapy dog," Kara said, not sounding entirely sarcastic, which surprised Doug.

At the sound of his name, Hooper's ears turned but he stayed where he was. "Nothing wrong with that," Doug said. "He's only five years old and in great condition, but if he ever reaches the point that he no longer qualifies to be a police K-9, he can always spend his later years as a therapy dog." And Doug would be happy to work with him that way, too. "Plus, he can visit hospitals unofficially now."

"Right. Okay, go ahead to that class as long as you file a report about what's going on at the ranch and if there's any further evidence of who posted those signs."

"That's the other thing I wanted to talk to you about. No evidence has been found yet, but Elissa is going to put together a list of people she was in contact with over the past month or so. She may do some online research about any she considers potential enemies, but I also want to talk to Gil Jonas about doing some additional research in official police data banks."

Officer Gil Jonas was one of the youngest officers in the Chance Police Department. He had been at the head of his class when he had trained for the job—and started it soon after he'd graduated from college with a degree in information technology.

That made him the department's part-time Technology Officer—not entirely official yet, but he probably would be sometime in the future. For now, if there was any kind of issue involving computers or technology, he was the go-to guy. He also was good friends with Percy Relgin, who owned Cords and Clouds, Chance's technology retail store.

He would be better skilled, and faster, than Doug at this research.

"Good idea. I'll let Officer Jonas know you spoke with me, and he's to spend as much time on this as he feels is necessary. I'll call him now and tell him to expect you."

Doug thanked his boss and he and Hooper left. Doug realized it was probably a good thing to be a member of a police department tied to a relatively small town like Chance, where everyone seemed to give a damn about everyone else. It also didn't hurt that the department's higher-ups apparently still felt like they owed the K-9 Ranch and its owners, since Amber herself had in essence been the person to find her father's killer and stop potential destruction of the ranch.

Whoever was leaving those threats might not know that, or might not care. But Doug was determined to bring that person down, both to help the venerated ranch—and to make sure nothing bad happened to Elissa.

As a result, he quickly made his way up the steps with Hooper to the second floor of the building, where Gil Jonas's office was. He was one of the few entry-level police officers with an office of his own—because his techie skills were so needed by the department.

Doug soon knocked on the closed door. "Come in," called a somewhat tenor voice. As Doug entered the very small room with Hooper, Gil stood behind his desk, a good thing since it was covered with open laptop computers and Doug otherwise might not be able to see him. Gil wasn't the tallest cop in the department. "I'll bet I know why you're here." The junior officer grinned.

Gil wore black-rimmed glasses that bisected his long and somewhat doughy face. His uniform shirt was white, like everyone else's, but it was either brand-new or Gil had just ironed it, since it appeared stiff and wrinkle-free. His smile revealed glowing teeth that suggested he brushed them often with a lot of whitening toothpaste.

In all, he appeared to have decided that, since he was a geek, he might as well look like one.

"I'll bet you do, if Assistant Chief Province got in touch with you. Did she tell you about the case Hooper and I are working on?" Doug looked down at his dog, who was once more sitting on the floor beside him.

"Yeah, the K-9 Ranch. It'll be fun to work on something connected with that place. I like dogs, too."

"Good. Maybe you can come watch a class sometime, or a therapy dog session. But for the moment, we need to ensure that some threats leveled against the ranch and a new employee are stopped, and the perp is caught." Doug quickly described what had been happening to and around Elissa, then said, "Ms. Yorian is now putting together a list of people she's seen or talked to since all this started. I'll want you to check all official databases for the names she comes up with to see if there's anything we should know about."

Gil's grin broadened even more and he clasped his hands in front of him as if he was gearing up to plant them on his keyboards. "Great assignment!" he exclaimed. "For right now, till you've got some of those names, I'll look into Ms. Elissa Yorian herself, in case I find anything of interest."

That idea had passed through Doug's head but he figured there would be nothing useful...maybe.

"Sure," he said. "And keep me informed of your progress."

Gil's head tilted. "I suspect you don't want me to find anything about Elissa," he commented shrewdly. "You like her."

Damn. Once again, Doug realized, he must be acting too obvious about his feelings toward Elissa. Of course this geek was smart, but since he'd caught on that quickly, others might do the same—if they hadn't already. Maisie and Kara certainly had.

"Sure, I like her," he replied. "And I'm a cop. A K-9 cop, and Elissa is, among other things, a dog trainer, so she likes dogs, too. It's part of my job to try to protect people who appear to be in danger, and I don't want anything bad to happen to her—or anyone else, for that matter."

"Got it," Gil said. "Nothing should happen to a dog lover, especially one who's the subject of apparent threats. I'm with you. And I'll do my part to stop it."

"Great," Doug said. "I'll be in touch again soon." Then, Hooper at his side, Doug hurried out of the office.

The next morning Elissa woke bright and early and began her usual walk with Peace around the small employee houses, and even around the rear of the main ranch house—a nice, long circuit that provided exercise for both her and her dog. When they stepped outside, Elissa figured, as usual, that her dog would alert her if someone was around who shouldn't be, although as a therapy dog Peace was more likely to let Elissa know so the pup could go get petted.

Even assuming whoever was threatening her stayed away, this was going to be a busy day. First were her plans for breakfast, when she would address with Amber the possibility of her job becoming full-time.

Plus, she would hopefully see Doug soon after that. He'd called her early in the evening yesterday to ask how her list of friends, acquaintances and students was coming along, and she'd been able to confirm that she'd been working hard on it and believed it was nearly complete. He'd said he had the department's technology officer ready to search any official websites that made sense, if she decided to check further on anyone she knew, which she was glad to hear.

She'd also be glad to hand him a printed list of people, though she would also forward it via email. But being in his presence again, even just so he could observe or participate in another class somehow made her feel warm inside. Relieved, since he had tacitly designated himself her protector.

And that wasn't all, she admitted to herself. She simply liked being in his presence. A lot. Too much.

Well, she'd tamp it all down again once he'd done as he'd promised—and she had no doubt that he would succeed. Once whoever was harassing her was stopped, she could go back to admiring Doug like any other cop and not feel there was, or ever could be, more between them.

Notwithstanding that kiss…

They were now behind the main house and Elissa glanced at the cars parked in the driveway there—Amber's and Sonya's, she figured. Evan's remained near the house at the end of her row.

It was a lovely August day, even a little cool this early in the morning, but it promised to be a fine environment later for her first official training class for future therapy dogs. And she could easily teach other dogs the basics this way, too.

After Peace and she had been out walking for a while, it was time to get ready for breakfast. But first, Elissa wanted to take Peace for one more jaunt around the row of houses. "Come," she told her dog.

They passed the house where they now lived and the next one. Ranch hand Orrin popped out the front door of his place and startled Elissa, but Peace's only reaction was to try to go greet him.

Elissa just waved and got Peace to heel around Evan's house and on the way back to their home. It was definitely time to get ready.

Which Elissa did. Quickly. In a short while, Peace

once more leashed at her side, they arrived at the main ranch house, where Amber opened the front door at the first knock.

Sonya had breakfast ready. Evan joined them and the ranch's head trainer seemed pleased when Elissa broached the subject of her possibly becoming a full-time employee—and giving basic lessons to pet dogs as well as those designated to hopefully become therapy dogs. Evan seemed happy enough with the idea, since he had been hoping to hire an assistant or two, and he'd be able to schedule additional classes that way. Of course he would also need to work with her first on his preferences for training dogs who were pets, but she was definitely a willing student—assuming it was all right with Amber.

Even more fortunately, Amber also was in favor of the idea. "We do have a waiting list of people who want to come here to Chance and take at least a few classes with us. Chance is too small a town to provide all the students we hope to teach, but our K-9 Ranch has a great reputation, so we're always getting inquiries and new students for Evan—and there are places here and nearby for visiting students to stay." She shared a smile with Evan that seemed to include more than kudos for being a good dog trainer.

Elissa felt a small zing of envy pass through her and shoved it aside. She had no need of that kind of relationship, at least not now.

Before they finished the delicious omelets and coffee that Sonya had prepared, a knock sounded on the door. Elissa's class wasn't supposed to start for another hour, so she figured it wasn't one of her students. Evan, seeming right at home, was the one to answer it this time.

It did turn out to be one of her students—sort of. Doug, in police uniform, soon entered the kitchen with Hooper.

"Good morning," he greeted them heartily, looking at everyone but Elissa. It included Peace, though, who wagged her tail as she greeted Hooper. "Hope you don't mind our coming early, but Hooper's really eager for some lessons, and so am I. Plus, I've got a case I'm working on that'll keep us busy this afternoon so I figured it wouldn't hurt to come early."

"Glad to see you," Sonya said. The older woman gestured toward the table where everyone sat. "And the timing is good. We still have some food left, so please join us."

Why wasn't he looking at her? Elissa wondered as the others started talking about the weather and the rain storm predicted for sometime next week. She felt a little hurt. It didn't matter if he'd come there for reasons not connected with her and her situation—only, why else would he really be there? He already had a dog who was well trained in the basics and, although he'd expressed interest in Hooper learning therapy dog skills, Elissa had figured that to be an excuse to stay closer to her—to investigate the threats against her, that was all.

But now she didn't know what was going on.

He'd moved an empty chair and sat beside her. Of course that could have been because there appeared to be more room to her left than elsewhere. He'd only managed a glance and small smile at her that didn't last long before he'd looked away and begun conversing once more, first complimenting Sonya on her omelet—as Elissa had already done.

No other contact with her, nor any looks.

Until… Hooper stood and headed toward the kitchen door, and Doug followed him. Doug had made a gesture under the table that Elissa had seen. Had that been some kind of signal to his dog?

"Hey, Elissa. Why don't Peace and you join us on this outing? It'll be quick."

"Sure," she said, and stood—as she wondered what this was about.

Why not invite the others, with Bear and Lola, too?

What was on Doug's mind?

She had a feeling she was about to find out.

Chapter 16

Doug, with Hooper, preceded Elissa and Peace outside. He wasn't happy about what he needed to discuss with Elissa—although it could explain some of what she was going through.

Sure, she'd mentioned it, mostly as the supposed rationale for her being fired from her nursing job. But the situation as researched by Gil, then passed along to Doug, was worse than Doug had anticipated.

He'd called Maisie to discuss it briefly with her, wanting to get another cop's take on it—and his sister's, too. His wise sister had all but scolded him for just accepting what Gil had found without talking to Elissa about it.

Doug realized she was right. So now it was time to do just that.

"What's going on?" Elissa asked once they had stepped off the ranch house's front porch, walking slowly toward the fenced area containing Hal, Lucy and Rex, the three young German shepherds being trained as police K-9s. "Have you found something to identify the person who's been stalking me?"

"I don't know, but I need more information from you. Tell me again what your head nurse accused you of when she fired you—or allowed you to take a leave of absence." Doug knew he sounded cold, accusatory. But there apparently was more to the story than Elissa had revealed even to him.

"Why?" she demanded. "I already told you none of it was true." But her voice had turned hoarse.

He wanted her to be telling the truth. What was found online wasn't always accurate, and the information Gil had provided to him hadn't been in an official database like that maintained by the Department of Motor Vehicles or even the National Crime Information Center database.

But if it was true, it could explain a lot.

"Just describe it to me again," he insisted, though after turning away from watching Hooper beside him and looking down into Elissa's shattered expression, he had an urge to hold her tightly against him as she spoke.

Even if what he'd heard was true, he was still attracted to her.

"All right." Her voice was soft and shaky as she repeated that she'd been accused of allowing Peace to act aggressively toward some of the kids they'd been trying to help in therapy sessions, and criticizing the patients instead of really holding helpful meetings—which she'd mentioned before but not in detail. "I guess one might even have accused Peace of biting him. But my dog is sweet and loving. You've seen that." She scooted sideways toward where Peace sniffed a nearby bush and hugged the dog against her legs—without looking at Doug.

"Yes, I've seen that—but that's today. I don't know what either of you did before. And here's what I need to know. Did Peace, or any other therapy dog you were working with, push or scare one of the kids you were working with out a window?"

Elissa gasped. "No. Oh, no, not me or Peace. I was aware of that situation but never learned many details. We had worked with that child a few times a while before it happened, then stopped and others took over. But I can assure you we were not involved with what happened to him."

Doug felt himself relax inside—just a little. "Maybe not, but your name is the one Gil apparently found on several social media sites being accused of at least negligence in that situation, if not more."

Elissa quickly turned her head, though not before he saw tears streaming down her face. But crying wasn't evidence that she was telling the truth.

Neither was his attraction to her.

And yet—not only did he want to believe her. He *did* believe her.

Rightly or wrongly, he moved and wrapped his arms around her. "Assuming you're telling the truth, you have a major problem with your reputation to deal with."

"I guess so," she gasped. "And to be fair, I need to let Amber know. If she fires me—well, I'll understand." She gave Doug a swift hug, then backed away from him, wiping her eyes. She somehow looked resolved now. "I'd better do it right away since we have students on the way for today's class."

"Okay." Doug couldn't fault her for her reaction. "But one thing Gil hasn't found, or at least he hadn't when I talked to him before, was the name of the child who died."

"Tully Willmer. He was about ten years old, I think. He was apparently a troubled child, and everyone tried to help him with his mental health issues—including us for a while before we were told by a head nurse to stop and let some of the other therapy dogs try to help, which was fine since we hadn't been as successful as I'd have liked. He lived at home but his mother often brought him to the hospital for therapy sessions, canine and psychological. But…well, I don't know what really happened, but I heard about it. No one wanted to talk much about it, but apparently he may have tried to push a dog out the window and wound up falling himself."

"But neither you nor Peace were involved?" Doug needed assurance that was true.

"No, but…well, we didn't discuss it, so I'm not sure who, if anyone, was involved." She looked toward him, a puzzled expression on her lovely face. "When my boss said there were bad vibes going around regarding Peace and me, she didn't mention that situation, either. As I said, we didn't talk about it. It can't be why whoever is after me is doing this—can it?"

"Well, as I said, your name and Peace's did appear when Gil found something about the kid's death. It's one more thing I guess we'd better add to the equation, just in case."

"I guess," she echoed sadly. "And…well, I'm going to tweak the list of people I'd been in contact with just so you and Gil know which ones were therapy dog handlers who were around at that time. But why would anyone say I was involved—unless, maybe one of those handlers I considered a friend actually was involved but wanted to lay the blame somewhere else?"

"That's what I'm wondering," Doug said.

And it was.

A lot more research was needed.

Elissa hadn't paid attention to how fast time was passing till she saw some cars start up the driveway from the street below the area where Doug and she and their dogs stood.

"Oh, no," she said. "It's time for my class. And I need to talk to Amber."

"You can talk to her afterward." Elissa liked Doug's reassuring tone. "Meanwhile, I'll relate our conversation to Gil and have him dig deeper into who may have posted what."

"Thank you." Elissa knew her gratitude resounded in her tone. If they weren't out there in the open, with students beginning to arrive, she would have given him a big hug for not accepting as true what was apparently on the internet about her.

And maybe another kiss like the one they'd shared…

But she was focusing on his niceness rather than the horror of the situation. She didn't know if any of the dog therapy handlers or their dogs had actually been there when Tully had died, although rumor had it that the boy had said he'd wanted to hurt one of the dogs.

If any handlers or dogs had been present, then which had been involved? Dianne Doriene and her dog Sparta? But she and Elissa had been good friends—before. Surely she wouldn't start pointing fingers at Elissa that way to cover herself.

But she had been nasty the last time they'd seen each other…

There were other handlers, too, who'd brought their therapy dogs to the hospital.

One of them—someone just learning how to train and work with therapy dogs—Elissa knew had to be innocent: Adellaide Willmer. She'd been Tully's mother, and she had apparently taken on therapy dog work in his memory. At the time she'd learned about that, Elissa had nearly wept with the sweetness of the gesture.

But had it been sweet or had the grieving woman planned some kind of agenda for revenge? If so, against who—Elissa? If so, why?

Surely, Adellaide couldn't be the one behind what was going on with Elissa—could she?

Unlikely. She'd been around the hospital enough to realize Elissa knew virtually nothing about her son's death.

The first car had reached the top of the driveway and parked near the main house. Kim Boyd got out of the sedan and opened the back door for her Dobie, Barker, to get out. Paul Wilson was the next to park and get out, with Ollie, his French bulldog mix. Then came Jim Curtis, with Bandit.

As they approached Elissa and Doug, a fourth and then a fifth car drove up the driveway and parked. Jill Jacobs exited the first of those newly arrived cars with Astro, her Jack Russell terrier. It would be interesting to see how the energetic little dog reacted to the basic commands Elissa would be working on today. And whether he calmed down enough to allow people to stroke and play with him, which was critical for him to become a therapy dog and wasn't a skill that was completely teachable.

Doug's sister Maisie got out of the final car with Griffin.

Elissa had already figured that she would work with them today on a flat area adjoining the driveway.

It was time to get started.

Her students were here.

Could her class clear her mind from the terrible information Doug and she had been discussing? It had to.

Even if this was her only actual class with this group, she intended to do it well.

Standing at the edge of the flat, paved area in front of the ranch house where the new class was to be held, Doug was curious about how Elissa would run it—and how the students and their dogs would do.

As before, a couple of the students ran up to the dogs who were already there, including his Hooper, as well as Griffin and Peace, and greeted them effusively. He considered ordering them to back off but, heck, neither his dog nor Maisie's was on official duty here and friendliness and affection seemed to be the key to therapy dog work.

He watched as Elissa greeted the students, with Peace once more beside her, and asked a few general questions about each dog's training to date, including after the introductory class.

She was dressed casually, as was everyone else, yet her attitude made her seem more formal—and clearly in charge. She was definitely a pretty woman. She seemed quite interested in each person's responses to her questions. But of course she cared about people as well as dogs. Why else would she be a nurse—or therapy dog handler?

So why were there so many issues about her? Doug wanted to believe her. Did believe her. And yet the more he heard, the more he couldn't help wondering what, if anything, could be real.

Letting her dog push a kid out a window? Pushing him herself?

He forced his mind back to the present. Their previous class here, before the hospital demonstration, had been mostly to introduce the students to the background and concept of therapy dogs and to provide more information about how they could be of great use in helping people. People who primarily had issues that presented mentally, such as fear of others or fear of a medical or other situation in which they found themselves, or even just a hint of depression.

He'd enjoyed showing off Hooper's excellent training and suspected his dog wouldn't be showed much in this upcoming class that he didn't already know, if anything. Same with Maisie and Griffin. But it would still be interesting to learn more about the basic commands therapy dogs were supposed to obey, as well as how those commands worked into the healing they provided.

"Okay," Elissa finally called as Amber, Sonya and Evan walked out of the ranch house and crossed the porch toward them. "Time to get started." She motioned for the class members to join her along one side of the paved area while the folks from the ranch arranged themselves at the opposite edge. "First thing, as I've mentioned and showed you before, you and your dog need to work as a team—and your dog needs to recognize that. We'll be going over some of the basic but critical commands today, and it's important for them to know to obey you, but it'll be because they want to and not because you'll punish them if they don't. That definitely doesn't work for therapy dogs. They need encouragement and love to be able to convey that to your patients in the future."

Elissa looked from one face to the next as if trying to read whether they understood and were on board. Or maybe to make sure they knew she intended to make sure they followed her instructions.

"Okay, please line up," she said. "Peace and I definitely have that kind of relationship. We'll demonstrate the most basic commands, then, one at a time, I'll want you to work with your dogs and show whether they know the commands already."

No doubt about Hooper and Griffin, Doug was sure. Those two might be K-9s with lots of special training and skills, but they were also part of Maisie's and his family.

Apparently, Elissa was more concerned about her other students, those not paired with trained K-9s. Maisie and he, with their dogs, stood closest to her, but she moved away to face them all again. She briefly had Peace demonstrate some of her skills. Then she said, "First, let's have…Barker show his stuff." She gestured toward the Doberman mix and his owner Kim.

Kim looked young to Doug in her shorts, tank top and flip-flops, but even kids could train dogs. And Dobermans, though they could be aggressive, were smart, so he anticipated this trial would go well.

He wasn't disappointed.

Over the next several minutes Elissa told Kim which commands to direct to Barker. Sometimes she spoke them out loud, and at other times she showed a gesture to Peace, who obeyed them either way perfectly. Between each command, Elissa waited a few seconds while Kim told Barker what to do then rewarded the dog with a whole lot of praise and hugging, and a little treat.

Barker did fine with "sit," "stay," "down" and other directives, even "roll over." But he didn't seem to get "shake." Doug wondered how important that was but figured shaking paws could be meaningful to engage the subject of a therapy session and allow that kid or needy adult to believe the dog wanted nothing more than to be in his presence and play with him.

How would Hooper do? Griffin? Perfectly, Doug felt sure.

"That was wonderful," Elissa called to Kim when they were done. "There are more commands we'll go over, and we'll try them in different venues, even stressful circumstances, but Barker's definitely off to a good start."

Next in the spotlight was Astro, Jill Jacobs's Jack Russell terrier. Doug wasn't surprised when the dog hardly obeyed a single command. "Sit" was the only one he appeared to pay any attention to, and then he ignored Jill when she told him to stay. In fact, he seemed determined to ignore her and run in circles around the training area until Elissa told Jill to attach his leash again. Praise or other rewards? They definitely weren't earned, even though Jill tried to show the little fireball dog some love with hugs—when she could grab him close to her.

"Looks like we have some work to do here," Elissa said when they were done.

Jill, who appeared to be in her early thirties—and

clearly unhappy—nodded. "Like I said last time, I really hope you can help me learn a way to slow him down safely and act like the sweet, loving dog he is."

Or that Jill wanted him to be, Doug thought. But of them all, he suspected Astro might be the only dog who wouldn't become an acceptable therapy dog.

Next was Jim Curtis, with Bandit. Jim was the most senior of the handler students, and his Lab mix was already well trained in the basics, though Bandit probably had lots to learn as a therapy dog. Still, he seemed likely to succeed.

Then came Paul Wilson, with Ollie, his French bulldog mix. Paul looked more in his late thirties or early forties and wore slightly dressier attire than everyone else, consisting of a nice button-down shirt over his jeans. Seemed a bit too dressy for a dog training class, but guidelines weren't strict on clothing.

Doug was a bit surprised, though, when Ollie, too, didn't seem to obey the rules, at least not much. French bulls were trainable with practice and patience, but maybe Paul hadn't spent enough time with him.

And Paul as a trainer? Doug couldn't really tell. Although the guy did provide praise each time the dog obeyed, he seemed a bit remote, maybe even confused. Doug wondered how close he and his dog were.

In fact, after Ollie complied with "sit" and "down," and somewhat with "stay" but only for a few seconds, Paul approached Elissa looking rather embarrassed. "Sorry. I just adopted Ollie and thought he'd had some training first. I've done some work with him but he doesn't always seem inclined to do what I tell him. That's actually one reason we're here, not just to turn him into a therapy dog. I'll be happy if he learns to listen and obey those commands."

"Me, too," Elissa said. "Just be sure he recognizes that you're new best friends." She aimed a smile at Paul, who smiled back—which irritated Doug. Was flirtation a part of her class? "And be sure to work with him to interact gently and caringly with other people. That's the most important thing."

Doug was glad when Elissa walked away from Paul toward the last two people in the class—Maisie and him. Not surprisingly, Griffin obeyed every command with no hesitation, earning praise from everyone, including the ranch folks at the edge of the training area. And Maisie made it clear how much she loved him and how good he was.

Then it was Doug's turn, and Hooper's obedience surpassed even Griffin's. Doug found himself heaping even more praise than usual on his dog.

"Good job," Elissa said when they were done, smiling at him. "Now, everyone, we're going to start at the beginning again, and each of our dogs will work on 'sit' even if they know it. It's important that, in a therapy assignment, the dogs listen and sit and stay calm even at first, to help ease any fears the patient has. And of course, we'll ramp up the love and encouragement."

That part of the lesson continued for twenty minutes. All the dogs, even Astro, seemed fine with following that command. Staying worked reasonably well with them, again except for Astro, and Ollie didn't appear to mind staying as long as he wasn't required to do so for more than a minute.

And so forth. The class continued for about an hour, and Doug was amazed that, as Elissa wrapped things up and prepared to tell them all when the next class would be, he felt a big sense of accomplishment—a sense that should have belonged only to Elissa. But he felt proud of her.

The four non-cop class members left soon afterward, thanking Elissa profusely and promising to work hard with their dogs so they should all have perfected the commands by the next class, which would be in three days. All these people lived in Chance or not far away. Although this class had been on Wednesday, a weekday, the next one would take place on Saturday, which was easier since three of the four members had day jobs and had had to take a bit of time off that day, as before.

As they all stood near the base of the house's porch, Elissa told Amber she wanted to discuss scheduling with her, possibly to make the timing better for potentially larger classes. But she also glanced toward Doug as she spoke, and he heard what she wasn't saying.

As she'd mentioned before to him, she wanted to tell Amber about the latest issue—the apparent social media posts claiming she was involved not only in poor therapy issues, but possibly a child's death.

He wanted to be there with her. He'd make sure of it.

But first, he had to talk to Gil to see where his research stood.

Chapter 17

Elissa wasn't sure how so many mixed emotions could flow through her this way. She was definitely pleased about how her class had gone this morning. Sure, most of the dogs needed more training in the basics, as did their owners. But she felt certain they'd all learn enough to continue: the owners to feel confident in their dogs and show it, and the dogs to obey more commands pertaining to therapy training and demonstrate their caring natures toward people—although Astro, at least, might require some special hands-on work from her, which was fine.

She'd felt ecstatic about the class, happy to watch Maisie and Doug show off their well-trained and clearly beloved dogs…and now couldn't help the misgivings and more that she felt as she, Peace beside her, followed everyone remaining toward the house.

She knew she had to tell Amber about the latest accusations against her before she did anything else.

She'd hoped to at least have Doug's backup, but he had walked away with Hooper. A necessary doggy outing? Or was he also walking away from her?

She didn't feel comfortable waiting to find out. Evan headed back to his house since he had a K-9 training class scheduled at the ranch that afternoon he wanted to prepare for. That left Elissa with Amber and Sonya, and they all walked up the steps onto the porch, including Peace. Sonya had her cell phone in her hands and seemed to be texting. Maybe that would give Elissa an adequate excuse to talk only to Amber. Her mother appeared a lot more suspicious of all that was going on around Elissa.

But before Elissa could take Amber aside and figure out how to start this latest difficult conversation, Sonya turned to them and sent a big smile in Elissa's direction. "Hey, dog therapy specialist. I just learned of a special assignment for you."

"Really? What?" Elissa knew she should bring up her issue first, but she couldn't help being curious.

"I just got a text from Petra. We'll need to call her for details, but I gather a new patient who's just been admitted to Chance Hospital is a senior who's depressed and needs some cheering right away. Could you go there this afternoon?"

She wished. She really wanted to just say yes—but she had to let them know the latest accusations against her.

"Maybe, but before I can agree to it, I have something new to tell you about. Another untrue accusation and it's—"

"It's definitely fishy," said a voice from behind her as footsteps sounded on the wooden steps they had just walked up. Doug was joining them with Hooper.

"Fishy how?" She had to ask.

"Our tech support guy at the department has been looking into the allegations, and from what he's found all the nonsense on social media has come from unidentifiable sources—at least not identifiable yet by him, and he really knows his stuff."

"But what are the allegations?" Amber asked. Her eyes appeared suspicious and, after everything else that had happened, Elissa could understand why.

Taking a deep breath, she revealed the situation at the hospital where she had worked in San Luis Obispo, and the death of the young boy soon after seeing a therapy dog to help his mental health. "I heard about it while I was there and was never really certain which dog and handler had been working with him closest to the time of his death. No one really talked about it much."

"But it wasn't you and Peace." Amber made a statement, but a question was in her voice anyway.

"Not then, though we'd had a couple of sessions with him weeks earlier." Elissa felt her eyes tear up. "But now, in addition to everything else that's been happening—"

"Someone's accusing Elissa of somehow causing the boy's death, too," Doug broke in. He now stood beside Elissa on the porch with the dogs at their feet, but he maneuvered around Peace to put his arm comfortingly around Elissa, though only for a moment. Still, that brief touch helped to calm her. "However, like I said, the allegations are coming from very suspicious sources."

"I just wish—" Elissa began then stopped. What she

wished was for all of this to go away. But it wouldn't just happen because she wanted it to.

If only she knew some positive steps she could take to ensure it would end—right away.

But for now… "I wish it would just stop," she said in a voice that sounded somewhat strong, at least to her. "Since it's been continuing, I can understand if you lose trust in me. As I said before, if you want to tell me to leave the Chance K-9 Ranch—well, I'd hate it, but I would go. And, Sonya, if you don't want me to follow up with Petra's patient, I'll understand that, too."

To her surprise, Sonya was the first to respond, and in a positive way. "The heck with all that nonsense!" she exclaimed, although she looked at Doug. "Your tech guy says it's nonsense, right?"

"Right," he confirmed.

"Well then," Amber said, "no issues here. I like how your class went this morning, and if you want to go with Peace and help that needy senior at the hospital this afternoon, do it."

"Thank you all," Elissa said, relief flooding her. "I won't let you down."

Turning to look at Doug, she found him smiling at her.

And hoped she could make good on that promise… particularly with the man who had been helping her so wonderfully.

If he'd had any genuine doubts about Elissa making up the stuff going on around her, Doug didn't now. In his brief conversation with Gil, he'd heard how confused yet determined the tech expert was. "It's one of those situations where things apparently got routed through servers all over the country, maybe all over the world," the techie had said. "Genuine posts can usually be linked to a source, or even a person, but not these accusing Elissa of having something to do with that kid's death."

"So why would someone do that?" Doug had asked, although he suspected he knew.

"Obviously he doesn't want to be linked to it, to have his—or her—identity discovered."

They'd talked a few minutes more. Gil had sounded somewhat stumped when Doug asked if he could, in fact, figure out who'd been doing that.

"Possibly," he'd said, "but it'll take a long time, a bunch of research—and I'll need to get the okay from some higher-ups to spend that time while I'm on duty. I'll work on it, too, when I'm not at the station if I can't figure it out here, but it'd be better if I can continue here with what I'm doing."

Doug had assured him he'd head to the station in a short while and the two of them could then seek that okay. He'd also had to convince Gil there was a good reason for a local cop to do this, a good connection to the town of Chance: the threats to the K-9 Ranch. It wasn't all about Elissa, he'd assured the techie—who blatantly asked Doug if he had something going with the lovely, sexy and possibly threatened woman.

"Don't I wish," Doug had told him—unfortunately somewhat truthfully. "See you soon."

Could Elissa be doing all this herself? No way, Doug thought now as he headed back to the station.

Although, for his own peace of mind, he might inquire about her technological skills...

* * *

Elissa drove Peace to the hospital with her, separately from Amber and Sonya since she wasn't sure how long she'd stay there, and the others wanted to return to the ranch in time for Evan's class that afternoon. She was excited about engaging in a real therapy session without it being part of a class this time, although she would again have observers. Perhaps, given more notice, she would have invited the prospective handlers she was teaching now to watch. It would have been another good experience for them. But this time, she and Peace would do it all themselves, without an ulterior motive like teaching anyone, and with the idea of comforting a person really in need.

Although, as she parked in the hospital lot, she decided that, as a new teacher of therapy dog handlers, she could use this as a lesson of sorts even though her students weren't invited here.

Remaining in the driver's seat, she called back to Peace, "We'll get out in a minute, I promise." Then she pulled out her phone where she'd already programmed in her students' numbers in case she needed to update them on a class time or something else.

Now, she texted them.

Peace and I have been asked to do a therapy session with a senior at the Chance Hospital this afternoon. I'll describe it at our next class. Therapy dogs are in demand!

She considered sending the same text to Doug and Maisie but they were a different kind of student. And with their relationships with dogs, they wouldn't be surprised at this latest event.

She'd let them know later—and in some ways would look forward to contacting Doug about it.

"Okay," she said to Peace when she was through. "Let's go inside."

Like last time, she and Peace walked from the parking lot to the front of the hospital and into the lobby area, with Amber and Sonya along now. Also like last time, Peace got a lot of stares and quite a few smiles. Elissa had, of course, tied her identification scarf around her neck.

Once again, the young receptionist, Rona, was at the front desk. Elissa asked for Petra and Rona called her then came around to greet Peace.

Petra soon appeared in her blue scrubs, and first greeted Sonya, then Amber and Elissa. "Thanks for coming," she said, also bending to pat Peace's head. "Please follow me."

She told Elissa that the area where most senior patients were given rooms was on the third floor. "This particular one, Florence, has been in heart failure. Her treatment appears somewhat successful, but she's sure she isn't going to survive—and her resulting depression could make that a self-fulfilling prophecy. Her family says she likes dogs, so your therapy was the first thing that came to mind."

"Peace and I will definitely do what we can," Elissa said.

"Judging by your performance last time, I'm optimistic that you'll be of help. I'll take you there now."

They rode the elevator and were soon in the hallway outside the room Petra said was occupied by Florence and another older woman who'd also had a heart attack but was due to be discharged later that day. "The doc-

tors paired these two together in the hopes that a roommate with positive results would help Florence's state
of mind, but that unfortunately hasn't been the case."

Petra knocked on the door but pushed it open before
either patient said anything. As Peace and Elissa, as
well as Amber and Sonya, followed her in, Petra first
approached the thin, smiling lady with soft gray hair
who sat and watched television on the bed on the left.
"Hi, Millie. You ready to go home today?"

"I sure am. Can I take that dog with me?" Her gaze
had landed on Peace and her smile broadened.

"Nope, sorry," Elissa said. "But you can definitely
give her a hug." Peace had done this often enough that
she knew what to do when Elissa pointed toward the bed
and said, "Go." The sweet dog hurried over and, standing on her hind legs on the floor, nuzzled at the bed's
occupant, who laughed and patted her head.

Elissa noticed that Sonya and Amber stayed near the
door, as did Petra. After a minute Elissa said, "Good
dog, Peace. Now, down." Her dog obeyed and then
Elissa pointed to the other bed. "Peace, go."

Once again Peace obeyed the command and in moments was standing on her hind legs with her front paws
on the room's other bed. It was occupied by a woman
who appeared much older and definitely frailer than her
roommate. Her hair was short and white, and her eyes
were closed. She had small breathing tubes in her nose
hooked by a clear hose to an oxygen tank on a platform
beside her bed, and on her other side stood two women
who might be family.

"Hi, Florence," Elissa said to the patient. "I'm Elissa,
and this is Peace. Peace is here as a therapy dog, and
she loves to help people."

"I really hope she can help our mother," the older of the two standing women, in a straight black dress, said in a low, pessimistic voice. Her brown eyes were sad and her mouth grim.

"Yeah," said the other, who resembled her sister but was dressed more casually in jeans and a T-shirt.

"Okay, then." Elissa approached the bed, too, where Peace remained standing and wagging her tail but not otherwise attempting to get Florence's attention. Elissa reached over and lifted the woman's bony, wrinkled arm nearest to the dog. She laid it back down carefully on the bed, watching the woman for her reaction as Peace nuzzled it.

In moments the woman's eyes opened and she turned her hand over to place it under Peace's chin. She made a noise that sounded somewhat questioning.

"Florence, Peace would love for you to pet her, if you'd like. If not, she can just stay here and keep you company. In fact, maybe we could get her a bed on wheels so she can lie down beside you." Elissa glanced questioningly at Petra, who remained at the door behind her with the others. The head nurse nodded and disappeared into the hallway.

Amber approached Elissa and said softly, "I know it's quick, but we'll leave now. This has been great so far."

The two K-9 Ranch women left after a goodbye wave from Sonya to Elissa.

When Elissa looked back at Florence, she was amazed and pleased when the woman said, "Peace?" Florence lifted her head to look at the dog as she moved her hand to pat Peace's head. "Peace. Beautiful dog."

Elissa heard a soft gasp from one of Florence's daughters. They both were smiling and both had tears in their eyes.

Thank you, one mouthed to Elissa.

A first session like this, with a person who had a difficult medical condition, tended to be short. But since Florence's condition might not be as grave as the patient thought it was, Elissa planned to stay for twenty minutes unless told otherwise by Petra or someone else. The head nurse returned fairly quickly with an assistant helping her to wheel in a bed. They placed it right beside Florence's on the side opposite the oxygen tank, arranged some sheets over it and then helped Elissa get the dog onto the bed.

For the next twenty minutes Elissa found herself grinning along with the woman's daughters as Florence talked to Peace in brief but loving terms, stroked the dog, laughed as Peace licked her, and moved over so Peace could get close to her on her own bed.

This was one wonderful therapy session, Elissa thought.

She felt in tune with her dog, as she knew the best therapy dog handlers did. Likewise, she believed Peace also on some level knew what her handler thought and felt. Plus, Peace clearly adored people and seemed to thrive on lavishing doggy love on them.

Elissa used her phone to take pictures after getting the daughters' okay, and Florence nodded about it, too. She told them she might post the pictures on social media to help promote the therapy dog classes she was giving at the Chance K-9 Ranch.

Online stuff. Elissa would be glad Doug could see that and not just the accusations against her.

"That's fine," said one of the women. "If you can get other dogs to help people this way, we're thrilled to have our mom as an example."

As Peace continued her therapy duties while Elissa

watched, she discussed timing of future sessions with Petra and the daughters. The consensus was for her to come every other day, if possible. Once again, the staff would ensure that the patient's hands and clothes were cleaned. Elissa then exchanged contact information with the daughters, too, whose names were Pat and Fae.

Eventually, the timing was right for the session to end. Though Florence appeared to want more time with Peace, she looked exhausted. Plus, that twenty minutes Elissa had allotted was now over—the maximum time she had figured would work best for a first session.

"I won't get to see Peace again," said Millie from the other bed after Elissa had said goodbye to Florence but promised to return soon. "I'm leaving this afternoon. But I'm so glad I got to meet her—and I'm really happy that she was able to help Florence so much."

Pat and Fae had expressed similar thoughts and Petra, who'd left for a while but returned, did the same. "Good job, both of you," the nurse said as they entered the hallway and shut the door behind them. "Thanks so much. I'll let our administrators know how well this worked out. I know not everyone was happy about the presence or training of therapy dogs here, but I'm sure now it will be fine."

"That's great," Elissa said, feeling thrilled. No matter what had happened to bring her here full-time, she now truly believed she—and Peace—belonged. "We'll look forward to working more here, including visiting Florence again."

It was time to leave now. Elissa had an urge to call Doug to tell him how well things had gone—but that would only be appropriate if they actually had some kind of relationship.

Although she could let him know, as she had with her other class members, that Peace was now acting not only as a trainer of other therapy dogs, but also as an actual therapy dog here.

Yes, that would be a good reason to contact Doug—and Maisie, too. Later.

Elissa stopped at the reception desk again, this time to say goodbye for the day to Rona.

"Yes," she said in response to Rona's question, "things seemed to go great. Hopefully you'll see us here again soon, and often."

"Wonderful!" the young lady exclaimed, adding to Elissa's good feelings.

As Peace and she walked out the front of the building and around the pathway to the parking lot, Elissa thought again of Doug, who'd been supporting her emotionally through some rather ugly stuff. Why not share something good with him now, as she'd previously considered?

Later, she reminded herself. Maybe when Peace and she had returned to the ranch or—

She'd reached her SUV and walked around it to the driver's side, ready to open the rear door to let Peace inside.

And stopped. And gasped.

Attached to the side mirror was another of those damned signs. A small one. But it looked very much like the kind that had appeared at the K-9 Ranch.

This one read "Therapy dogs and handlers are crap. You and your dog will pay."

Chapter 18

The call came while Doug was in his office with Maisie. They were seated at their desks, their dogs at their feet, and his sister had been telling him about her latest assignment—accompanying some officers on a raid of a potential illegal narcotics sales facility.

Griffin was definitely a skilled scent dog. He had alerted on some very large stashes in what was supposed to be—of all things—an exercise gym and health club. Health?

"Some of the guys in charge have connections with other similar facilities," she had been saying, "so you and Hooper can help check them out."

He'd been about to confirm they'd be glad to help when his phone rang. He pulled it from his pocket.

Elissa.

"Hello?" he said somewhat cautiously. He had already talked to Gil about the internet references to Elissa and the confusion about their origin. He intended to talk to her about it—but not this soon. Not while Gil was trying a few more avenues to get answers.

"Doug? Doug, I need your help."

His heart immediately started racing. "What's going on? Where are you?"

She hadn't finished her description of the latest sign and where it was before he stood, his eyes meeting Maisie's. "I'll be right there," he said into the phone. "For now, go back into the hospital lobby where there are people around and wait for me."

He barely had time for a brief explanation to his sister before he'd grabbed his uniform jacket, attached Hooper's leash and ran out the door.

The hospital wasn't far from the station but he drove there in case he needed wheels for his part of the investigation. He immediately saw Elissa's SUV in the parking lot and grabbed a space near it. He and Hooper first circled the vehicle on foot.

The sign was still there. Unsurprisingly, she'd been smart about it. He called the station to have a crime scene investigator sent there.

"Stay," he told Hooper. His dog could guard the SUV while he went inside for just a minute—and found Elissa.

Sure enough, she was in the lobby as he'd instructed her, sitting in a far corner of the busy room with Peace lying on the floor at her feet. She looked pale and frightened, staring down at her hands folded on her lap.

He was a little surprised she was by herself since she now knew some people here—but maybe it was better this way. Without knowing who had hung that sign, or the previous ones, trusting no one seemed a good decision.

He rushed over to her. For a few seconds when he stopped right in front of her, she didn't even look up. But when Peace stood and started nuzzling his leg, Elissa seemed to shrug off her fright, at least a little.

When she met his eyes, she immediately stood and threw herself against him. He gently put an arm around her and gave her a brief hug before stepping back. He was in uniform. He was on duty and had an investigation to conduct.

But what he really wanted to do was to hold her close and comfort her.

"I saw what you're talking about before I came inside," he told her. "I've called in to get an investigator sent over. Let's go out and wait, okay?"

"Okay," she said then looked him in the face once more. Some color had returned to her skin and her expression now seemed more determined than scared. "Thanks for coming. Now, please, get whoever is doing this."

Okay. She had to get hold of herself. Even if Doug wasn't there, she needed that. She could do that. She had Peace with her. Her dog might not be a police K-9, but even as a therapy dog she would protect the human she loved—or at least bark and growl at anyone menacing her.

But as they followed Doug back to the parking lot where Hooper sat stiffly beside her SUV, Elissa knew that her renewed sense of courage was largely because of Doug's presence…and not entirely because he was a cop about to investigate the latest threat against her.

Peace seemed to recognize that Hooper was on duty. She wagged her tail but did not approach her K-9 buddy.

"Okay," Doug said when they stopped beside her SUV, "tell me exactly what you did this morning, and when and how you did it."

He had been with her when Sonya had passed along the request that she conduct a therapy dog session with an ill senior at the hospital, and she told him that was mostly what she had been up to. "I even told my students about it by text, just to let them know how in demand therapy dogs and their handlers were. I didn't include Maisie or you, though, but only my new students without a background in training dogs."

She described all that had occurred in the hospital room with the ill lady and how she had responded. And how, when the session was over, Elissa had simply led Peace back to their vehicle to head back to the ranch—and discovered the sign.

"It was horrible," she finished. "But I took a picture with my phone."

She noticed a couple of official police vehicles arriving. Doug soon spoke to the occupants and they discussed how to check out her SUV and the sign and any other evidence they could find.

Which Elissa found sweet and kind. She hadn't been physically hurt by all that had been going on in her life, even though she had most likely lost her beloved job. Even so, she felt horrible. Scared. Angry—in a futile kind of way.

Doug soon joined her. "We may have a break here." He pointed up toward some power poles. "Security cameras. Maybe we'll be able to see whoever did this. Anyway, right now I want to take you back up to the ranch while the investigation is conducted. We'll get your vehicle home to you later, when all this is done."

"But I hate to put you to any more trouble," she said, while at the same time feeling relieved that not only would she be leaving this difficult scene, but that she'd be in Doug's presence a little longer.

"Believe me," he said, looking so deeply into her eyes that she felt herself flush—and wish he'd never look away. "It's no trouble."

Tension resonated in his SUV, especially since Doug spent most of the time on the phone, using its Bluetooth connection to talk to the investigators.

At least that way she could hear what was being said.

One investigator had taken possession of the sign. He had dusted her vehicle for fingerprints and said he would do the same with the sign when he returned to his office. He had gone into the hospital and spoken with its security staff, who were sending him the footage taken by their cameras during the pertinent times.

Soon they headed up the ranch's driveway. "Let's stop at the main house first," Doug said after he parked. "I don't think Amber or the others here are involved with all this, but I want them to know what happened— and that the Chance PD is on it, and not just its K-9 unit. It hopefully will be safer for you if they're aware you're home, too."

"Okay." Elissa appreciated his reasoning and had no problem letting her bosses know of her presence. But she also wanted to be alone for a while.

As it turned out, they were all in the yard watching Evan present a K-9 lesson to handlers from another police force and their dogs. This wasn't the time to let them know what was going on. But at least they would know she was back.

Doug and Hooper accompanied Peace and Elissa to her house, where she unlocked the door and promised to lock it again behind them. She expected Doug just to leave.

He didn't. Instead he asked her for a bottle of water, which she provided, getting herself one, too, and making sure the dogs also had a drink. Then he accompanied her into the living room. And immediately pulled her into his arms. Then he kissed her—hard and long and so deeply that she nearly grabbed his hand to lead him to her bedroom.

"This has to end," he finally said throatily as he pulled back.

Confused, she asked, "The kiss?"

"No. These threats against you."

"Absolutely." Although, deep inside, she realized she now had a tiny, ridiculous reason to thank whoever was doing this. She was spending more time with Doug… No, that was even worse than a ridiculous thought.

He drew her close again and once more they kissed. He was clearly sexually attracted, too. She could feel his hardness against her. Could she—should she—take advantage of his soothing, sexy presence now and—

His phone rang. He pulled back immediately and answered it.

"Yeah?" he said in response to whatever his caller said. "Interesting." He talked for a while longer and Elissa felt sure it was someone involved with investigating the latest threat.

He looked at his phone's screen a couple of times

before hanging up. Then he looked at Elissa, who'd sat on the couch near where he still stood.

"They got a video of the person who left the sign, but it's blurred. I'll show it to you in case you can recognize it. But one thing is clear. The person was a woman."

"Interesting," she said. "I assumed, with all the threats and online stuff, that it had to be a man."

He showed her the video. Something about the woman seemed familiar but Elissa couldn't identify her, not with the blurry, dark pictures. A hint of a question and possibility passed through her, though. She didn't want to even mention it since it seemed so absurd.

But maybe she could follow through and at least ask some questions...

No easy answers, damn it, Doug thought as he finished his conversation with the crime scene guys and hung up.

But he needed to return to the station. Press them a bit more, and Gil, too. Look for more answers. Fast.

First, though— Well...he hated the idea of leaving Elissa there alone, even with Peace. The dog really was much too peaceful. Ha, ha.

"Sorry we couldn't just nail the person through that security footage but I've got to get back to the station to follow up. You'll be okay here on your own?"

"Sure." But he could tell she was just putting on a brave front.

"Okay. Just stay here, doors locked. I'll remain in touch and let you know if we find anything else."

"Fine."

He initiated one more big, sexy kiss then he and Hooper headed out the door.

* * *

All right. It was absurd. But the accusations on the internet claiming she'd harmed kids, combined with everything else, had given Elissa an idea—one she had firmly suppressed before.

She might wind up just tearing at her target's old wounds, making them even more painful again especially if she was wrong, but she needed to at least contact the person she had in mind.

Adellaide Willmer was working on becoming a therapy dog handler in San Luis Obispo.

She was also the mother of Tully Willmer, the boy who had died by falling out a window after his therapy dog session. And Elissa and Peace had worked with Tully months before his death. Adellaide had accompanied him then. Elissa therefore knew Adellaide, though only slightly. She had contacted the bereaved mother at the time to express her condolences.

She had later seen Adellaide at the hospital starting her therapy dog work.

Her tormenter was a woman and Elissa couldn't rule out the person in the indistinct security footage from being Adellaide. And what person was more likely than one with anger and hurt and vengeance on her mind?

A bereaved mother looking for someone to blame? One who had brought in a therapy dog that hadn't wound up helping her son?

Why Elissa and not one of the other handlers? That was a good question—one that might make this whole idea absurd, especially since Adellaide herself now shared a connection with therapy dogs.

But it wouldn't hurt to talk to Adellaide. Maybe she

had other ideas about who was doing this—assuming it wasn't her.

It would be better to talk to her in person but Elissa had no intention of returning to SLO, especially not for something like this. Instead, not having direct contact information, she called the restaurant where Adellaide had once mentioned she worked as a chef—and was pleased to have Adellaide come to the phone nearly immediately.

Elissa hadn't spent much time figuring out how to ask her questions, but she did so as subtly as she could. Instead of bursting right out and demanding whether Adellaide was her harasser, she began by inquiring how the woman was. How her husband Perry was.

And got some interesting answers. Very interesting. And surprising. And worrisome.

When she was through, she knew she needed to head to downtown Chance—but she at least called Doug first.

He didn't answer his phone, so she supposed he was in a meeting. Nevertheless she left a message, telling him she'd come up with some information she needed to share with him. Maybe they could get together for dinner—in town, since that was where she was heading.

To entice him, she said, "I had a new idea about who my harasser could be—but when I talked to her she led me in a different, though similar, direction. I'm going to check on someone else now. Don't worry. I'll be careful. But if you happen to be able to join me in the next twenty minutes, here's the address." She recited it, then hung up.

And she was careful. She of course took Peace with her, and she'd invited Doug to meet her at her goal. Most likely, she would wait till he arrived. It would

218 *Trained to Protect*

make more sense for a cop to question the woman she wanted to talk to.

Elissa already had the information about where to find the woman, which she found both scary and fascinating.

It was Jill Jacobs, one of her students. Jill lived on a busy Chance street in an area containing quite a few apartment buildings. Elissa arrived, parked and exited her SUV with Peace, walking up and down the street, staring at the building in question, wanting—but also not wanting—to go inside.

She finally did, but just into the lobby area, which was unlocked but empty.

That's when her phone rang. It was Doug. "What the hell are you doing, Elissa?" he demanded.

"I've got to talk to someone whose name I was given. It's Jill from my classes, and I'm in her apartment building now. I've more information to tell you and—"

"Wait right there. I'm on my way."

She promised she would wait inside the building lobby. He was right. He was the cop, and just because she was angry about what had been happening to her and now had the possibility of putting it to an end, it was his job.

He joined her there quickly. They went outside for a few minutes with the dogs, and when Doug heard what she had to say, he grasped the point right away.

"You could be right," he said. "I'll get an investigator here soon and go talk to Ms. Jacobs."

"Please...could I at least listen?"

Doug glared at her. "And exactly who here is the police officer?"

"You are," she said softly. "But who here is the victim in all this?"

His look softened and he shook his head gently. "You are. Okay. I'll see what the situation looks like, and then determine if there's a way for you to observe—although not much is likely to happen. Not now, at least. Maybe just some questions. That'll have to be enough."

"It is," she said. "Thank you."

His backup, including one other officer plus Maisie and Griffin, arrived within ten minutes. In the meantime people, who were likely residents, strolled into and out of the lobby appearing puzzled, but no one attempted to stay.

Jill's apartment was on the third floor and they used the elevators. Soon they were outside the subject's apartment. Doug knocked on the door. "Jill Jacobs? This is the Chance Police Department. We need to talk. Please open your door."

Nothing except Astro's shrill barking.

"I have her phone number," Elissa whispered to Doug. "Do you want to call her or have me call her?"

"Go ahead. We don't know if she's home, even though her dog apparently is."

No answer.

Doug called out to her again as other tenants opened their doors and were shooed back into their units by Maisie and Griffin.

Still no answer, but Doug tried the doorknob.

Surprisingly the door opened. Doug motioned for Elissa to stay back as he and the other cops entered the way she had seen people acting like cops on TV did, guns drawn.

Elissa recognized Maisie's voice when she called, "Looks like we have a homicide here!"

Elissa wasn't permitted to enter even if she had wanted to. But she soon learned what was happening—somewhat.

Jill Jacobs was, in fact, home. She had been murdered there.

Elissa was not told any of the details.

But Doug soon exited and faced her. "Were you up here before? Did you go inside?"

"No!" She felt shocked that he would even ask.

She was even more shocked at his follow-up. "I can't tell you any details, Elissa. But there is a possible murder weapon there, as well as some other evidence. And—"

"And?" she prompted.

"It appears as though you were the perpetrator."

Chapter 19

Yes, it damn well appeared that way, Doug thought angrily more than once that late afternoon.

He was back at the station with Hooper. It was late in the day. Maisie and Griffin were there, too. Maisie had been the one to take charge of Elissa and her dog and bring them here.

No, Elissa wasn't under arrest...yet.

But there were plenty of questions that needed to be answered before she could be released—assuming she wasn't guilty. He believed for now, at least, that whoever had killed Jill Jacobs had also tried to frame Elissa. That made sense considering what she'd been going through and the kind of evidence found against her at the site.

But he recognized that it could be his blasted attraction to the woman affecting his brain and not reality.

Maisie had taken Elissa and Peace into an interrogation room. Doug had spoken briefly with both the chief and assistant chief about the situation and what he had seen at the murder site—though he hadn't gone into detail, especially not regarding the evidence that seemed to point to Elissa. They had undoubtedly heard about it already.

"Hi, Doug," said a voice from behind him. "You ready? I understand you'll be with me during this interrogation."

Doug turned to face Detective Vince Vanderhoff, who looked at him strangely through his glasses, as if he wanted to interrogate this fellow policeman, as well. But Doug got it. His attempts to help Elissa, though they were also for the benefit of the K-9 Ranch, had probably been a discussion point around the station—and if not before, then they would be now. And having a superior tell a detective what other cop would join him in an interrogation probably wasn't among Vince's favorite things to happen.

"I'm ready," he confirmed, and they both, along with Hooper, walked down the hall to the interrogation room. Vince asked a few questions to bring himself up to speed on what Doug had seen and experienced earlier, and Doug gave what answers he could.

Fortunately, the chief, Sherm, had agreed with Doug's request to be physically present during Elissa's interrogation. Doug knew their suspect better than anyone else in the department and might come up with some questions, or answers, to help in the interview.

Whether they would help the detective or Elissa most remained to be seen.

The hallway held several doors leading to meeting rooms that mostly had one-way mirrors, allowing cops to observe through the window. As far as Doug knew, no one would be watching Elissa's interrogation from outside, at least not this time.

Vince opened the door and walked in, and Doug followed with Hooper.

Elissa sat at the rectangular table in the middle of the room, with Peace lying on the floor and Maisie in the chair beside her. She must have left Griffin in their office. The two women were talking animatedly, and Doug wished he was in on the conversation.

Presumably, they weren't discussing this murder, since Maisie would know better than to talk with a suspect about it. But were they conversing about the threats against Elissa? Something unrelated? He supposed he would find out from one or the other later, and the subject probably wouldn't have any effect on the results of this interrogation.

"It's time for me to leave." Maisie rose as she caught Doug's eye.

He nodded. "See you later." The unspoken meaning of his words was that he would be on the spot to tell his sister all that went on in this room while Elissa was being questioned, just as he could count on Maisie telling him what they'd talked about first—both as siblings and as cops.

Vince took Maisie's spot nearest Elissa at the table, and Doug sat on a chair across from her. Peace wagged her tail and traded nose sniffs with Hooper.

Doug couldn't quite read Elissa's gaze but thought he saw both anger and pleading there, though only for a second. She turned to face Vince.

The detective began fairly coolly, telling Elissa that

she wasn't under arrest but could have an attorney present if she wanted.

"No, I'm fine," she said, and Doug hoped she was right.

Vince then asked if Elissa knew Jill Jacobs. "Yes," she responded. "I just met her recently, though. She is—was—a student in my class at the K-9 Ranch where I'm teaching therapy dog handlers." She shook her head. "This is so sad, and so confusing."

Doug thought about telling Elissa just to answer the questions and not volunteer extra comments or information, but maybe her going further would show the high level of her cooperation. He knew that any attorney representing her would tell her to keep it simple, though.

"Confusing how?" Vince prompted.

Over the next few minutes Elissa described what had brought her to Jill's apartment that day as Vince continued to ask questions.

Doug got the answers he was looking for—sort of.

Once she had heard that the person leaving the threatening sign on her SUV had been a woman—one she didn't recognize when he showed her the dark and blurred footage—she'd started thinking about women who might be angry with her. Since she'd most likely lost her job at the SLO hospital, she doubted anyone from there who might have been jealous or unhappy with her for any reason would continue to harass her like that. The same thing applied regarding any competition from her dog therapy work around her former home.

"But as I thought about the therapy I conducted there, something came to mind," she said. "Something I considered way beyond logical—but there it was." She de-

Linda O. Johnston 225

scribed the situation she had mentioned before—a child who had died by falling out a window after a meeting with a therapy dog. "Peace and I had had a couple of sessions with the boy, whose name was Tully Willmer, a while before his death, but others holding dog therapy sessions at the hospital had seen him since. I was in touch with a couple of them at first, and both indicated that Tully's mother, Adellaide, had unsurprisingly been distraught.

"When I saw her recently, she was working on becoming a therapy dog handler herself, which I thought was a poignant way to deal with what had happened—but not if it was a cover for something else."

Elissa then described the brief phone conversation she'd had with Adellaide earlier that day. She'd still sounded sad but determined to handle her sorrow. Adellaide had also described breaking up with her husband Perry, a successful computer software engineer who had remained furious about the loss of their son—and had immediately found a new girlfriend. One who had recently moved to Chance, California, and acquired a dog.

That girlfriend was Jill Jacobs.

Doug shuddered internally as he heard that. It gave Elissa a motive to kill the woman, if she believed Jill had been threatening her. Self defense? Maybe. But it would be hard to prove.

On the other hand…where was Perry Willmer? Could he have killed his new girlfriend with the idea of framing Elissa?

Or what about supposedly calm Adellaide?

Either made a lot more sense to Doug than Elissa.

The interrogation ended with a display of some of the evidence—including one of Elissa's business cards as a nurse and therapy dog handler in San Luis Obispo. Her eyes grew huge and she looked at him. "Could the person who broke into my home in San Luis Obispo have stolen some of my cards? I hadn't checked the drawers in the table in my spare bedroom, which I sometimes use as my office. That's where I kept them."

"It's a possibility." Doug glanced at Vince to make sure he was listening.

And since the murder weapon had been a scalpel—something a nurse could get hold of easily—the idea of someone, possibly Tully Willmer's father or mother, framing her if they thought she might have been involved in their son's death, made sorry sense.

After the interrogation ended, Vince asked to speak with Doug outside the room. "The evidence pointing toward Elissa also seems to point to the possibility she's being framed. I'm not going to arrest her now, but neither will she be off my radar."

"Got it," Doug said, "and I agree." He felt relieved—sort of. But if she wasn't arrested and the killer knew it, Elissa could be in danger of worse than the harassment she'd been receiving.

The kid's father and mother had split up. Both had been, and probably still were, angry—notwithstanding whatever the mother was doing at the hospital now. The mother might have been responsive and calm when Elissa had spoken with her, but that didn't mean she wasn't guilty. The Chance PD would have to request that the San Luis Obispo PD follow up on her.

The father, Perry Willmer had started seeing Jill—and now Jill was dead. Thanks to him? Why?

And if Willmer had done it, whatever the motive, he

clearly wasn't afraid to kill. Elissa might be the next target.

Or the mother's, if she was the guilty one.

While Vince went to let Sherm and Kara know the results of his interrogation, Doug reentered the room with Hooper to stay with Elissa.

Both she and Peace stood at his entrance. "Am I under arrest?" Her voice shook.

"You're not off the hook," Doug said, "but there's enough information to indicate that someone might be trying to frame you for the murder, so you'll be released soon. And I'm driving you home."

It was early evening. The remainder of the afternoon had seemed to fly by with all the questions and hinted-at accusations that fortunately hadn't governed everything. But Elissa still felt relieved.

Doug, who had removed his uniform jacket, had been thoughtful enough to stop at a sandwich shop to pick up something for dinner. For both of them, Elissa noted. Although since the sandwiches were take-out, that didn't necessarily mean Doug planned to stay with her long enough to eat. But at least it was a possibility. She needed some company now. Friendly company.

Elissa didn't attempt to express to Doug how glad she was to be out of there. She figured he knew.

He'd insisted on driving Peace and her home. "I'll come get you tomorrow to retrieve your car." Maybe. She understood from what he hinted at that it was also being searched by crime scene investigators. They might be looking for anything that could tie her to the crime—a scalpel or two, or some additional business cards, or whatever else they thought of.

Not that they'd find any. Not unless whoever killed Jill had also planted something in her SUV.

She also didn't mention to Doug how relieved she was that he appeared to believe in her innocence. Neither had she acted on her urge, when they'd reached his vehicle, to thank him by throwing herself into his arms and kissing him. Despite their earlier kisses, he was still a cop and she had changed from being a victim of some nasty but not necessarily life-threatening attempts at intimidation to being a murder suspect.

But on the ride back to the ranch, with their dogs both lying on the back seat, she talked to him a bit about her earlier discussion with his sister, who'd asked about Elissa's further plans for her therapy dog handler classes. Maisie's interest had seemed real, yet Elissa had a sense she was also probing to see if Elissa might admit to something regarding the death of her student.

She hoped she could find a way to convince Maisie of her innocence, as her brother appeared to have accepted it—or at least not totally rejected it.

Elissa also talked to Doug about her theory—which she suspected was now at least partly his, too—about all that had been going on with her.

Not that she understood why, but if Perry Willmer actually was the person who had been tormenting her as some kind of payback for his son's death, she might be in real danger now, assuming he'd been the one to murder Jill. But if so—why? Just to get at her? She had never met the man. Tully's mom Adellaide had been the only one who'd taken him to dog therapy sessions. And Elissa had only provided a couple of those sessions.

Perry had supposedly been dating Jill. Could he have

killed her for an unrelated reason to what had been happening to Elissa—a new love affair gone bad?

Or was the killer Adellaide—because of jealousy or something else? But their conversation, which had seemed sincere, hadn't led Elissa in that direction.

"Adellaide said her ex had gone nuts after their son died," Elissa said as Doug drove her from town and toward the road that led to the ranch. It was a nice August evening, warm but not too hot. Her own temperature was heated, though, with nerves and concern. "She didn't exactly deny that she had been a bit crazed, too. But she seemed to feel some relief that Perry wasn't with her any longer, even though she admitted that the idea that he'd found a new girlfriend so quickly had hurt."

"We can't take her off our suspect list in that girlfriend's murder," Doug said. "Sure, Adellaide is in San Luis Obispo, not here, but you were planning on commuting from there. It's not that far away."

"Of course. But she seemed to be trying so hard to find some new stability in her life by helping other people, with therapy dog handling. Unless—"

"Unless that's just a ploy to make it appear as if she wasn't attempting to get revenge against her husband for dumping her."

"And if that's her attitude—well, she might also want to get some kind of revenge against someone who'd been working with her son, although I'm not sure why she would choose me to go after."

"We'll definitely have her checked out," Doug said. "Perry, too."

They were nearing the driveway to the ranch. Elissa was both glad and sorry. She was free, at least for now.

Doug appeared to trust her. But she had a lot of concerns about being by herself there. Once more, she would let Amber, Sonya and, most especially, Evan know she was there. Evan, former military and current police K-9 trainer, would be a good person, with his dog, to have on her side watching for anyone who might come after her.

They passed the ranch house and turned onto the narrow lane to Elissa's place. Doug parked in front, and though Elissa half assumed he would come in with Hooper to check it out, she was relieved when he did so. After taking a short walk with both dogs, they entered the house—but not before Doug and Hooper walked around it and then preceded Elissa and Peace inside after she unlocked the door.

As they walked from room to room, neither dog alerted on any scent that shouldn't be there.

Elissa brought out some food and both dogs dug in.

Then, together, she and Doug sat at the kitchen table with the bag of sandwiches and a bottle of beer for each of them. Elissa wouldn't overdo, but a small amount of alcohol to help blunt some of the extreme emotions she felt sounded good.

Before they ate, though, Doug brought out his phone and, pressing the speaker button, called Amber first. He told Elissa he intended to call Evan next but that turned out to be unnecessary since he was at the main house, eating dinner with Amber and her mother. Doug quickly related what had been going on, and after everyone had expressed their concern, Evan promised to keep an eye on Elissa's home.

The sandwich tasted bland to Elissa, most likely because food wasn't the main thing on her mind.

She wished things were different, that this kind cop who had been helping her actually felt he could completely trust her. But even though he didn't, he hadn't walked away when she had been all but accused of committing a murder. Instead he had kind of taken her side—although she recognized that could change in an instant if another piece of evidence, even false as the rest, turned up.

They didn't discuss all that, though. Instead, Doug told more humorous stories about their uncle's influence over Maisie and him during their childhood, and Elissa felt herself finally begin to relax. He watched her with his hazel eyes sparkling—and there was an additional sparkle in them as she reacted and laughed. His expression suggested he was interested in her as more than a table companion…and a suspect.

Which made her insides simmer. Inappropriate? Yes. But she realized she wanted this man. Not just because he was helping her, but because he was one highly sexy guy.

Soon they were finished eating. He'd told her more about how Maisie and he had wound up here in Chance after training as K-9 officers in Riverside. Their conversation was drawing to an end.

What now? Was he about to leave?

He stood to help her clear the table, and she waited for him to say good-night. She could at least request that he and Hooper accompany Peace and her for a last walk outside in the near darkness, but after that he would leave. That was right—but she wanted oh, so much for him to stay.

When the beer bottles were disposed of and dishes

were in the sink, Doug turned to her and Elissa braced herself for the beginning of the end of the evening. Only—

Suddenly she was in his arms. Had she initiated it? Had he? It didn't matter. His mouth was on hers and the kiss was even hotter than those she had experienced with him before. His tongue probed into her mouth and she encouraged it, teasing it with her own.

Below, she felt the hardness of his erection through his trousers, pushing against her, and she moved her own body closer against him. His hands stroked her back, then downward until he grasped her buttocks and she gasped slightly, moving to do the same.

His expression, as he looked down at her, was full of heat and desire. He opened his mouth but before he could speak, she anticipated, or at least hoped, what he was going to say.

"My bedroom is just down the hall," she managed to tell him. He knew that. He and Hooper had examined her house multiple times, including tonight.

But this wasn't merely informational. It was an invitation.

"Let's go," he responded. He grabbed her hand, and she was both amused and excited when he was the one to lead the way.

The dogs followed, but Elissa figured they would settle down and sleep once they were in the bedroom. She and Doug, on the other hand, wouldn't sleep, at least not yet.

As soon as they entered the small room with its single bed covered by a thick beige comforter, they both moved as if according to a plan, kicking off their shoes, then reaching to remove the other's shirt.

Hers came off first and she found herself lying on the

bed with Doug beside her, kissing her face as his hands moved down, down, gently pulling off her jeans. But she didn't allow him to undress her fully. Not until she had done so with him, removing his trousers and then his briefs and baring an erection that made her dampen and crave what they were about to do even more.

She reached for his arousal even as she moved her hips to allow him to finish undressing her. His hands never stopped moving—and soon he was also kissing her everywhere that was now exposed, moving downward until he reached the place where her craving was now a center of hot, demanding passion.

She cried out even as she tried to pull away enough to return the favor, but he didn't let her. Instead he grabbed the pants she had helped to remove, reached into a pocket and pulled out a condom. He began to do it himself but she reached out and helped to fully sheathe him.

And then he kissed her again as he gently yet firmly thrust inside her. He drove into her even as she moved to help draw him in and out. Their mouths met again and then…

As Elissa reached her climax, he did, too, calling out her name even as he tensed against her also rigid body.

After a while, as he moved off her but maintained his hold on her heavily panting form, he laughed a little, clearly out of breath.

"You may not kill with a scalpel," he managed to say, "but you just might be able to get a guy breathing so fast that he dies from hyperventilation."

Chapter 20

Okay. Had that been a wise move? No. The woman was still a murder suspect. Even if she was innocent, she was deeply involved with the case, and Uncle Cy's strong advice reverberated through Doug's mind even as he reached once more for a clearly willing Elissa.

He was here. He was hooked, even if only for the moment. He wanted more—and so, apparently, did she.

"Oh, Doug," she murmured more than once.

"Tell me what you want next," he responded—and she did. Of course he obliged, even as she did even more to arouse him and keep their passion at amazing heights.

She was warm and soft and one extremely sexy lady, and her eagerness to continue with what they had started only drove him further and made him more eager to please…both of them.

But exhaustion set in. His, and hers, too. Snuggled

together beneath the coverlet, they fell asleep—until Hooper awakened Doug with a small woof.

He glanced at the time. It was late. Even if he stayed the night, which seemed best, they still needed to take the dogs out once more.

"Hang on, Peace," he heard Elissa say as she moved away from him. Soft light entered through the window at the back of the room, from somewhere on the ranch property. He could see her. Her lovely, still-bare body. And as he, too, rose, she looked at him, as well.

They both laughed. "Guess we're under orders from the dogs," he said.

"Yes, we are. And if you need to leave…"

"Hey, if you want to kick me out, fine. Otherwise, I'm staying."

She managed to pull on her jeans and shirt—but no underwear that he'd noticed. He did the same thing. "I don't feel like kicking you out," she said, and he felt his smile broaden.

Their venture outside didn't take long since both well-behaved dogs were ready to accomplish quickly what they needed to.

And when they went back inside…well, their clothes came off again quickly. They engaged in one more fantastic heated encounter.

Afterward, when Elissa left the bedroom for a short while, Doug remembered to call Maisie to make sure she didn't worry about his not coming home.

"I can guess where you are," she said dryly. "Just make sure there are no hidden scalpels around."

They had already discussed how Doug believed—or wanted to—that Elissa was being framed, so that was supposed to be a joke.

"No problem. I've got my weapon here." Which he did, although he had left it in the kitchen.

He said good-night and hung up. Soon, Elissa and he were both ready for bed, and they fell asleep naked and in each other's arms.

Elissa's eyes popped open early the next morning. She heard Doug's soft, deep breathing beside her, along with some snores from the floor near him—Hooper. She found herself smiling. Then frowning.

What had she done? What had they done? Oh, physically she knew very well what they had done last night. But what effect would it have on the rest of their relationship—the cop-civilian part of it? The cop who, no matter what he told her, suspected her not of merely being a possible victim, but also a murder suspect.

She must have moved at least a little, for Doug's eyes opened, too. He came awake immediately—a cop thing?

He turned to prop himself up on his elbow and looked at her. "Good morning," he said. "Did you sleep okay?"

"Very well," she responded, knowing her smile had to appear sexy, the way she felt inside. "I was worn out."

"Me, too."

They talked briefly about their plans for the day. Doug had to report to the station for duty.

Elissa had intended to make another venture downtown to the hospital to hold some dog therapy sessions, since it was Thursday and her next class wasn't to be until Saturday.

How would her class handle the death of one of their fellow students? Her therapy dog handling skills might wind up being directed toward helping the remaining students deal with the loss.

And what about her? Was she in danger? How could she be sure without knowing who had killed Jill or why?

Well, for now—

"I'll just get in touch with Amber and see if there's anything I can do here at the ranch," she said. "Maybe I can work with the dogs in training to be K-9s, or see if Evan is holding classes I can watch or help with, or... well, whatever. Unless..."

Unless you arrest me, she thought, no matter what happened between them last night.

"Unless I tell you otherwise." Doug's head was cocked a little as if he was guessing what she was thinking.

"Yeah," she responded, looking down. The movement attracted Peace, who put her adorable golden head on top of the bed. Elissa petted her dog, but her mind didn't concentrate on that.

No matter how wonderful the night had been, this was a new day—one in which her reputation, and even her freedom, remained in jeopardy.

And in the light of day, would Doug remain on her side?

"One reason I need to head to the department," he said from behind her, "is to see where things stand in the investigation. But I really don't like the idea of your being alone."

Neither did she. But she said, "I'll be fine," hoping that was true. She stood, gave Peace another pat and then grabbed clothes from the room's closet.

Soon they were fully dressed, Doug in his uniform shirt and trousers, and her in a casual outfit.

"Ready to take the dogs out?" he asked.

Doug was only partly amused when Amber and Evan, both also walking their dogs, caught up with Elissa and him in front of her house, on the sparse lawn on the other side of the driveway. "Busy time," Amber said, undoubtedly referring to the dogs' needs to come outside. But her look, eyebrows raised and slight smile, suggested she was referring to how busy the humans might have been inside the house.

Not that he felt embarrassed. Instead he had an urge to let the whole world know what Elissa and he had been up to—despite the possible threat to his job. But it would be unfair to her to even hint at the wonderful sex they'd had, though Amber and Evan undoubtedly could figure out what they'd been doing.

An idea came to him. Nothing outrageous, but it made a lot of sense: to tell these folks his concerns for Elissa's safety and encourage them to keep an eye on her when they could.

"Hey, I think you two need to know what's been going on—or more of it than you might already know. Can we talk?"

"Have you had breakfast yet?" Amber countered. "We can talk there."

Doug shot a glance toward Elissa, who nodded and said, "That would be great. Thanks."

They headed to the main house, where Sonya was already preparing breakfast. It was simple that day, just cereal and coffee, but she'd made plenty of coffee and just laid out a couple of extra bowls while giving the dogs a few treats.

When they were all seated, Doug decided to start talking before the others asked any questions.

For the next few minutes, while eating a bowl of crunchy, not-too-sweet cereal with a little bit of milk, he described what had happened, in case they hadn't heard about Jill Jacobs's murder.

Of course they had but still had questions. Elissa kept looking at him in a way that suggested she wanted to know what he was going to say before he said it, but this was far from a time to point any fingers at her.

"One thing you need to know," he finally said, "is that some evidence found at the crime scene could implicate Elissa in the murder, although so far we also believe it could have been planted to attempt to frame her. I'd like to believe in Elissa's innocence and I'm sure you would, too."

He nearly bit his tongue at that, especially after aiming a glance at her and seeing the hurt on her face, at least for a moment. It wasn't exactly a ringing endorsement of her innocence. But he couldn't do that—yet. Not even here.

"We absolutely would," Amber said, scowling at him. Good. Elissa at least had one person on her side—a person who also happened to be her employer.

"In case anyone wants to hear from me," Elissa said, "I am innocent." She punctuated that with a substantial gulp of coffee from her cup, and Doug resisted the urge to get out of his chair beside her and give her a reassuring hug.

"I figured," he said. "And since that's the case, whoever is attempting to frame you might be unhappy that you're not under arrest yet. You could be in danger. You'll hopefully be safe here at the ranch—"

"And we'll try to keep an eye on her while she's here," Amber stated with no hesitation.

"That's exactly what I was going to ask. Thanks."

"And thank you, too," Amber said, "for trying to protect our new employee."

After breakfast, Elissa and Doug played for a while with the young dogs in the den who were being trained as K-9s. They also provided some quality time petting the other dogs in the house, Bear and Lola, while the other people provided attention to Peace and Hooper.

Soon, though, it was time to say goodbye to Doug and Hooper.

Just for now? Elissa assumed so. She hoped they would get together again as…what? Lovers? Sure, or at least friends. And hopefully not because some other false evidence showed up and Doug came to arrest her.

With Peace, she walked Hooper and him to his SUV, still parked in front of her house.

As he used the remote on his key ring to open the doors, she said in as bright a tone as she could muster, "Thanks for coming…and staying. And for trying to help me."

His tone was a whole lot sexier as he returned a grin to her, his smile all but stripping the clothes off her, and said, "And a big thank you to you, too."

She couldn't help smiling back, but neither could she make herself ask what she really wanted to know: when would they see each other again, for whatever reason?

He seemed to hear her anyway. He drew closer, pressing his large, hard body against hers as he leaned down, apparently oblivious that he was sort of out in public, wearing his uniform, and about to kiss her. "You be careful," he said. "I'll check with you often, and you can call me anytime. I know Amber and Evan will be keeping an eye on you, at least somewhat, but that doesn't mean you'll be safe." Before she could reply, he bent and the kiss they shared was reminiscent in heat level to those they had engaged in earlier.

She felt forlorn when he pulled back. "See you soon, I hope," was all she could manage to say.

"Count on it. Oh, and by the way, I'm looking forward to your next class. I'll be there with Hooper, and I'd imagine Maisie and Griffin will come, too."

"That would be great. It'll be Saturday at ten in the morning," she reminded him, wondering if that would be the next time she would see him. This was only Thursday.

Even if it was, she would at least have that to look forward to.

She stood there waving, Peace at her side, as Doug drove along the narrow lane toward the driveway that led to the road. And then he was gone.

But when she turned she saw that Amber, Evan and Sonya, and ranch hand Orrin, were all on the ranch house's front porch, talking. She had nothing in particular to do, so she headed that direction and joined them.

"Peace and I don't have another class to give till Saturday, and for right now we're not going off on any therapy sessions on our own." She didn't need to tell them why that would be a bad idea, although she really hoped things would change and they could do so again soon. She continued, "So if any of you have anything we, or either of us, can help with, let me know."

She watched as Amber and Evan traded glances— and felt a familiar twinge of envy at the caring emotion she saw there, even though there was nothing particularly emotional happening here and now.

"Actually, there is something you can help with,"

Amber said, turning back to Elissa. "Evan has a class scheduled early this evening for general dog training, and it always helps to have an example to show the students what he's talking about, in addition to Bear. Care to give a demonstration?"

"I'd be glad to," Elissa said, relieved that she would be at least a little busy—and contributing, in a small way, to the success of her kind and understanding employer. "Just tell me the time and Peace and I will be there."

Chapter 21

Saturday morning arrived much quicker than Elissa had anticipated.

Maybe it was because she had been kept so busy over the past couple of days, thanks to Evan and Amber.

She had known almost nothing about how cops were trained to work with K-9s. But she had enjoyed watching Evan demonstrate to a few classes of police officers who'd brought their own nearby departments' dogs some of what he considered to be advanced moves. That included scenting out bad guys and having the dogs attack ranch hand Orrin in a protective suit, acting as what they called an *agitator*. Orrin helped Evan a lot, and this was one of the most frequent ways.

Plus, Elissa had helped to arrange which student and their dog was up next and what exercise they would engage in. Highly interesting and enjoyable.

She'd had fun working with the ranch's K-9s even more—German shepherds Lucy, Rex and Hal—who stayed mostly in the den when not outside in the area within the chain-link enclosure inside the large plank fence surrounding the ranch. In training here for months, the three shepherds knew basic commands, and Evan was working to familiarize them with even more of what the visiting K-9s already knew.

Elissa regretted that she couldn't visit Florence again in the hospital with Peace. But it was safer to stay here. And she would at least be able to give her therapy dog class soon.

Besides, she remained busy in other ways.

She completed her list of people she didn't always get along with, as well as her computer search for information about them, and emailed it to Doug to pass along to his station's computer guy. No one stood out as a particular problem, though.

Much more fun, she even got to play the role of a handler a few times and loved it. Not that she intended to get involved with training K-9s other than here. But she hoped Doug would let her work with Hooper at least a little.

Doug. He had called her a couple of times on Thursday after he'd left and come to take her out to dinner that evening, which had evolved into further time together... But he hadn't stayed overnight. There was a major investigation that Maisie and he and their K-9s had to dig into on Friday, pretty much all day. Even so, he had managed to call her several times then, too, asked if she was okay and if she was hanging out with the people they trusted at the ranch. She'd been able to say yes with certainty. She had even managed to sound calm and neutral when talking with him, hoping not to bring to mind—too much—all the fun they had engaged in when alone together.

She didn't know when that would happen again. If ever.

But now it was nearing nine o'clock. Her remaining students were scheduled to arrive soon, and she was outside with Peace for a walk on the ranch's grounds—after again having had breakfast in the main house with Amber, Evan and Sonya.

They were definitely wonderful people, and were keeping their promise to Doug to keep an eye on her.

So close an eye on her that she relished this moment walking alone outside with her dog. Of course she'd told them where she'd intended to go—to the area enclosed by chain-link fencing since the ranch's K-9 students were inside the house. That was where she would hold her class.

Assuming her students showed up—any of them.

"We'll see," she said softly to Peace, who was busy sniffing bushes off the side of the narrow road leading to her house. From there, Elissa could look down on the fenced area in question. She intended to have each student, in turn, act as a hospital patient needing the kind of therapy only a loving dog could provide. They would all additionally take turns being the therapy dog handler on duty.

Her remaining students. She had spoken with each of them over the last two days. Paul and Kim had called her after hearing what had happened to Jill. Elissa'd been the one to call Jim. Yes, he'd heard but didn't know what to say. As long as the class was being held on Saturday, he'd planned to attend—and ask any questions then.

All of them had sounded rattled. And concerned. And had asked whether Elissa believed the murder had anything to do with her training Jill to become a therapy dog handler.

In some ways, Elissa worried that the answer was yes. Maybe anyone associated with her was in danger.

She had merely told the students to be careful, but that she didn't believe Jill's attack had anything to do with this class.

With her? That was another story, but she didn't mention it to them.

"Guess we'd better go inside and get ready," Elissa said to Peace and then gave the command, "Come." Of course her smart and obedient dog did so, remaining leashed at her side as she turned toward their house. That's when she saw a car pull off the road below and onto the driveway: a black SUV with a light on top that wasn't lit now, but it confirmed who was arriving. Doug. And maybe Maisie with him.

Instead of going to her home, Elissa walked to the main ranch house to wait. In moments, Peace was able to greet his friends Hooper and Griffin, since both officers and their dogs got out of the SUV.

"Thanks for coming," Elissa said as, side by side, they faced her—dressed in their uniforms and looking all cop. Even Doug looked all professional, his handsome sexiness not hidden but certainly not at the forefront of his appearance. Maisie, who resembled a feminine version of her brother, seemed even friendlier than he did at the moment.

Was there something Doug hadn't told her?

Was she going to be taken into custody this day?

Apparently not at the moment, at least, since they

both approached her, even as another car started up the driveway. Amber and the others in the house must have heard the cars since they came out onto the porch. After saying hi to Elissa, Doug and Maisie joined them.

In a minute, Elissa greeted Kim, with Barker. And shortly thereafter, the other two students also arrived.

The three of them seemed uncomfortable standing there with their dogs at the base of the ranch's porch. They glanced at each other, then away, as if all were uneasy even trying to speak about the loss of their barely known classmate.

Elissa realized it was up to her to address this very sad, very frightening, elephant on the ranch.

"Before we get started," she said, facing them as Peace sat on the dry turf at her side, "I know you're all aware of what happened to our other student, Jill Jacobs. We've all briefly discussed it, plus the media has provided some information and updates." The three students nodded at her, still without looking much at the others.

Elissa glanced up at Doug and Maisie on the porch. "I'm sure none of you is surprised that the Chance PD is giving their investigation high priority." Both Doug and Maisie nodded as the students looked up at them. "I gather there's nothing they can talk about publicly right now, but I've seen that they're looking into a number of possibilities." *Like whether I could be the killer.* But she wasn't about to mention that—although she figured they all knew she was a suspect.

"Now," she finished, "let's go ahead and start today's lesson. I'd like to dedicate all our wonderful efforts to Jill as well as our combined wishes that she could be with us today and through the entire class."

"Hear, hear," Kim said, and the youngest of the students made a gesture to her Dobie. In response, Barker did exactly as his name implied: barked, as if he agreed with his owner.

Jim Curtis just nodded and his Lab mix Bandit sat at his side, leaning against his leg as if he recognized some emotion on his master's part.

Paul Wilson looked at Elissa, shaking his head while holding Ollie, his French bulldog. "Good idea," he said. "But this is so sad."

"I agree," Elissa said then heaved a big sigh.

"Do you know where her dog Astro is?" Kim asked.

"No, but I wish I did," Elissa said, glancing toward the porch.

"Jill's parents came up from Ventura to help deal with the situation," Maisie said. "They're taking Astro home with them, or at least, that's what I heard."

"Oh, good." Elissa felt relieved. Even though she didn't know Jill's family, surely they would take good care of her dog in her memory. "So…please follow Peace and me to the exercise area and we'll begin our lesson."

Their minds might remain filled with thoughts of their missing classmate, but life had to continue.

Elissa just wished that she knew what Doug, who'd remained so remote and silent, was thinking.

So far, Doug admired Elissa's attitude and her approach to her students regarding their deceased classmate.

She had addressed the situation in a way that would hopefully keep the others thinking about their own safety. Since no one knew the motive for Jill Jacobs's homicide, it remained unclear whether anyone else was in danger.

But she had also given them reason to continue with their classes—and to be cautious with their lives.

Now, with Maisie beside him and their dogs accompanying them, too, he followed the group off the porch and down the hillside to the fenced class area. He'd said hello to Amber, Sonya and Evan, and they, too, headed in that direction.

Everyone should now behave as if things were normal. Or so he believed.

And in fact the class did seem to go well. At the beginning, Elissa had the students demonstrate how their dogs were learning the basic commands. Then, one by one, she had them each pretend to be a patient in a hospital or nursing home, while someone else's dog provided therapy.

She told Paul to act as if he had been in a bad car accident with a beloved family member injured, too— and had Kim's dog Barker nuzzle him where he sat on a folding chair Evan had brought out for the class.

Next, Paul's dog Ollie helped to cheer up Jim, who was ostensibly a patient in a long-term-care facility with no family around—although Ollie seemed a bit energetic to help a supposed senior. If that kept up, he might not qualify as a therapy dog, the way Elissa had described it.

And finally, Jim's dog Bandit was instructed to help Kim as a hospitalized new stroke patient who had a good chance to get better if her mindset improved. Doug enjoyed listening when Elissa described how, similarly to this exercise, Peace had helped hospital patient Florence, who had been mostly unresponsive, to react.

All seemed to do well. Elissa also seemed pleased.
A good class.

He was glad he was watching it.

He was glad he was watching sexy and skilled Elissa.

Now, if only he, or his fellow cops, could find the
killer and get Elissa off the hook.

Assuming she was, in fact, innocent.

The class appeared to go well, or so Elissa thought
as she observed her students chatting in the enclosed
instruction area after the last exercise while their dogs
traded sniffs once more. At least she hoped so.

She had a sense that the different therapy dog aspects of the class were extremely important that day.
The new handlers themselves were in need of therapy
dog assistance, thanks to the sudden and terrible loss
of their class member.

They helped each other. She helped them, too—and
at the same time received some degree of therapy herself.

Of course she could have relied on her wonderful
Peace for that. Had relied on her. But the extra help
was useful, too.

It also didn't hurt having Doug—and Maisie—here
with their dogs. They participated in the class, too, with
both dogs doing everything they were told and then
some.

Same went for the two K-9 cops.

And Elissa had felt Doug's gaze on her nearly all
the time.

Her bosses observed the entire class, as well, standing just outside the gate to the practice area. They

smiled and clapped and cheered now and then when one of the dogs did exactly as directed by his or her owner.

Elissa dared to allow herself to feel…well, happy. Somewhat. And, possibly, free of all the suspicions against her while she worked there.

They would undoubtedly return later, and she would have to deal with them. But so be it.

"So what do you think?"

She turned quickly to face Doug. She had been concentrating so much on observing her remaining three students that she hadn't noticed Hooper and him move away from the inside of the gate area where he'd stood with Maisie and Griffin, near where Amber, Evan and Sonya stood outside. And now he'd joined her.

"I think it's going well," she said somewhat cautiously, not knowing if he was leading up to something.

"So do I." He leveled a calming yet sexy smile on her that added to her feelings of at least temporary relief.

Before she could say anything else, her three students approached, their dogs leashed beside them. They all stood facing Doug and her on the rough terrain of the training area.

"Thanks so much, Elissa," Kim said as Barker sat at her side, panting slightly. Elissa believed this Dobie mix would be the best therapy dog in the class, but she wasn't about to mention that with the others around.

"Thank you for coming," Elissa replied. "And thank you, too, Barker." She held out her hand and the dog responded by lifting his paw. Grasping it, Elissa laughed.

"When will our next class be?" Kim asked. "I don't live far and could come any day after four."

"Same here," Jim said. "Bandit is really having a

good time here and I think he'll make a good therapy dog someday, don't you?"

"I do," Elissa said. With Jim's advancing age, she thought his Lab would be a particularly good fit at providing therapy sessions at senior or rest homes. "I think what we'll do is have one or two more classes here, and then I'll see if I can work out a lesson at the hospital or another venue near here where we can work with real patients."

"I like that idea, too," Paul said. "But I'm just not feeling sure that Ollie is getting it yet." He looked uncomfortably toward Elissa, his light brown eyes appearing concerned. As usual, he had gotten dressed up more than his classmates, and his white shirt was wrinkled now after his training efforts.

"Let's give him a while longer," Elissa said. "Next time I'll try to spend a little more time with you and Ollie and see if that helps."

"I'd really appreciate a private lesson soon, if possible. I'd be glad to pay extra." The guy didn't appear comfortable asking, but it wasn't as if Elissa didn't have time on her hands.

"Well, okay," she said. "When would you like it? Before our next class? I'm thinking the class should be on Wednesday again, but later in the day. Would you like your private lesson tomorrow, maybe? Or late Monday?"

"I'll need to check my calendar since I've got a bunch of stuff going on, but tomorrow might work out fine. I'll call you after I get home, okay?"

"Sure," Elissa said. Extra money for an extra class? Since she only had this one job now, even though it was beginning to expand, she wasn't about to object. Part of it would go to the ranch anyway.

Soon all three students and their dogs got into their cars and headed down the long driveway. Elissa figured Doug and Maisie would leave soon, too. They had both come in the same vehicle, so Doug would need to go when his sister did.

But first, Amber invited them all into her house for some tea and scones and discussion.

Which sounded good to Elissa—especially when Doug asked to see something in her house as Maisie and Griffin followed the rest of them to the ranch house.

Once inside her front door, Doug said, "Everything okay with you?"

"Sure," she said, knowing her quick affirmative probably implied something else to him.

"I'll take Maisie home soon and come back this evening, if you're okay with it."

This time she knew her response had no negativity to it at all. "I'm definitely okay with it."

Chapter 22

While waiting for Doug to return that evening, Elissa visited the ranch house to talk over how things had gone at her class, and Amber and the others all seemed pleased—including Evan, the more experienced dog trainer.

She couldn't have been happier. Well, that was an exaggeration. She'd have been happier if Doug had been able to stay.

And if she wasn't a murder suspect...

Later, at dinnertime, she'd insisted on ordering pizza for everyone, her treat. And, happily, Doug and Hooper arrived a short while before it was delivered.

They'd enjoyed the meal with everyone else...then gone to her home with their dogs. She'd stated, while with her dinner companions, that Doug and she wanted to discuss the lessons. Which they did—but that wasn't all, and she knew she wasn't fooling anyone.

On the walk to her house, Elissa made herself ask about the status of the investigation into Jill's murder. Doug indicated that there was, unfortunately, nothing new. Or at least nothing new he could reveal to her, she figured.

As soon as they shut the door behind them, Elissa put all her uneasy thoughts aside. She moved toward Doug as he edged closer to her—and the kiss they shared ignited what she had hoped would happen that evening.

And that night.

But morning came too quickly.

"Will I see you tonight?" she asked Doug as she saw Hooper and him to his SUV after their inevitable but too short dog walk.

He was dressed in casual clothes, which he had worn on his return to the ranch the previous night. He looked down at her with hazel eyes both lusty and concerned. "Count on it." He pulled her into his arms. They engaged in a hot but too-quick kiss. Then Doug helped Hooper into the SUV and they drove off.

Elissa knew she was counting on it.

Doug hated to leave her, but at least, when he reached the department after eating breakfast and changing clothes at home—Maisie had already left—he checked in with those fellow cops still strongly engaged in the Jill Jacobs murder investigation, including Gil and his online search for any answers.

He even called the detective who had become his contact at the San Luis Obispo PD. They had agreed to search for Perry Willmer, but no one had located him yet for an interrogation. His apartment had been cleaned out, which was a good thing for Elissa, since he remained a possible suspect. Although there'd been some light speculation as to whether she might have done something to him, too.

Everything remained a vortex of big questions, which definitely didn't take the pressure off Elissa.

Yet something just didn't seem right.

Sure, he cared too much about her, despite his initial attempts to keep his emotional distance. Now that they had shared such amazing physical contact, he knew he was feeling a lot for her in more ways than he'd ever anticipated. Plus, he was constantly worried about her—and her safety.

"Hell," he said aloud in his office just as Maisie and Griffin walked in the door.

"Does that mean you didn't have fun last night?" his sister asked with a snide grin.

"Just the opposite." Doug was seated at his desk then, looking at today's assignment on his computer. Both Maisie and he would be working on three burglaries that had occurred over the past couple of days in some Chance retail establishments—two chain clothing stores plus one fast food joint—to have the dogs check remaining scents to determine if they all had the same perpetrator...and, if possible, who that suspect was. That should be an almost enjoyable exercise for their K-9s' skills.

But he wasn't going to get away with last night's visit with Elissa. Maisie approached him. His older sister regarded him with an unflinching gaze with eyes that so resembled his own. She still looked great in her police uniform, even with her jacket now over the back of her chair. Her light hair was combed just so, and she appeared to be the perfect cop.

One who was about to chew him out.

Instead she said, "I'm worried about you, bro. And I know you're worried about Elissa. I'm giving her the benefit of the doubt—for now, probably because I know you care so much. But until we have answers in that Jacobs murder—"

"I know," he said. "I need to be careful and stay as detached as possible."

"Which I gather isn't so detached."

Ah, his sister knew him well.

When he didn't respond, she said, "Okay, then. We need to get our K-9s working. But tell you what. I'll give Amber a call before we go to thank her for letting us observe and even participate in those therapy dog classes. And oh, by the way, if she could just continue to keep an eye on Elissa for us to make sure she remains safe, that would be great. Especially if Amber lets us know if anything appears to be wrong."

Which Doug knew could be interpreted that his sister and he both were worried about Elissa…or that they wanted her actions observed and reported in case she did anything to implicate herself in the murder.

Doug had had to leave right after they'd taken the dogs for their early morning walk. Elissa understood.

She didn't have to love it.

After watching his SUV go down the driveway and turn onto the road, she'd directed Peace on a path away from the ranch but toward the rest of the houses in her row, and even past Evan's. He might see her, but she wouldn't be as potentially visible to Amber and Sonya. She hadn't seen anyone else on the ranch when Doug and she had been out, not even Orrin.

Now, she took her time returning to her house. She just needed a bit of "me and my dog" time before starting any assignments her bosses might have for her.

But as she passed Orrin's house on the way back to her own, her cell phone rang. Since she had programmed her students' information into her phone she knew immediately who it was: Paul Wilson.

"Hi, Elissa," he said. "Do you have a little time this morning to work with me on Ollie's training? Around ten thirty, maybe?"

Elissa had glanced at her phone for the time. Nearly nine thirty. If she saw him in an hour she would still have the rest of the day if Amber came up with something for her to do, like work with Evan on any classes he had that day.

"That's fine," she said. "Come on over."

"Can we work inside your house? My dog just seems to be more relaxed inside and maybe he'd do better there."

"We'll give it a try," she responded. She wondered if she should ask Amber or someone else to be there to act the role of a person needing dog therapy, but decided to wait to learn Paul's questions first. After they hung up, she decided to call Amber to put her on notice that she might be needed later. Amber sounded amused and said she would be sure to have someone available if Elissa called again.

While waiting for Paul, Elissa ate a quick breakfast, fed Peace then sat at the kitchen table again, placing her laptop on it. She got online and started researching websites that had therapy dog demonstrations, including descriptions of training problems and their solutions, just as a reminder to herself.

One link brought her to a police K-9 site, which reminded her of Doug—as if she needed a reminder.

She wondered what he was up to that day. And if she was the topic of any of his conversations—as a murder suspect.

She almost called him, although any excuse would be flimsy. He didn't need to know she was giving a private lesson to one of her students. Since Amber knew, it wasn't as if there was any big secret about it. And it wasn't as if the well-dressed Paul and his French bulldog Ollie were particularly dangerous.

A short while later, though, Elissa heard a noise behind her and saw that Peace had risen from where she'd been sleeping on the kitchen floor and run to the door to the hallway.

"Peace?" Elissa called. What was she up to? Her dog also started barking as Elissa stood and hurried after her. And stopped immediately as she saw that Paul Wilson stood there in the narrow hall, his left hand holding Peace's collar as the poor dog jerked back and forth as if she was strangling.

"What are you doing?" Elissa cried, dashing over to her dog.

The good thing was that Paul let go of the collar.

The bad thing was that he quickly grasped Elissa around her throat and started compressing it as if she was the strangling dog with the collar around her neck.

"Calm down." He sounded as if he spoke through gritted teeth.

Feeling as if she was about to pass out, Elissa attempted to comply, even as her mind frantically sought some way to push away. To run.

To call Doug for help—as if that would do any good with him so far away, in downtown Chance.

She allowed herself to go limp, even as she heard Peace growling in a threatening tone she had never heard before.

She wanted to reassure her wonderful pup before she did anything to make this man harm her even more. But she couldn't talk.

Until suddenly she felt a hand patting the side of the jeans she wore. Paul yanked her phone from her pocket and she heard it drop then the sound of it being ground against the floor. Only then was her throat released. She felt herself slide to the floor, grasping at her neck and gasping for air.

Paul moved until he was kneeling, facing her. He held a scalpel in his gloved hand and he pointed it toward her.

A scalpel? Did that mean—

"Let's go into the living room," he said. "We'll talk there."

After being allowed to smell a shirt brought from another crime scene, Hooper had alerted on a scent around the cash register of the first clothing store they had visited and followed it out the door, then stopped.

Doug figured the thief had gotten into a car there— along with the few hundred dollars' cash stolen from the store.

He wondered whether Maisie and Griffin were having the same degree of success—if you could call it that. They'd located that shirt at another crime scene but hadn't yet been able to determine its owner.

Doug had no doubt that one dog or the other would

pick the perpetrator out of a crowd or a lineup or whatever, when they figured out some possible suspects to investigate.

For now, though—heck. He wanted to talk to Elissa. Maybe invite her out for dinner that night. Celebrate the fact that, when he had gone into the station that morning, those who were investigating Jill Jacobs's murder still weren't prepared to arrest Elissa. Yet.

As some fellow officers grouped around Hooper and took his picture, nose down to the ground, because they enjoyed watching the K-9s work, Doug pulled his phone out of his pocket to call Elissa.

Strange. The call went straight to voice mail. He tried again. Same result.

Maybe she was doing some kind of dog training lesson with Evan and had turned off her phone. That made some sense, if they didn't want any interruptions.

But Doug wanted to know for sure. And so he called Amber to see what was going on at the ranch that day that involved Elissa.

And learned she was going to be giving a private lesson to that guy Paul, one of her students.

That was probably just fine. Doug recognized that the worry he felt after hearing about it was simply because, despite all his intentions of not getting too involved with the lovely, sexy woman, he was hooked. He should just back off.

But he was a cop. Backing off wasn't in his vocabulary.

And so, dumb as it might be, he waited just a few more minutes while the crime scene investigators finished their photos of Hooper on the scent.

"Let's go boy," he said to his dog.

* * *

At the man's direction, Elissa sat on the black-fabric couch in her living room. He pulled a chair up directly across from her and sat facing her.

He was definitely her student Paul Wilson—although he looked quite different.

For one thing, he had hold of Peace's leash and held the sweet dog's head against his leg, with that scalpel only an inch or so away from her neck.

His legs were jeans-clad now, despite how dressed up he had always been while attending classes. He wore a plain navy T-shirt and had dark blue tennis shoes on his feet.

But it wasn't only his clothing that looked different. Elissa hadn't paid much attention to his looks before, only noting that he wore glasses over pale cheeks and had medium-brown hair that was clipped fairly short.

No glasses now, and his face was anything but pale. Its redness all but glowed, as if the blood inside was about to burst out.

But his eyes. They were the hardest thing to look at. They were so dark, as if his pupils had been dilated medically, and they were glaring at her as if trying to assault her by their fury.

Would anyone on the ranch come to help her? But even if Paul had been seen, Elissa had already told Amber that he was coming for a class.

Since he didn't say anything at first, she was nearly afraid to, scared that if she said the wrong thing, whatever it was, he would immediately stab and kill her beloved Peace.

But then he smiled—and she almost preferred his glare to the nasty and threatening grin he now wore.

"So here we are, Elissa Yorian, you murderer."

Elissa could only blink at that. Her? What about him? Or hadn't he murdered Jill?

"I know what you're thinking," he said, barking a laugh. "But you see, you started it all. You killed my son Tully."

Elissa felt startled. "Then you're Tully's father? And I didn't kill him." They had been wondering where Perry Willmer was, even had San Luis Obispo police looking for him—and he'd been here in Chance for at least a week.

"Oh, yes, you did," he replied in a too sweet voice. "A damn therapy dog killed him, and you're the first of the damn therapy dog handlers he saw."

She wanted to express both condolences and an explanation that his poor son's mental illness had apparently been what had killed him, not pet therapy or any of the therapists. But she didn't want to goad him into anything that would result in his harming Peace or her any more than they were already likely to be harmed by his actions.

"I'm sorry you feel that way," she said.

"Yeah, yeah, yeah. You're about to go into the standard spiel that the damn shrinks always did around Tully—that he had some issues they could help by therapy sessions and getting him to talk and to act different. Well, forget it. You're not going to convince me otherwise. You started what happened to him. If it wasn't for you, he'd not have been with that other dog and tried to push it out the window—and fallen himself."

Strangely, or maybe not so strangely, Perry's eyes teared up. Elissa tried to come up with a way to soothe him.

But before she spoke again he continued. "Well, I can't bring him back and neither can his witch of a mother who's getting into doing the damn therapy dog stuff herself now, I heard."

"I believe she's trying to help people in Tully's memory." Elissa hoped that wasn't offensive, but she hoped to use the idea of doing something good in Tully's memory to get this man to back off.

But Perry rose, fortunately not hurting Peace but aiming the scalpel at her. "Forget that. And don't think you can con me into leaving you alone *in Tully's memory.*" His tone, while speaking those last three words, sounded taunting.

Elissa swallowed but didn't speak again. Not then.

"Okay," Perry said. "Here's how it is." He sat back down, this time releasing Peace but still pointing the sharp edge of the scalpel toward her.

The good thing was that he provided an explanation of all that had been happening to and around Elissa.

The bad thing was that his admissions made it clear that he did intend to kill her.

"I dumped Adellaide," he said. "She didn't blame anyone for our son's death. But I did. I knew exactly who was responsible." He glared at Elissa. "She was sad, but she didn't have the sense to get even. Well, I did. I did my research. Even though I hadn't been the one to attend those damn sessions with Tully, I knew you were the first to ram them down my boy's throat. I knew you needed to pay for that. The rest was simple. I wanted to threaten you first. Scare you. Make other people know what kind of witch you are."

His rationale, such as it was, wasn't a surprise to

Elissa, but once more, despite her beginning to shake—or maybe because of it—she said nothing.

"When you weren't home, I broke into your house and stole the kind of stuff you wouldn't notice, like some business cards I could toss around where it would make the most trouble, though I wasn't sure where then. I'd later heard that a cop and K-9 checked the place out, but that was okay. I'd also worn a strong cologne to cover my own scent before I locked your damn dog in the kitchen, in case I ever saw it again."

There had been some question as to what Hooper had been tracking when he'd been in her house. Doug had concluded it was the smell of fear, but maybe it was that unusual scent, Elissa thought.

"Plus," Perry continued, "I made sure I had a good alibi for when I was actually at your place. And so far, no one has questioned me about it—and you won't get a chance to tell them."

His grin was evil. Elissa wished she could do something to erase it.

She wished she could do *something*…but she didn't move.

Perry wasn't through. "I was worried when I realized, after asking dear Amber some questions before signing up here, that the same cop and dog might be at your classes. I'd already decided to attend them, both to keep an eye on you and to give myself a reason for being in Chance." He chuckled then and shook his head. "I acted all lovey-dovey to the damn police dog, so even if he did point to me, people would assume that was because I gave him treats. I told Jill to do the same thing, and I made sure I included that one, too." He nodded toward Peace.

Elissa was glad her dog was now lying on the floor near the wall by the drape-covered window, not moving. She yearned to do something to at least get her out of the room while she was okay. But Elissa was afraid to move.

"But they're so much bother—you can see why I hate dogs," Perry nearly shouted, glaring at Peace but not getting any closer to her...now. "And you'll love this, since you want to help kids so much. I found out who the other parents were whose kids were tortured by your miserable therapy work in SLO. There were a couple I trusted, and I asked the right kinds of questions that led them to see how rotten you and your dog were. That you'd hurt other kids, too. They wound up telling the right people at the hospital—which is why you got kicked out, at least for now, though you should have gotten permanently canned. Anyway, that's also how I first heard you were going to teach more of that stuff in Chance, damn you."

His ongoing rant now made it clear he knew he could, and would, stop her.

He could turn on the charm when he needed to, so once he knew where Elissa was headed, he'd seduced a woman in Chance who'd wanted to train her dog for therapy work. "It was easy to convince Jill that I wanted Ollie to do it, too—though that joke of a dog will have to go once I take care of you. I don't need him as a burden wherever I end up."

Poor Ollie, Elissa thought. Poor Jill. And she recognized where he was going with this: poor Elissa and Peace.

And—oh, no, possibly poor Amber and Sonya, too. "And those damn K-9 Ranch people who ignored my warning and hired you anyway? Well, they're going to be sorry, too—and not just because they'll feel sorry that you died here."

Enough, Elissa thought. But how was she going to stop him?

Doug, she called in her mind, wishing she could call him with her now-gone phone.

Just the idea of never seeing Doug again—before she died—created an ache deep inside her, as if Perry had already used the scalpel on her.

Perry was still talking, though. He seemed to need to explain himself, whether from pride or fury, she did not know—but it was fortunate, since it was buying her some time.

Yet she still didn't know how to save herself.

She did know he was unbalanced. And as he described himself further, she learned that he was a skilled computer tech, so posting the anonymous accusations online about her killing Tully had been simple. Plus, he had eventually, also anonymously, contacted even more of the kids' families Elissa had had therapy sessions with, as well as some he'd already talked to, and demanded that they accuse her, too, to the hospital…or risk their kids being attacked somewhere unexpected and maybe killed.

All had complied.

Then, more about Jill. "She was a nice lady. Pretty. Good in bed. Sympathetic enough about my loss of Tully to help me any way she could. And she understood what I wanted. She pretended not to know me in class because I asked her to. She's the one who attached those signs to the ranch gate and your car, because I told her to. That helped keep the damn K-9s off me, since they

couldn't have smelled me there even if they weren't
fooled by the games I played with my scent. Too bad I
didn't also have her overdose on cologne, too, though
that might not have helped, either.

"But she knew too much and also could have caused
K-9 reactions when they were around and smelled her,
so we both hugged those damn dogs. But that wasn't
enough." The disturbed look in his expression intensi-
fied. "I had to kill her—and make sure it was at a time
you'd be around so you would be blamed for it."

When he paused to look at her, she simply said, "I
see." Which she did.

"Okay, I might as well let you know how things are
going to go now. I wanted to make sure you knew why
you're about to die, and your damn dog, too, which is
why I'm telling you all this. So I'm going to kill you
with your nurse's weapon of choice, a scalpel, like I did
with Jill. Your dog, too. And then I'm going to sneak
out of here and come back with Ollie soon for our 'lesson.' There'll be a record of my call to you earlier asking for one and you might have told other people about
it, right?"

His glare demanded an answer and since he wanted
her to say yes she considered saying no. But she simply
nodded. She wondered, though, if he'd been successful
getting onto the ranch property without being seen by
people or scented by any dogs.

Even if he had been, that wouldn't save her life.

Would he also be able to get away and act out his
scenario?

"No one will know Paul Wilson and Perry Willmer
are the same person and I'll just get to see their confusion when I come here later for my lesson and am

shocked to find your body instead. And then, finally, my poor Tully's death will be avenged."

That's awful, Elissa thought. Smart? Maybe.

But she had to be smart, too.

How was she going to save Peace and herself?

Chapter 23

Doug hoped he appeared like an overly cautious cop attempting to act professional, though maybe all he really was doing was finding an excuse to go see Elissa during a busy day at work.

But he had nevertheless told Maisie what he was up to, and why. She didn't understand, maybe, but neither did she give him a hard time.

"Your intuition is hard to beat sometimes," she'd said. "Just keep me informed."

In his car, speeding in the direction of the ranch with Hooper in the back seat, Doug tried calling Elissa again. Immediate voice mail again.

Then he called Amber once more. No, she hadn't seen Elissa since that morning, though she'd talked to her, and Elissa was giving another lesson that day to one of her students. Amber was working now on some financial stuff for the ranch—but she could head over there with Lola and say hi, if Doug wanted.

No, he didn't want. If everything was okay, no use pulling Amber away from her work, when she clearly didn't want to be disturbed. And if everything wasn't okay—well, he certainly didn't want Amber in danger.

Surely, Elissa's giving another class that day should be fine, right? Doug had met the remaining students. Yet—

He thanked Amber and said goodbye. Should he call Evan? The former military K-9 officer and current police K-9 trainer would be in a better position to help. But Doug couldn't avoid figuring he was overthinking this and would look ridiculous if he got someone else, especially Evan, involved.

Even so—he called Evan. "I'm in town right now buying some dog food and treats at Pets and Products," he said. "Want me to get you some for Hooper and Griffin?"

"No thanks." Doug said goodbye. He would get to the ranch before Evan, even if he asked him to head there and why.

His intuition, as Maisie had called it, and not necessarily reality.

Fortunately the ride wasn't long. It didn't hurt that he turned the light on the top of the car to flashing, although he turned it off again when he reached the base of the ranch's driveway.

This was all probably an exercise in absurdity. Even so, at the top of the driveway he parked near the ranch house and got Hooper out of the car there. In case something wasn't right at Elissa's, no sense making it obvious that a cop had arrived.

And if all was well, he would look even more absurd in her eyes.

Even so, just in case, he put Hooper's official bulletproof K-9 vest on him, then softly said, "Heel." Of course his wonderful dog obeyed.

He headed up to the ranch house and walked in the shadows between it and Elissa's nearby place. As they approached it, Hooper sat on the dry turf and stared forward, alerting to something.

To what?

Doug wasn't sure, but he suddenly felt as if his impulse to come up here and check on Elissa was justified.

He would soon confirm it—or not.

No answer had come to Elissa's mind yet. She felt paralyzed by shock and fear, but that wasn't like her.

At least Perry hadn't moved from the chair facing her. His scalpel remained poised, its point aimed now toward her throat as he continued to talk—rant, in a way, about how false it was for people to think they were helping others in stupid ways like claiming they would heal all the hurt inside them if they touched and talked to stupid dogs.

Elissa forced herself not to react to that. Dogs weren't stupid. They were smart and loving and—

Hey. Her thoughts had led her to glance at Peace, who had remained lying near the window without moving, as if she'd somehow sensed that getting close to her human mom could result in harm to both of them. A few minutes ago, while Perry was talking, Elissa had also made the gesture that meant "stay" so Peace would remain still for her own safety—at least for now. She was a good dog and knew to obey.

But she'd just sat up and started wagging her tail.

Fortunately, Perry was still engaged in his rant against dogs and dog therapy and hadn't noticed. But… the way Peace's ears moved while her tail wagged—similar to how she acted when there was another dog around she liked, especially Hooper.

Surely that didn't mean…but Elissa was hopeful. If not Hooper, something was causing her dog to react. A scent or sound of some kind of help?

"So that's how it is," Perry said, apparently finishing his nasty tirade. He stood and Elissa's heart raced even more as he brandished the scalpel toward her. "Now let's finish this so I can get out of here for now. It'll be oh, so sad to find your body later." His nasty grin told her just the opposite was true.

But he wasn't going to "find" her body. Not if she could help it.

She had to do something—especially in case she was just imagining that help could have arrived…

"You're not going to get away with killing me," she all but shouted. "You're already being sought for questioning in the murder of Jill Jacobs, so if something happens to me, the police will work even harder to find you—and they'll succeed. They're smart. They'll recognize that you're Perry Willmer pretending to be a guy named Paul Wilson—and this time you won't be able to play games to make officers believe the Chance K-9s are reacting to Paul as a dog-loving person rather than a suspect they're looking for."

"Shut up!" Perry took a step toward Elissa, who prepared to run, hopefully fast enough to avoid him—but recognizing how unlikely that was in this small area.

Peace barked, startling Perry. Elissa prepared to do

whatever was necessary to save her dog—just as another dog leaped into the room through the door to the hallway: Hooper.

"Attack!" called a familiar and very welcome voice.

The K-9 immediately leaped onto Perry, knocking him over and grabbing the arm that wielded the scalpel in his teeth as he snarled.

"Get off me, you damn mutt," Perry screamed, writhing on the floor.

But, fortunately, it was too late. Doug stomped into the room, gun drawn.

"Drop the weapon, Willmer," he shouted. "When you do, I'll call the dog off."

Perry fought a few more seconds, to no avail. The scalpel suddenly fell to the floor.

Doug immediately kicked the scalpel away. "Hooper, let go," he said. Hooper obeyed, and then Doug grabbed Perry, turning him over to cuff him.

The man started cursing and attempting to get up anyway, till Doug said to Hooper, "Take hold," which the dog did, standing on the man's back and grabbing one of Perry's arms in his mouth, though not chomping down.

Perry suddenly lay still. Hooper didn't move, but Peace hurried over to Elissa and sat beside her as she dropped to her knees to hug her beloved and now safe dog who had tried to help her.

She wished she could do the same with Doug, but he remained busy, clearly on duty. Still holding his weapon pointed at Perry's head now that he wore handcuffs—and clearly avoiding the possibility of harming Hooper—he pulled a phone from his pocket with his other hand, pressed a button and told whoever answered where he was and what was going on—presumably the department's dispatcher, since he asked for backup and a crime scene team.

Then he looked at her. "You all right?"

"I am now," she said, not thrilled at how her voice shook. "Thank you."

His smile didn't appear to be simply the look of a cop after successfully bringing down a bad guy. There was caring in his expression, and relief, if Elissa read it correctly. "Any time," he said. "But promise you won't get into this kind of situation again."

It was Wednesday evening, three days after Perry Willmer had come forward using his real identity and attempted to exact further revenge for the death of his son—on the wrong person.

If anyone, Elissa had concluded, Perry should have blamed himself. A child who had a horrible father like Perry had probably suffered throughout his short life before ending it himself.

She sat at a table at the Last Chance Bar with Doug and Maisie, sipping Shiraz from a tall glass while patting Peace, who lay on the floor beside her, with her foot.

Of course the K-9 cops had brought their dogs in, too. Maisie had given those K-9s some biscuits she'd had in her purse, and their server had brought over a water bowl, so the dogs were now as well treated as their people.

Elissa, Doug and Maisie continued to discuss what had occurred a few days earlier as well as the time since then.

"I still don't really understand how you happened to be at my house right then," Elissa said, and not for the first time. His explanation, that something hadn't felt right, didn't give enough detail. At least he had told her how he had entered the house. As a cop, he'd been prepared to kick down a door if necessary—but fortunately it was obvious which door Perry had jimmied open despite it being closed then. He'd easily entered there.

"He just missed you," Maisie said with a grin, taking a drink of her gin and tonic.

Though that was supposed to be a joke, Elissa felt warmth spreading through her at the idea. She looked once more at Doug.

"Well, maybe that, too," Doug conceded, also smiling. "But call it intuition or concern or whatever, but when you didn't answer your phone when I tried calling a few times and it kept going straight into voice mail, I wanted to check on you."

"Right," Elissa said.

Perry had been arrested and charged with a number of things, the most serious being the murder of Jill Jacobs. But he was also charged with assault with a deadly weapon and more regarding his attack on Elissa.

She had related to Detective Vince Vanderhoff her entire conversation with Perry, or as much as she could remember considering how frightened she had been. That included what he'd said about threatening the parents of other children who'd had therapy dog sessions at the SLO hospital where she'd provided some of them. The San Luis Obispo police were cooperating and questioning all of those people.

Elissa's name would hopefully be cleared.

Plus, Adellaide Willmer had agreed to come to Chance to be questioned about her ex, as well. From what Elissa had heard, Adellaide had sounded shocked, when she was contacted, about all that Perry had allegedly done, although she seemed willing to discuss him and their relationship—and had given the impression that Perry had always been difficult and even acted mentally deranged sometimes.

They talked about that, too, over their drinks. Then Doug said, "So once this is all resolved, you'll be cleared of wrongdoing against those kids, too. Guess you could get your job back at the San Luis Obispo hospital, right?" He sounded casual, but there was a look in his eyes as he regarded Elissa that caused her to think he really wanted a negative answer.

She gave it to him.

"I possibly could, but I've got other ideas." She had pondered the options, even wondered if her employers there might consider apologizing now that the truth was known. She decided not to follow up on that, though.

"What ideas?" Doug asked, his tone now suggesting he was very interested.

"Well, I called Sonya's friend Petra yesterday, the head nurse at the Chance Hospital, and went in to see her. We talked about more dog therapy sessions and training, and I asked her about whether I could apply for a nursing job. I told her about all that had been going on and my reason before for needing to take a most likely permanent leave of absence from the last one, and she said they'd been looking for a new pediatric nurse. No guarantees yet, but she sounded as if they might officially interview me first, then possibly make me an offer."

"Hey, that's great." Maisie lifted her glass to toast Elissa. Elissa clinked her wineglass against it, as well as against Doug's mug of dark lager. His grin bisected his handsome face as if he was really pleased.

Well, so was she—especially at his reaction.

"Plus," Elissa said, "I've related all of this to Amber, Evan and Sonya. They sounded shocked at what happened, and poor Amber apologized for not helping me. I assured her I realized she couldn't have imagined what was going on. Anyway, they're happy I'm okay—and though they're fine if I go back to working part-time for them, they made it clear they want to work with me more with classes for future therapy dog handlers. They were really apologetic about half the members of my first class.

"Evan promised to teach me more about general dog training, too, so I can be his assistant at first and then give classes of my own later. They might have their computer person record some of my lessons for the ranch website. And they both might want my input on therapy dogs and their handlers in the book they're writing."

"So it sounds as if you will be in Chance for a while," Maisie said, looking at her brother.

Elissa hadn't been sure at first, but she definitely liked Maisie now.

And Doug?

He gave a mock scowl toward his sister as if to get her to stop her teasing, then said, "Looks like Chance still needs our K-9 handler skills, so I'll be around for a while, too."

"I'm counting on it," Elissa said.

A short while later they'd all finished their drinks. Doug paid the bill despite Elissa's offering to and then they all walked outside with their dogs beside them.

"So I guess Griffin and I will be on our own tonight," Maisie said to Doug as they stopped beside her car in the parking lot. Both Murrans had driven there separately, as had Elissa.

Elissa hoped Maisie was right—but figured her brother would follow his sister home to avoid any embarrassment.

The opposite was true. Instead, Doug edged up beside Elissa, after getting Hooper to sit beside tail-wagging Peace on the pavement, and put his arm around her, hugging her against his hard body. Elissa felt her insides warm immediately, believing Doug would in fact accompany her home—and not because she was in danger anymore.

"You got it, sis," Doug said. "You're on your own tonight. I definitely have some plans, as long as they're okay with Elissa."

He looked down at her and the way her body had reacted before was nothing compared with the sexual awareness that now pulsed through her.

"They're definitely okay with me," Elissa said, and felt her smile give way to a very heated and welcome kiss as Doug's mouth came down on hers.

They got into their separate cars and met again at Elissa's home, where they first took both dogs for a walk.

"You know," Elissa said as they stopped while Peace and Hooper sniffed grass along the sidewalk, "I've been wanting to thank you again for helping me, not only by saving my life—which I can't tell you how much I appreciate—but also for believing in my innocence enough to stick up for me. A lot. Even when I'm sure you had some doubts." She looked up at him and was suddenly back in his arms.

"You're very welcome," he said against her lips. "And there's something I'd like to talk to you about now, too."

"What's that?"

He stepped back and looked down at her. "It's... well, I really care about you, Elissa. Maybe even more. And I can't tell you how glad I am you'll be staying in Chance."

"I care about you, too, Doug. I'm also glad I'll be here. Do you suppose our relationship—" She didn't finish, since Peace had moved forward and was pulling on her leash. "Heel, Peace," she called. And of course her dog obeyed, but Elissa was sorry the moment had ended.

Or had it? Doug was suddenly close to her again, with Hooper by his side. "You were saying...our relationship? Yeah, let's talk about that."

"Yes," Elissa said, "let's." He acknowledged the possibility of a relationship, too. She couldn't help smiling.

And suddenly she couldn't wait till they entered her house...together.

* * * * *

*Look for more books from award-winning author
Linda O. Johnston coming soon.*

*And don't miss the previous title in the
K-9 Ranch Rescue miniseries:*

Second Chance Soldier

*Available now wherever
Harlequin Romantic Suspense books are sold!*

Get 4 FREE REWARDS!

We'll send you 2 FREE Books <u>plus</u> 2 FREE Mystery Gifts.

Harlequin® Romantic Suspense books feature heart-racing sensuality and the promise of a sweeping romance set against the backdrop of suspense.

FREE Value Over **$20**

ROMANTIC suspense

When Liz James is threatened and her daughter kidnapped, she turns to Harley Maxwell for support. Fortunately, he's an undercover cop who, for sixteen years, has been tracking the man who kidnapped her daughter. Will Harley's quest for revenge overshadow his chance at love with Liz?

Read on for a sneak preview of the next book in the Undercover Justice miniseries,
Undercover Passion *by Melinda Di Lorenzo.*

Liz asked, "Can I really trust you, Harley?"

He felt his eyebrows knit together in puzzlement. "Trust me? With the gun? It's a legal licensed firearm. And I'm fully trained. But if you're not comfortable…"

"No. That's not what I mean. I'm sure that you wouldn't do something reckless."

"I definitely wouldn't. So what do you mean?"

"I mean if I tell you about what happened today, can you promise not to go to the police?"

The question made him want to roll out his shoulders to relieve a sudden kink. If she was about to confess to some involvement with Garibaldi, he wasn't sure he wanted to hear it.

Because you already decided she was innocent based on the feel of her lips?

He shoved off the self-directed question and went back to work on her leg, cleaning it more thoroughly this time than he had on top of the roof. "That's a tough question to just give a yes or no to."

"Is it?" she sounded almost disappointed.

And he had to admit that he felt something similar. With her tempting lips and all, he really didn't want her to be on the wrong side. It was the only small positive that he thought had come out of the current sequence of events. Knowing that her store was under fire had led Harley to infer that she couldn't be involved with Garibaldi. The possibility that whatever crime had been committed at Liz's Lovely Things was a third party seemed unlikely.

But not impossible.

He chose his next words carefully. "I think of myself as a decent guy, Liz. One who does the right thing whenever possible. So as far as trust is concerned…you can count on me for that, every time."

"And if it's not a black-and-white situation?" she asked softly, opening her eyes and directing a clear, serious look his way.

He met her gaze. "I think a lot of things fall somewhere in the gray spectrum, actually. You have to sort through it to figure out what's right and what's wrong. But doing things that could result in people getting hurt…that's a hard limit for me. I wouldn't ever endanger Teegan, or ask you to do anything that might. The cops are the good guys."

She bit her lip, looking like she was trying to hold back tears. Harley couldn't help himself.

Garibaldi be damned.

He pushed up and reached out to fold her into an embrace.

Don't miss
Undercover Passion *by Melinda Di Lorenzo,*
available November 2018 wherever
Harlequin® Romantic Suspense *books and ebooks are sold.*

www.Harlequin.com

Need an adrenaline rush from nail-biting tales
(and irresistible males)?

Check out **Harlequin Intrigue**®
and **Harlequin**® **Romantic Suspense** books!

New books available every month!

CONNECT WITH US AT:

Facebook.com/groups/HarlequinConnection

Facebook.com/HarlequinBooks

Twitter.com/HarlequinBooks

Instagram.com/HarlequinBooks

Pinterest.com/HarlequinBooks

ReaderService.com

**ROMANCE WHEN
YOU NEED IT**

SGENRE2018

Love Harlequin romance?

DISCOVER.

Be the first to find out about promotions,
news and exclusive content!

Facebook.com/HarlequinBooks

Twitter.com/HarlequinBooks

Instagram.com/HarlequinBooks

Pinterest.com/HarlequinBooks

ReaderService.com

EXPLORE.

Sign up for the Harlequin e-newsletter and
download a free book from any series at
TryHarlequin.com.

CONNECT.

Join our Harlequin community to share
your thoughts and connect with other
romance readers!
Facebook.com/groups/HarlequinConnection

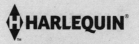

HARLEQUIN®

**ROMANCE WHEN
YOU NEED IT**

HSOCIAL2018

lover in you!

Earn points on your purchase of new Harlequin books from participating retailers.

Turn your points into **FREE BOOKS** of your choice!

Join for FREE today at
www.HarlequinMyRewards.com.

Harlequin My Rewards is a free program (no fees) without any commitments or obligations.

MYR18

THE WORLD IS BETTER WITH

Romance

Harlequin has everything from contemporary, passionate and heartwarming to suspenseful and inspirational stories.

Whatever your mood,
we have a romance just for you!

Connect with us to find your next great read, special offers and more.

f /HarlequinBooks

@HarlequinBooks

www.HarlequinBlog.com

www.Harlequin.com/Newsletters

HARLEQUIN®

A *Romance* FOR EVERY MOOD™

www.Harlequin.com

SERIESHALOAD2015